Skip to the End

Skip to the End

MOLLY JAMES

FOREVER

NEW YORK   BOSTON

Copyright © 2022 by Molly James
Reading group guide copyright © 2023 by Molly James and Hachette Book Group, Inc.

Cover design by Mel Four Design & Illustrations
Cover copyright © 2023 by Hachette Book Group, Inc.

Forever
Hachette Book Group
1290 Avenue of the Americas, New York, NY 10104
read-forever.com
twitter.com/readforeverpub

Originally published in 2022 by Quercus in Great Britain
First U.S. Edition: August 2023

Forever is an imprint of Grand Central Publishing. The Forever name and logo are trademarks of Hachette Book Group, Inc.

The publisher is not responsible for websites (or their content) that are not owned by the publisher.

Forever books may be purchased in bulk for business, educational, or promotional use. For information, please contact your local bookseller or the Hachette Book Group Special Markets Department at special.markets@hbgusa.com.

Library of Congress Cataloging-in-Publication Data
Names: James, Molly, author.
Title: Skip to the end / Molly James.
Description: First U.S. edition. | New York : Forever, 2023.
Identifiers: LCCN 2023008693 | ISBN 9781538739273 (trade paperback) |
    ISBN 9781538739280 (ebook)
Subjects: LCGFT: Romance fiction. | Magic realist fiction. | Novels.
Classification: LCC PR6110.O56 S55 2023 | DDC 823/.92—dc23/eng/20230324
LC record available at https://lccn.loc.gov/2023008693

ISBN: 9781538739273 (trade paperback), 9781538739280 (ebook)

Printed in the United States of America

LSC

Printing 1, 2023

For all the people who need more kisses in their life

Skip to the End

1

We're lying face to face, pillow to pillow, heart to heart.

The lights are dim and I can hear the faint sound of waves dragging and sighing over the sand.

His kiss is just a breath away. And yet I must resist. It's crucial that I don't venture beyond this tantalizing, tingly "Will-he-won't-he?" stage. I'm attending a wedding on Saturday with a school reunion element and I have to be able to sound convincing when my former classmates ask, "So, Amy, are you seeing anyone?"

My plan is to give an enigmatic smile and confide, "There is someone but it's very new, so I don't want to jinx it."

If I kiss him, I won't be able to say that.

"Well?" he husks, eyes flitting around my face, looking so amorous I can almost feel the sensation of his eyelashes, lips and fingertips glancing over my skin.

I take a breath, hyperaware of the exaggerated rise and fall of my chest, giving away my attraction. I want to tell him yes. One word and his face would light up; he might even whoop. But I hold back, needing to be absolutely certain. This is a big commitment. I can't afford another bad decision.

He sighs and rolls onto his back, sensing I need a bit of space.

My eyes linger on him, studying his profile, thinking how amazing it would be to get to know this man from every angle.

"This does feel really good," I concede.

He nods, turns his head toward me. "Firm but yielding."

"Mmm," I say, snuggling deeper. "I could lie here all day."

"Do you want to try the memory foam one again, just to be sure?"

I'm just a girl, lying on a bed, asking a guy to sell her a mattress.

And I want to buy one, I really do. I've been searching for the perfect fit, something that will prompt a contented exhale when I recline at night, something that responds to my contours and cradles and supports me, something that gives me sweet dreams. I would also prefer one that doesn't require a rope and pulley system to get me upright in the morning. I don't think that's too much to ask, just that one perfect mattress. Sold to me by Mr. Right.

This may be an unconventional way to find romance, but it turns out few men are as attentive as mattress salesmen, especially when you're in the market for a luxury, hand-tufted number.

I was going to wait to make my purchase until I was in my

first flat as an actual owner but my quest for a characterful yet airy nook hasn't progressed as I'd hoped. When a coil pinged through the worn fabric of my old hand-me-down mattress and skewered me like a corkscrew, I decided I couldn't wait any longer to sort out my bed situation. But even that has proved quite the trial.

The first place I visited, the middle-aged salesman was way too creepy and hovering. When he eyed my boobs and said he could tell I wasn't a stomach-sleeper I headed for the door, but en route he caught me looking enviously at the couple spooning on the Sleepeezee.

"We do offer body pillows." He hurried after me. "Studies show that by replicating the emotions associated with hugging you can allow your mind to stop racing and enjoy a sense of peace."

I looked at the long, cotton-covered columns waiting for a human companion and then back at him.

"Do they come in the shape of Jason Momoa?"

The second place had more pine bed frames than mattress options so today I went straight from work to a superstore a little way out of town and that's where it all came together: a spacious showroom flooded with natural light, soothing ocean sounds playing in the background, a female salesperson already with a client but cheerily letting me know her colleague would be out any second. I just wish she'd given me a heads-up about his eyes so I could've been more prepared: *Just so you know, they are really blue. Like, Bradley Cooper blue.*

I didn't hear the first thing he said because they were so

jewel-bright they put me in mind of the phrase, "If you're going to rise, you might as well shine!"

"Sorry, what was that?"

"I'm Matt," he repeated.

"As in mattress?" I replied without thinking.

He burst out laughing and it was a lark from that moment on. To him, mattress construction was a form of wizardry—when he led me over to the display cubes to show me a cross-section of the inner layers, I found myself peering with genuine interest, while also trying to guess at the full form of the tattoo playing peek-a-boo with his shirtsleeve.

One minute I was learning about the medical explanation of dead arms, the next we were discussing Stephen King novels (of course, his favorite is *Misery*). Between the bed samples we did impressions of our morning zombie walk to the bathroom and shared the weirdest things we've cried out in our sleep. ("I can't, I only have three legs!")

"Did you know that swear words feature eight hundred times more often in sleep talk than daytime talk?"

"Really?" I gasped. "That totally plays into my fear of falling asleep on a plane and shouting something X-rated."

"You should probably travel with a roll of gaffer tape."

"Yeah, that's always a good look. Hostage chic."

He handed me a different pillow to try. "There's even cases of teens sleep-texting now."

"Like they don't have enough problems," I said as I stared up at the ceiling. "If I had a kid, I'd bring them up in the wilderness.

Though I'd need to pack a stack of these pillows—how come it's so springy?"

"That one's talalay latex—breathable, hypoallergenic. It's actually made from the sap of the rubber tree—perhaps you could become our supplier, if you do end up moving to the wilderness?"

It was all so much more fun than the usual date treadmill of, "Sooo, what do you do? Where are you from? Any restraining orders I should know about?" I didn't know what he was going to say next and, like a deft doctor distracting a patient before a jab, instead of feeling self-conscious as I tested the mattresses, I found myself lying comfortably on my side, chatting away as he sat on the edge of the next one along. When the female sales-person clocked out and turned out the lights in the other sections, I felt excited by his proximity, not intimidated.

"Have you ever had a customer ask a bed-related question that made you blush?" I asked, knowing full well I was inviting a sexual reference.

"There was this one eighty-year-old woman who was con-cerned that memory foam might impact sexual performance, since it lacked the trampoline qualities of a traditional mattress…"

I chuckled along. "What about…has a customer ever asked you to lie down beside them, you know, to help them judge if they would be disturbed by their partner's movement?"

He nodded. "Karen prefers not to, but I don't mind." His head then tilted to the side. "Why, do you require that service?"

Did his voice just get lower?

I bit my lip and then said, "I suppose it would be good to know, for future reference…"

So here we are, lying face to face. And it just feels so natural, like we're under an invisible duvet and he might at any moment reach over and switch off the bedside lamp. This is what I've always wanted—someone I can talk to after all carnal desires have been sated. Someone whose eyes dance when they look at me. Someone who gives me best friend security and a bountiful heart.

I don't know how it's possible to feel more comfortable with this stranger than any of the men I have ever dated, but I do.

Now all I have to do to preserve this charmed feeling is slide off the mattress, take his card and tell him I'll be back on Monday to make the purchase. I'd buy it right now but it's already past closing. Besides, I want the excuse to return after the wedding.

"I've definitely found what I'm looking for," I say as I get to my feet.

"Excellent choice," he confirms. "I actually have the same one at home."

It's a sign! Or a line…Either way, it gives me a kick to think our bodies have similar taste. Perhaps we too will create the perfect blend of plush and firm…

I smile back at him, so happy to be sent off to the wedding with a little pocket spring in my step. "See you Monday!" I sing-song.

As I move toward the exit he calls after me, "Actually, I think Karen probably locked the door when she left. Hold on while I set the alarm, I'll walk out with you."

My heartbeat quickens. We're about to cross from the workspace into "anything goes" territory. I look out across the empty showroom.

"Wouldn't it be funny if people were allowed to test the beds overnight and this became one big dormitory?"

No reply. I think he's out of earshot.

Clunk.

The last light shuts down, the soothing ocean soundtrack ceases and the alarm begins beeping as he makes his way toward me.

My nerves flair. What will I do if he asks me to go for a drink? I don't think I can resist.

Be elusive! I tell myself, stepping to the side so he can unlock the door. *Keep him waiting a few days more...*

"After you." He ushers me through.

As he jangles his keyring and secures the building, I look down the street toward the tube station. "Which way—"

I don't even get to finish my sentence. He's swept me into the adjacent alley.

I go to speak but his eyes tell me everything I need to know. My legs feel weak with lust and I fall back onto the wall for support.

His lips are warm and ardent, triggering mini fireworks all over my body. I'd forgotten how thrilling this could be! As I respond I hear him moan lightly and I pull him closer, clasping him to me, feeling his belt dig into my hip. I dial up the passion, desperate to ward off the inevitable but it begins, as it always does when I experience a kiss with someone new…

Blackness, a warp-drive surge as my mind gets catapulted from this delicious, heady, all-things-are-possible moment to the very end of our potential relationship. There are times when the visions are muddled or take a moment to decipher but this one is crystal clear.

I struggle to prize myself out of his grasp but he mistakes my wriggling for ardor and leans heavily into me. I wish I could just go with it and sate my cravings but I go the other way and slap him. Hard.

"Wh—what was that?" he reels.

"*You've got a girlfriend!*" I exclaim.

He looks horrified. "What?"

"You heard me!"

"Oh my god." He looks stricken. "Did she send you here?"

"No, I…" I fumble for a response. Usually I pass off these flashes of insight as female intuition, mostly because premonitions are such a hard sell, especially in amped-up moments like these when I'm welcoming a man's attention one minute and rejecting him in the harshest manner the next. They already think I'm half psycho. When the truth is, I'm half psychic. Well, not even half. And not exactly psychic. It's complicated.

In this instance, Mattress Matt and I were in a bar, he was nuzzling at my neck, whispering in my ear and then a petite brunette appeared on the other side of the table, angrily tipping it forward so the cocktails crashed and spilled into our laps, all the while howling, "How *could* you?" over and over again.

I know this sounds absurd, coming from someone who gets sneak peeks of future events, but I did not see this one coming.

"You seemed so nice," I sigh, crushed to my core.

"I am nice!" he protests, hand rubbing at his smarting face. "You were just so…"

"What?" I snap.

His shoulders slump. "So lovely and funny and… unexpected."

The way he looks at me, so sincerely, I can't help but wonder— was there anything in the vision that could suggest he was not meant to scramble up and beg forgiveness? Anything to hint that his girlfriend was awful and snarky and dragging him down? I close my eyes and re-conjure the vision, reliving the profound hurt in her eyes and the way her hand instinctively went to her belly. And then I blanch.

"Oh my god—is she pregnant?"

"What?" he startles. "How do you—"

"*Is she?*" I cut in.

He looks terrified and then hangs his head. "Yes."

I feel stunned. Yet how can I be surprised? There's nothing new here. If I had to sum up the last twenty years of my love life in one word, it would be *disappointment*.

9

I shake my head and then push past him, catching sight of a black cab as I stumble out into the street.

"Taxi!" I yelp at the yellow light.

It duly screeches to my side, the closest I'm going to get to a knight in shining armor. Better yet, the driver is a woman.

"Thank you so much for stopping!" I say as I climb into the back, reciting my address before glancing back at Matt. He emerges from the alleyway, looking emotionally beaten to a pulp.

The cabbie gives me a sympathetic look in the rear-view mirror as we pull away. "You two just break up?"

I nod.

"I'm sorry, sweetie. Were you together long?"

I sigh as I slump deep into the seat. "Just a few minutes."

2

Ah, home sweet place-I-can't-wait-to-move-out-of.

I first viewed this low-ceilinged, squeaky-floored one-bedroom on a winter evening, thinking it was just the January miseries making it feel dingy. I pictured throwing open the windows come spring and setting a little vase of flowers on the sill, but the sun never seemed to find me. I didn't know about prioritizing south-facing and natural light back in those days. Still, the low rent has helped me save up over the years, and as soon as I find the right spot to buy I'll be out of here.

I drop my bag on the pink velvet chaise and head for the kitchen. Much as I'd like to slug back some rum, I'm saving all booze consumption for the wedding so I reach for what's left of my blackberry gelato. My hand lingers on the fridge door handle as I take in the photos held in place with retro housewife magnets.

"Hello, friends!" I smile at my two best girls—May and

bride-to-be Charlotte—and two best boys—Gareth and Jay (May's twin brother).

Though Jay has been threatening to move to New York since *Pose* first aired, we've been a pack since school. Charlotte and May were first to pal up, making an unbeatable goal attack and goal shooter combo on the netball team. To this day May is all attack while Charlotte personifies seal-the-deal precision.

Jay and I bonded when we were cast in the drama department's interpretation of *The King and I*. Jay still loves to be the center of attention, while I've never been known to turn down a spin on the dance floor.

Gareth became our unlikely fifth musketeer a year later, coincidentally combining physicality with dramatic flair. I'm just about to relive his scene-stealing moment in PE when my phone rings, making me jump.

"*Kiss Me, Honey Honey, Kiss Me!*" Shirley Bassey entices.

I must remember to change my ringtone before the wedding. May put it on as a joke and I never got around to updating it. I think some part of me kept hoping that one day the right man would hear the invitation and respond accordingly.

"Hey, May!" I say, balancing the phone on my shoulder as I reach for a spoon from the drawer.

"I DON'T WANT TO GO!"

Excellent. Someone in a worse mood than me.

"Neither do I right now," I concede.

"You've finally seen the light about Marcus?" She brightens.

"There's still time for Charlotte to cancel, should we go to her now? One hour and this nightmare could be over!"

"May."

"What?"

"You've got to let this go," I say as I put her on speaker and recline on the chaise. "The poor guy has done nothing to warrant your distrust."

"*Poor* guy?" she sneers.

"Okay, rich guy. This rich guy has done nothing to warrant your distrust. Nothing."

"He's going to take her away from us. We already see less of her."

"We saw less of you leading up to your wedding."

"And too much of me during the divorce."

"I liked having you to stay!" I protest.

"Anyway, it's a slippery slope," she continues. "He'll have her pregnant before we know it."

"And then we get to be aunties!"

"Of a human that is half *his* DNA."

I set down my gelato and unclick the speaker button. "Can't you just be happy for her?"

"He's not good enough!" she rails.

"No one would be good enough for her in your eyes."

"What's your point?"

I sigh.

"Anyway," she huffs. "I know why I don't want to go, what's your excuse?"

I wasn't going to go into details about Mattress Matt but I feel any distraction from Marcus is probably a good thing.

"*Woman!*" May reels after I bring her up to speed. "That is a zinger!"

"I know. And before you offer, I don't need him to be punished in a cruel and unusual way. I just want to know how to face a dozen of our schoolfriends when they introduce their beloved husbands and wives and I stand there alone."

"Being single is nothing to be ashamed of."

"I know that, of course," I sigh. "I just can't carry it off like you. Plus, I've always been associated with romantic failure. I wanted to surprise everyone by being squared away."

"Maybe by Charlotte's *next* wedding..."

"Oh May!"

We veer off topic for a while and then as we go to wrap up, her voice softens. "I really am sorry about Matt. There has to be one non-dick out there for you."

"Yes, that's my goal—to meet the non-dick of my dreams."

"All you need is one good premonition," she reminds me. "I know it's been twenty years of disappointment but that light at the end of the tunnel is no use unless you keep moving toward it."

I was fourteen when I first heard about our family legacy, for want of a better term.

Mum and I had just watched the final episode of some Sunday night period drama when she abruptly turned off the TV and came and sat beside me on the sofa. "I need to talk to you about something."

"Yes?" I said, a little unnerved by the look on her face.

"Do you remember kissing Tommy Turner in the playground when you were seven?"

"Random!" I frowned. "Yes, vaguely. Little Tommy Turnip."

"Do you remember what you told me about it?"

I thought for a moment and then suggested, "That he smelled of apple shampoo and Plasticine?"

Mum chuckled. "Actually, you probably did say that. But do you remember what else?"

"No."

She took a breath. "You told me that when you kissed him, the sky went dark and you had a dream even though you were standing up."

I gave a shudder. "That sounds a bit *Sixth Sense*."

"You said you saw him with metal on his teeth and that you didn't like him anymore because he reminded you of Jaws from *The Spy Who Loved Me*, which you'd watched with Dad the weekend before."

"That rings a bell."

"Well, it wasn't a dream, it was a premonition. You had a premonition of him when he got braces."

I shifted positions. "I don't think I'll set up my Madame Zaza tent just yet—he had gappy teeth, just like me. It's actually one of the things I liked about him."

"Okay, that probably isn't the best example," Mum conceded.

"What I'm trying to tell you is that all the women in our family have a particular ability and that was your first experience of it. When we kiss someone for the first time, we get a flash of how the relationship will end."

I looked around for a half-drunk bottle of Baileys—she must surely be tipsy.

"I know it sounds far-fetched or delusional but it's true. It's been going on for generations, as far back as anyone can remember."

I studied her for a second. "Did it skip a generation with you?"

"No, I had it too."

"So you saw Dad leaving when you first kissed him?"

She looked sad and a bit uncomfortable. "Yes."

"But you married him anyway?"

"I had my reasons. The point is that the premonitions don't lie. You need to pay heed."

"Should I also beware the Ides of March?" I tried to lighten the mood.

"Amy, darling, I know this is a lot to process." She reached for my hand. "I've put it off for as long as I could because I didn't want you worrying, but I feel it's important for you to be prepared."

"You're serious, aren't you?" I withdrew my hand. "What if I don't want this to happen to me?"

"I'm afraid you don't have a choice. This is our family gift."

*

That night I stayed up fretting, swinging between "It's all a load of nonsense" and "What if it's true?" Which led me to three key questions by daybreak: how long does the premonition last? Do I see myself in the premonition or am I looking out through my eyes? What will the person I'm kissing think is going on?

My mum had replied calmly: "They are fleeting. Sometimes you are looking onto the scene like Scrooge in *A Christmas Carol*, other times it's more emotion-based—you'll see the other person and get a strong feeling of sadness or regret or anger, et cetera. As for the person you are kissing, they won't know anything—except that one minute you're receptive to them and the next minute you might be pushing them away."

"Right," I had replied. "So it's basically a big spoiler alert for the relationship. And I have to decide whether I want to experience the full movie based on a few-seconds-long snippet of the ending?"

"I hadn't thought of it that way but yes, it's exactly like that. You still get to choose what you do about what you see. You just don't get any say in the outcome."

This sounded super depressing to me so I shared the burden with my friends. Charlotte said it was like having a direct line to destiny and insisted I wait for someone I really liked to test it out. May and Jay were all for unleashing my "superpower" that day. I was equal parts terrified and curious but agreed it would be best to start with someone I wouldn't be hoping for a future with, so I wouldn't have to add crying to the mix. I really just had one criterion—I wanted it to be someone I could trust not to blab all round school if I started screaming or passed out. I studied each guy in our class and couldn't find one candidate. At least not one I actually wanted to physically kiss. An uneventful year passed and then new boy Gareth arrived. I never pictured myself with an outdoorsy type—compared to the techy stringbeans and cool-coiffed pretty boys I'd been eyeing across the school cafeteria, he looked as burly as a lumberjack—but I did notice that he never got sucked into any gossip or drama. If May demanded an opinion from him on a topic, he'd look vague and say he missed what she said because he was just thinking about pollen. Or orchid propagation. Or ferns. Apparently there are over ten thousand species of ferns. It's a wonder we were able to get his attention at all.

Then came the school outing to the local Christmas market. Gareth and I had been tasked with getting the hot spiced apple cider and, as we awaited our order, he casually pointed to the sprig of mistletoe hung above our heads.

My eyes widened—was my first kiss going to be straight out of a Hallmark movie? Just enough snowfall to catch on my eyelashes and a chaste kiss tasting of sugar-dusted pfeffernusse? Suddenly I felt ill-prepared—we'd had zero flirtation in the lead-up, barely even any eye contact. Nevertheless, I tilted my face and attempted a flirtatious twinkle. "Yes?"

"Did you know mistletoe is actually a parasite?"

My face froze, my heart beating uncomfortably in my chest. *What?*

"Birds eat the berries then deposit them onto the branches of another tree, where they proceed to suck out all the nutrients."

"Oh," I grimaced, deflated.

"As for the kissing part…"

I raised a wary brow.

"That comes from the legend of Norse god Loki poisoning another god with the berries."

"They're poisonous?"

"Yes, but in the story the poisoned god recovered and his people were so relieved that the mere sight of mistletoe would prompt a celebratory embrace."

This was at least ten years before Tom Hiddleston played Loki in *Thor* so there wasn't even that element to pep me up.

"Do you want my cinnamon stick?"

I looked at the dusty, twig-like scroll he was offering and that seemed like all the premonition I needed—we were never going to be romantically entwined. My shoulders slumped briefly but as we rejoined the rest of the group and I watched Jay use him as a buffer against the whistling wind, I realized I was perfectly fine—this wasn't a personal rejection of me, Gareth was just being Gareth. For years he showed more interest in hugging trees than women. It's almost as if he knew that Freya was on her way and he had no need for place-holders.

Valentine's Day brought with it an invitation to a spin-the-bottle party—the odds of getting kissed there seemed decent, if daunting. But things took a decidedly different turn and ultimately impatience got the better of me and I succumbed to the pestering of class stud Chas. In a tube stairwell smelling of stale wee.

The only thing worse than the setting was the kiss. You know those haphazard assaults that make you want to wipe your face after? When it came to the big premonition moment there was no fainting, no screaming; it was more a surge of blackness, not dissimilar to going into a dark tunnel, and then a fleeting vision, like passing through a station without stopping and trying to make sense of what you are seeing on the platform.

I didn't let on what I had seen. Chas had promised to take me bowling and I wanted to make some attempt at having a boyfriend, even knowing it would end. But I barely made it through two weeks of dating, with most of our interactions consisting of me saying, "Not now!" "Not there!" or "Not on your life!"

In my eagerness to move on, I got my premonition timings a little off and accused him of cheating with Alison Kirkpatrick before they'd even got together.

"Don't deny it! I saw the pair of you canoodling at that new cafe by WHSmith!"

"What are you talking about, Whole Latte Love hasn't even opened yet?"

"Oh," I sighed frustratedly. "Well, why don't you take her there, on me?" And then I gave him a fiver.

I can't say that things have greatly improved in the twenty years since then.

3

I'm dreaming that I am being lightly but repeatedly tasered. And then I realize my phone is buzzing on the nightstand.

I reach for it, squinting at the series of messages, rolling my eyes at each one—the first three are wedding guests who need to update their dietary preferences, including one woman who doesn't want any wedding cake.

The wedding cake is not compulsory, I tap back.

I know, she replies. *I just don't want to be offered any or I'll eat it.*

I flump back on the pillow but take some satisfaction in the next message—the couple whose last Instagram post was a gushing, "My life began when I met you!" are now insisting on being seated at different tables, with no direct sight lines.

Fortunately the venue is unphased by the updates. "We also have a selection of heels for those women who traveled in their flip-flops and forgot to pack their party shoes and Savile Row ties for the men."

I can see why Charlotte settled on this particular stately home.

All is well with the guest situation, I type, reassuring her that I am on top of my duties before I even ask how she's feeling, because that would be her priority despite it being the day before she says "I do."

We have a small problem with the mother-of-the-bride, she taps back.

I sit up and call her immediately. "What is it?"

"She's not coming."

I catch myself before I say "Thank god!" out loud.

"We were supposed to be having a special mother–daughter night before the wedding."

"Mmm-hmm," I say. Now's not the time to point out that this was only going to bring stress and puffy eyes. As Jay might say, these two were cut from very different cloth…

With her white-blonde river of hair, Charlotte looks like someone who entered the world aboard a Viking longship on a misty fjord, as opposed to in a hoarder's bedroom in a Kilburn high-rise. The clutter and chaos of her upbringing somehow birthed a world-class organizer, which only served to put her further at odds with her mother. The two of them were always pulling in opposite directions, with literal tugs-of-war over certain household items.

"But I might need it one day!"

"You already have seven of these that you don't use, three of which are broken and two are still in their original packaging!"

You get the idea.

Charlotte thrived with the structure of school and even streamlined a number of the office filing systems they still use to this day.

It was these skills that first attracted her husband-to-be Marcus. Charlotte was hired to take his firm's annual banking banquet to the next level and just hearing her say "Consider it done!" gave him goosebumps. He found himself making excuses to call so that he could revel in her decisive precision. When the time came to meet, he was already three-quarters smitten and watching her respond with calm efficiency to the non-stop queries from her staff finished him off.

The only downside to Charlotte, as far as he could tell, was her ethereal beauty, putting her in a different league. Marcus did the very best with what he had—barbershop shaves and bespoke suits, designer watches and convertible cars—but the aristocratic ties that had previously bagged him dates meant nothing to her, so for a while he was at a loss for how to impress her. Then one day they had to forgo a gala dinner to babysit his niece and nephew and it dawned on him that she was far happier at home in loungewear than being paraded around like arm candy. She also really, really liked how neat and tidy he was. So he took a chance and popped the question. I don't know what surprised us the most—how quickly she said yes or the fact that they would now beat Gareth to the altar. In just a matter of hours…

"I had thought I might spend the eve of my wedding in quiet meditation," Charlotte says, bringing me back to our current conversation. "But then I just started spinning out, worrying about everything and—"

"I'll come straight after work," I tell her.

"Really?" Her voice brightens.

"Well, it's going to be a wrench tearing myself away from my sagging mattress for your four-poster but I'll do it."

"Oh, thank you! Do you think we should invite May?"

Jeez! First her mother, now May? Anyone would think she's trying to sabotage the ceremony.

"She can't come."

"She can't?"

"No. She's getting a tattoo."

"The night before the wedding?"

"It's a much sought-after artist. In from Japan, for one day only." My lie gets more elaborate. I would feel bad if the alternative wouldn't be such a disaster. I picture May attempting to fill Charlotte's head full of doubts about Marcus and then, when that didn't work, locking her in the wine cellar. "Anyway! I should get ready for work!"

"Don't forget to bring your wedding outfit so you can come straight here," Charlotte instructs.

"And you don't forget to breathe amidst all your last-minute cross-checking."

"I won't," she sighs. "It's right here—number four on my list."

*

I gaze up at the wisteria-garlanded castle, all sandy stonework and chunky crenellations. I can picture Charlotte leaning out of the top turret window, her river of blonde hair accented with butterflies as she waves to her adoring courtiers. Hashtag real life fairytale. And then I try to think how I would feel if this was my wedding…

Nothing.

For someone who has premonitions, I've never been able to picture my wedding day. I can see Gareth in some rustic setting with as many woodland creatures as guests, May in an underground nightclub in Berlin for her second time around, and if Jay decided to settle down, sometime in his eighties, he would try to top having Liza Minnelli singing "Single Ladies" at the altar. But me…?

"I found a bottle of non-alcoholic gin!" Charlotte runs toward me whooping.

"You say that like it's a good thing," I say as I hug her.

"Well, it would be too weird to not have a drink but we don't want to be hungover for the wedding."

"Quite right," I say, noticing that her eyes are uncharacteristically shadowy.

"I've got fresh lemons and ice and we'll put on a face pack and pretend we're at a spa."

She takes my arm as she leads me through the arched stone entrance, dominated by a dramatic flourish of a staircase. To the right are the wedding rooms—one for the ceremony and one for the dining and reception. Charlotte won't let me see either.

"You have to wait until Gareth has completed positioning the flowers. The design is sublime."

"What's over here?" I point to the intriguing half-size door to the left of the stairs.

"That's the old snug bar. It's really cozy and characterful, lots of dark wood and booths to hide away in. People can step out of the fray if it gets too much with all the music and dancing."

I can't wait for the dancing. Especially as Charlotte has planned a sequence of tunes from our school years.

"And through here?" I take a step forward.

Charlotte stops me before I nose too far. "That's the owner's quarters so out of bounds. The ladies' and gents' are either side of the staircase."

"Got it." I look around. "This time tomorrow this is going to be a-buzz with people in their finery toasting a woman who looks just like Charlotte Dixon but is now Charlotte Davenport!"

She gives a little squeal. "Let's crack open the fake gin!"

I had felt a little dubious about spending the night in the honeymoon suite, lest that be my only experience of it in life, but thankfully Charlotte is saving that for Marcus. "It's in a turret, up this winding staircase with all these different levels. You'll see it as soon as my hair is done tomorrow. It's all on the schedule."

"Remind me how many times we have to chew our toast in the morning?" I tease.

She ignores me and instead leads the way to our shared room for the night. If this is just a basic room, I can only imagine the grandeur of her suite.

"It's funny how posh people can get away with really outlandish wallpaper that anywhere else would look bizarre," I note as I take in the tropical jungle design. In a world of Elephant Ear paint and rose gold everything, the rich jewel colors seem incredibly decadent.

"I hope you don't mind sharing the bed," Charlotte says as she prepares our drinks in heavy cut-glass tumblers.

"I might just curl up on this rug it's so plush!" I kick off my shoes and wriggle my toes in the soft teal textile. "Where are your things?"

"I already unpacked. My case is in the wardrobe."

You can tell a lot about a person by how they inhabit a hotel room. I have a gift for marking every available surface in a matter of minutes, even if I'm only traveling with a carry-on. With Charlotte, everything is tucked neatly away, her beauty products symmetrically aligned. May's the same way. She still has a key to my flat and sometimes makes an excuse to come over before I get home from work so she can re-color-code my wardrobe and untangle my jewelry.

Charlotte hands me my drink, we clink "To love in all its forms!" and then she leads me to the surprisingly modern bathroom where two sheet face masks are set on the marble countertop.

"Ooh, I've always wanted to use one of these but was too afraid to try one home alone."

"Afraid?"

"Not that my skin would react but that I'd forget I had it on, catch sight of my reflection and think some freaky masked killer had broken in."

Charlotte laughs and then positively snorts as we struggle to apply them.

"I think you've got yours upside down!" I feel hysteria kicking in. "No, that bit goes around your ear!"

"My ear? My ears don't need a facial."

"It's just to hold it in place."

"Where are my nose flaps?" she squeaks.

I try to help her but keep going limp from laughing. "Oh my god, are you on sideways now?" I ask, eyes streaming.

"Don't cry, you'll dilute the serum!"

Finally we settle, side by side on the giant bed.

"How are you feeling about your mum now?" I ask.

"Like I've dodged a bullet."

I smile.

"I didn't want to deprive Mum of her special mother-of-the-bride moment but it turns out she wanted no part of it. She doesn't really like to leave the house now. Marcus thinks she needs some professional help, but she's surely not that bad. Is she?"

It's a good thing the mask is hiding my expression. "That's certainly nothing you have to fix or decide right now." I try to move her on to cheerier topics. "Let's just try to savor this special time—the night before your wedding!"

"You know the only thing that would make this better?"

"Actual gin in the gin?"

Charlotte turns to me. "If we were having a double wedding—remember when we were fourteen and we swore that's what we were going to do?"

"Well, it's a good thing you decided not to wait for me for that!"

"Oh Amy!" she sighs. "I want so much for you to meet someone who loves you as much as I do."

I experience a little pang. "Thank you."

Her head tilts to the side. "Do you ever wonder about Rob?"

"Funny you should ask, I looked him up the other day—three kids and one more on the way."

"Oh."

Rob Mead is my longest relationship to date—six whole months. Of course, I knew from our first kiss that he was going to leave me but on this occasion it was for a job in New Zealand, not another girl. The way he was looking at me in my premonition of our airport goodbye was incentive enough for me to withstand knowing of the impending departure.

"That must have been so tough," Charlotte notes.

"It certainly imbued every moment with a sense of poignancy," I admit. On the one hand I wanted to make the most of him while he was here, and on the other I always felt like I was carrying around a sense of loss. "Plus, it was weird knowing that he got the job before he did."

"If only you could have bet on that at the bookie's." Charlotte sighs then gives a sudden shudder. "You know, I still get chills thinking about Mick."

I nod. "Me too."

We met at an indoor rock-climbing party. He was talking about a trip to Pembrokeshire to try it for real and when we kissed on our pub date I saw myself in a hospital bed. A nurse handed me a mirror to inspect the bruises on my face—I was all swollen and bashed up and my jaw hurt—had I taken a tumble? Was he injured too? But then in he walked and my whole body went cold with terror. He was the perpetrator. I remember my nails digging so deep into the nurse's hand that she ushered him straight out of the room. I was so freaked out by the vision that my hand was actually shaking when I reached for my drink. I excused myself from the pub saying that I felt a bit faint, which I did, and when he followed up with a text I went into graphic detail about my upset stomach so he would never see me in a romantic way again. It worked for me but I hate to think of the next girl he zoned in on. If only everyone who kissed him could see what danger lay ahead.

After that I went through what May called my "Kiss Me Quick!" phase—swooping in at the earliest opportunity because I felt I couldn't trust my judgment and needed some insight into the man's character before I'd even agree to go for coffee. Sometimes we would place bets on what the outcome might be—runs off with another man, wildly jealous, sentenced to life imprisonment...

Of course, it hasn't always been so extreme, there are milder reactions—basically when I like them less at the beginning and despise them less at the end. That feels more like a "Sorry, no dice. Thanks for playing, better luck next time." And, yes, I do get back hours of my life that I would have wasted on the wrong person but it's a bit like school—you might not like every subject but you end up with a well-rounded education. I've always felt I'm missing out on the practical aspect—the actual relationship with all its highs and lows. But would you keep turning the pages if you already knew how your love story was going to end? It's like putting a stack of money on a roulette number when you know you are going to lose. Or buying an expensive sweater that will no longer fit after three wears. Mind you, if I really fancied them, I did try to apply the sentiment "Tis better to have loved and lost than never to have loved at all," and do it anyway.

Charlotte giggles as we start to peel away our masks. "Remember when you tried the *Pretty Woman* angle?"

This isn't quite how it sounds—no thigh-high PVC boots required. I just wanted to have a physical encounter without all the spoilers so I told the guy in question that I had a fantasy about cutting straight to sex with no kissing. Crafty, right? I could be as oblivious as the next woman about what was coming next. But that just proved to be extremely uncomfortable in all senses of the word. If I'd kissed the guy in question, I would have seen myself making a hasty exit after an excessive barrage of grunts and commands. At least the sex worker motif paid off in that sense—the bedroom activities were strictly limited to an hour.

"I still think it's very cool," Charlotte says as we peel away our masks. "One day it will serve you well."

"Would you want to know about you and Marcus?" I ask as I rub the excess moisturizer into my skin.

"If I could go back to our first kiss?" She frowns.

"How about if you could kiss him at the moment you are declared husband and wife and know whether you were going to make your paper or diamond anniversary, would you?"

She looks freaked out. "Absolutely not."

"Why?"

"Because I love him and I'm happy and I don't want anything to spoil this feeling." And then she blinks as if the penny has finally dropped. "Oh Amy, I'm sorry. I never really realized."

"Don't be!" I wave away her concern.

She's quiet for a moment and then ventures, "You know, there is someone interested in you coming to the wedding…"

I roll my eyes. "Your cousin Elliot doesn't count."

He's had a weird crush on me since we were teenagers. Charlotte briefly moved in with his family when she was going through a rough patch with her mum and then felt obliged to invite him along when we went out as a group. He wasn't a bad-looking guy, definite boy band fodder, but whenever he came out with us I would feel his eyes upon me. I don't know if it was because my boobs were starting to kick in or, more specifically, *out* but there was something creepy about his stare and the way he always ended up sitting next to me. One time we shared a bumper car at the fairground and he repeatedly threw his arm across my chest on the pretext of protecting me from the moment of impact, never mind that he was the one hurtling us headlong into every available surface.

"I was thinking about his spin-the-bottle party the other day—"

"Let's not go there!" I cut in. "I still have nightmares about that near-miss." I reach for my faux gin. "I suppose I should be flattered that he's still interested twenty years on. But I'm not."

Charlotte gives a little smirk. "I wasn't talking about Elliot."

My head snaps round. "What?"

She purses her lips. "I promised I wouldn't say anything."

"Promised who?"

"The guy."

"What guy?"

"I don't know him well but he saw your picture when Marcus and I were working on the table plans and he expressed an interest. He made me promise I wouldn't say anything so he wouldn't feel self-conscious when he approached you."

"He's going to approach me? Do you think I'll like him?"

Her face falls.

"Oh great."

"You never know, though. Look at me and Marcus!"

I nod, trying to hide my disappointment. "So, talk me through the plans for the day again…"

Three times Charlotte rushes out to check on things in the out of bounds rooms and each time I pledge I'll go for a simpler ceremony. By the time we climb into bed I finally have a vision for my wedding day—a Vegas drive-thru.

We're just getting ready to turn out the light when Charlotte turns to me and says, "Amy, I want you to know that I'm never giving up on you finding your love. I might be getting married but I'm in this as much as you and I'm always looking out for your heart. Even when you want to give up, I won't."

A tear slides down my cheek, my heart hurting a little from the sweetness of this sentiment. "That's so kind of you." My voice wavers. "Now, please stop worrying about me and let yourself be happy."

"If you insist," she replies, turning out the lamp. But even in this shadowy light I can see the ruck in her brow.

I study her for a moment and then ask, "Why did you really want your mother to be here tonight?"

She gives a half-smile. "It's silly."

"Tell me."

She turns to face me. "When I was a little girl, she used to smooth my brow to try to stop me from overthinking. She always had the coolest fingertips...I thought maybe she'd do it one more time, so I could have a good night's sleep before the wedding."

"You haven't been sleeping?"

She shakes her head. "There's just so many details to think of—it has to be perfect."

I'd be wasting my breath arguing that point. Instead, I press my hand to the icy dregs of my drink on the nightstand. "Just relax now," I say in my best meditative voice. "Find a comfortable position, let the tension in your shoulders go. That's right,"

I say as she settles into the pillow. "Breathe in for seven, out for seven…"

And then I reach over and gently smooth her forehead, from the middle of her brows, sweeping up to her hairline, over and over again, until she falls asleep…

4

I wake to a note on her pillow.

*Slept like a dream! Thank you—best wedding gift
I could have asked for!*

I smile contentedly—well, that was a job well done!

*See you in the turret before the ceremony—I'll text as soon as my
hair is done. The keys to your new room are on the breakfast tray
outside the door under the silver sugar bowl.*

There's a breakfast tray?

I swing my legs out of bed and hurry to open the door. Set
neatly on a side table is an ornate tray straight out of *Downton
Abbey*. I reach to touch the silver coffee pot—youch, still hot.
How did they know what time I'd wake up? I wonder if they've

refreshed it every half an hour. The ensemble is heavy to lift but I make it back inside and then hesitate, feeling this could end badly if I try and rest it on the bed. Instead, I set it on the writing desk and then peer under the covers of assorted delights—fruit bowl, yogurt, a super-flaky croissant…There's also a second note.

One last thing! Could you call Gareth and ask if he can
bring one more table display? The owner's dog peed on one.
On the table. Don't ask.

I shake my head. I don't know how she copes, organizing events, being responsible for every microscopic detail. At least she's getting better at delegating, though that is especially stressful for the person she is putting her trust in as she has such high standards. I pour myself a cup of coffee, delighted to find the milk is also hot, and then pull the desk chair over to the window so I can look out across the grounds as I make my call to Gareth.

"Morning!" I sing-song.

"Well, you sound happy."

"I slept at the castle last night—filling in for Charlotte's mum."

"Ohhh," he says. "Is she going to be at the ceremony?"

"I don't think so."

"Mmmm," says Gareth—about the closest he'd ever get to bitching about someone.

"So. Table displays. Do you carry a spare?"

There's a moment's hesitation. "What happened?"

"You don't want to know."

"How many?"

"Just one. Well, I say 'just' one—I know each one is artfully crafted."

"That's okay, I can do it," he assures me. "I'll come over as soon as it's ready."

"Thank you so much! And sorry to hear that Freya couldn't make it. We haven't seen her in an age."

"Right," he says absently, his mind already on foliage accents.

"Okay, I'll let you go. See you later, propagator!"

He laughs. "See you, Amy."

It is a bummer about Freya. Swedish environmentalist by day and major drinker on a night out. I wish I could be as uninhibited as her—she's just so free and unconcerned with her looks, putting all her attention on Mother Earth. She likes stripy tights and wild swimming and never sugar-coats anything. Jay adores her deadpan delivery—he's always suggesting they do open mic night as a comedy duo at the drag club, though she has yet to take him up on his offer to be the au naturel Yin to his bedazzled Yang-a-Lang-a-Ding-Dong.

Freya has never minded a jot that Gareth has three close female friends, probably because the pair of them are such an indisputably good match. I mean, they met at a talk on cryptogam diversity at the Royal Botanic Garden Edinburgh, for goodness' sake! Gareth was working there at the time, following his degree in horticulture, and living with his dad. Freya was looking for accommodation and his father had a spare room that she moved into that weekend. We heard her name a lot and then one day they became a couple. I remember the four of us visiting one spring and them taking us out driving in the Highlands—one minute we were cruising along, the next they had screeched to a halt like they'd spied the Holy Grail. We'd watched with utter bemusement as they set about foraging for some special brewable leaf with not a care for the surrounding thorns and nettles. It was official, we'd concluded, "He's found his person!"

I always imagine their children will look and act like woodland sprites. The one glitch is getting them to live in the same country. Gareth is very invested in his flower shop in Battersea—his weekly window displays have started to be a thing and he wants to expand and open up a cafe. It's such a lovely idea—all herbal tisanes and health-giving elixirs custom-mixed to suit your mood. We even have a name—The Botanist. I see the decor as primarily white and green with a few velvet-backed chairs in primrose yellow and cornflower blue. The flower shop offers such a fresh, dewy fragrance, just breathing in would feel like a tonic. The bold USP would be no wi-fi, no mobile phones—you come here to sit and sip amongst the plants, maybe order a little snack from The Forager menu, and relax.

I adore the idea of working there at the weekend and doing all the branding for his launch, actually using my work skills for something meaningful, as opposed to a diet food that tastes as delicious as its list of chemicals would suggest. So selfishly I hope he doesn't relocate to Sweden, even if I can picture him perfectly in a cabin a-swirl with Northern Lights. Freya's work is holding her there for longer and longer periods which is why she won't be at the wedding, but she wouldn't care for all the excess anyway so perhaps it's no bad thing.

After breakfast, I answer all the last-minute guest queries and check in with Charlotte to see if I've missed any of her hand-written notes.

"There was just the two," she confirms. "I worry about your phone, one more crack to that screen and you won't be able to see any messages."

I feel bad. I promised I'd get a new one before the wedding for this very reason but can't seem to do the deed.

"It'll last today and I'll be with May most of the time anyway so ping her if you need me."

While Charlotte gets back to her eyelash extensions I have a long, steamy bath, which feels deliciously decadent after my claustrophobic shower cubicle at home, and then tend to my make-up, going for a warm glow, cat-eye flicks and an ultra glittery peach lip.

Okay. I think I might have to pare back that metallic shimmer and eyeliner wing but the lip gloss part works.

I reach for one of the complimentary glass bottles of sparkling mineral water. This is so much better than getting sweaty and grimy on a train in from my place. I'm going to save putting on my dress until the last minute so I don't catch it on anything as I drag my case along to the next room. I could go there now but I want to wait for May to arrive so we can be wowed together.

Or not.

Our room turns out to be an attic nook with a slanting, head-bumper of a ceiling and chaste twin beds.

"And so the relegation begins," May complains.

"It's cute!" I say, but as we prepare to change into our wedding outfits I feel the need to prop open the door with my shoe because it seems like the kind of place you'd send naughty children, only to forget about them for a decade or so.

Still, I'm extremely grateful not to have to trek back into London after what promises to be a night of great excess. Oh, and love and refinement, I remind myself as we hear the wafting strains of the string quartet. I adjust my posture—shoulders back, extend a swan-like neck...Suddenly it all feels rather grand and serene, bar the mocking peacock calls. I think they just heard the one about the bride who asked if they could be trained to fan out their tails on cue.

But who needs a peacock when you have Jay? While Gareth is in charge of the floral arrangements and May is security (should anyone other than her get out of line), Jay is head of neck-cricking, as everyone will be doing a double take at the sight of his outfit. I can say that with confidence despite having no idea what he's planning on wearing.

Mind you, May is giving him a run for his money in a sharply tailored lilac suit with satin lapels and cropped trousers, her blue-black hair shorn around the ears but flopping over her right eye. She winks at me as I strike a pose in my dress—the floaty, girlie incarnation of the same fabric.

"The structuring holding everything in place?" she asks, checking the side seams.

"Yup, feeling secure," I say, resetting my boobs and then twirling so she can see the silk flare out.

"Nice. And I'm glad to see you persuaded Charlotte to go for the nude heels."

"I caved on the lilac nail varnish, though—it is her special day."

"Is it?" May looks less than thrilled.

"Don't start," I say. "Is that your phone vibrating?"

She nods. "Tis her ladyship. Apparently she's found a pair of binoculars in the turret—says she can't see us at our designated spot…"

"Oh crap!" I say, looking at my watch. "We've got to run!"

We hurtle down the stairs, across the hall and down the front driveway, turning to wave blindly up at the turret.

"Smile, May, for god's sake," I elbow her.

"I'm trying!" she says through gritted teeth, then turns away with a sigh. "It's just that she was my first girl crush, you know?"

"I know," I nod in sympathy. "I think she was mine too."

May's head snaps to me.

"In a pre-teen crush kind of way," I explain. "Her hair was so pretty and swishy and she always smelled like candyfloss."

"You don't think you've been missing a trick all this time?" May ventures with a smirk. "I mean, you're kissing all these boys and seeing these terrible scenarios play out, maybe you ought to try something different?"

"I can't say it hasn't crossed my mind," I confess. "I used to look at you and Teagan and it seemed a far more harmonious existence."

"Until it wasn't."

"I know. I'm sorry that didn't work out."

"We should never have got married," she tuts as the first gaggle of guests appear on the horizon. "It was just so thrilling to think that we could. 2014 – suddenly all these same-sex couples are at it and we wanted to be part of the historic movement. We just got carried away with it all."

"Totally understandable."

"Word is that she's on the verge of doing it again."

"Really?" I grimace. "How does that make you feel?"

"Oh, you know, discarded, like I was a trial run. Jealous that she's moved on and I haven't – the usual." She shrugs.

"Oh May." I pull her into a hug and kiss the top of her forehead.

"Oh my god! Did you two get together?" Ex-classmate Clancy Hetherington scuttles up to us. "I always thought there was a certain frisson."

May and I exchange a look and then burst out laughing as she totters on her way.

"Something to think about!" May notes and then grips my

arm. "Oh my god, look. Is Melanie Barnes finally preggers? She's been trying since she was fifteen!"

We welcome a mix of familiar and unfamiliar faces, young and old, friendly and snooty. The majority are from Marcus's side of the family, which is why I think Charlotte ended up inviting so many people we haven't seen for years, just to make up her quota.

"I'm beginning to think some of these people are from a casting agency," May notes. "Nobody wears hats like that anymore."

When the third blast-from-the-past asks if May and I are now a couple, May cocks her head. "What if we are meant to be together? What if we've been here under each other's noses all this time?"

I roll my eyes. "You want me to kiss you, don't you?"

"Oh, go on! It would be hilarious to see how things would pan out between us!"

"No way."

"What are you afraid of—getting a vision of us all loved up with little hearts fluttering around us?"

"I know I'm not your type."

"Oh, what's a type anyway? Go on, I dare you!"

"It's not a party trick, May. You know the toll it has taken on me."

"I do know, and I'm not making light of what you've been through. I just think you need to take control of this superpower and show it who's boss."

"And how do you propose I do that?"

"You've got to stop being afraid of kissing people for fear that they'll disappoint you. You said that after mattress guy you were taking a break?"

"I have to, at least for a while."

"No," she asserts. "What you need to do is up your game. You know that business phrase 'Fail faster'? You make a mistake, you don't wallow in it or beat yourself up, you just move on. You kiss them, they're a dud, you yell NEXT!—maybe not out loud—and then you kiss the next and the next and the next."

"That sounds exhausting."

"But it's the only approach that will work. Speed it up!" She clicks her fingers at me. "You've got to be in it to win it."

"Remind me, when did you get your life coaching certificate?"

"It's the champagne. You know it always makes me extra bossy."

"They haven't even started serving it yet."

"That's sweet that you think I would wait to be served." She turns and holds my bare shoulders in her hands, targeting my pupils with her own. "Use today as an experiment. No club in the land has more willing candidates for romance than a wedding. People are at their most lonely and vulnerable. Take advantage of that."

"Um…"

"Or, you could look upon it as offering a service—give the guys something to brag about at the office on Monday. 'There was this one girl—total fox in lilac silk, killer cleavage—'"

Suddenly I take May's face in my hands and kiss her full on the lips.

There's a moment of stunned silence before she clamors, "Oh my god, what did you see? Tell me, tell me!"

"I couldn't possibly!" I taunt, though there is nothing to tell.

"What?" she shrieks.

"I'm serious—I'm taking that one to my grave!"

"Tell me, tell me *now*!" she implores.

I dodge out of her grasp and break into a run, squealing as I go. My plan was to divert from the gravel driveway onto the lawn and sprint over to the walled garden but no—the second I step onto the damp grass my heels sink down, locking me in place.

"Haha! Your girlish ways foil you again!" May is upon me in an instant, tickling me, insisting I tell all when suddenly I get an entirely different kind of premonition—a clear vision of me losing my balance, falling backward and ruining the lilac silk, Charlotte's bridesmaid line-up and all the wedding photos in one fell swoop. There's nothing supernatural about this, it's simply an awareness of gravity.

"Noooo!" I cry out, bracing myself for impact.

But instead of my bottom meeting with sludgy turf I collide with something a good deal firmer—a set of arms bearing me up and sweeping me off my feet like Superman. Only this hero is firmly earthbound, on his knees, looking like he is about to offer me as a sacrifice before the mocking goddess that is May.

"I think you may have missed your calling on the rugby field," she smirks at Gareth.

"You saved my dress!" I gasp in disbelief.

"At the expense of his suit, I fear." May points to his trousers as he sets me upright.

"Oh no!" I wail at the state of his mud-smirched knees.

"Don't worry about that." Gareth brushes aside our concerns along with a chunk of turf. "People would probably be more surprised if I didn't have dirt on me."

"I can't believe you got to me so quickly!" I didn't even see him arrive.

"I came from the house," he explains. "Had to drop off the flowers."

He then turns to May, who is inspecting him from assorted angles. "Can I help you?"

"You know, aside from your knees, you look remarkably clean." May squints. "Let's see your hands."

He holds them out for her assessment.

"Impressive. Did you get a mani?"

"I got a nail brush," he concedes.

"You clean up well, my friend."

He really does. Crisp white shirt, lilac satin tie, silver-gray suit jacket doing its darnedest to accommodate his biceps… But I'm pleased to see there's still a trace of the Gareth we know and love when it comes to the footwear—while the other men are in highly polished dress shoes, he's sporting gray suede desert boots.

"So, what was going on with you two anyway?" he asks. "You looked like you were playing kiss chase."

"Funny you should say that…" I arch a brow.

"She kissed me and she won't tell me what she saw," May pouts.

"She made me do it!" I protest.

"Oh, come on," May scoffs, "you know you wanted to!"

"May!" Gareth scolds. "It's like Me Too never happened!"

"Ooh!" May gasps, grabbing at my arm with undue vigor.

"What now?" I sigh.

"Kiss Gareth!"

Oh. My. God.

"Go on, Freya wouldn't mind!"

"I'm sorry, she's already on the booze." I wince as Gareth flushes pink and turns away, desperately searching for something to point to.

That something comes in the form of May's brother Jay, stomping up the driveway like he's on the catwalk, complete with booming Taylor Swift soundtrack.

"I thought he was joking when he said he was going to install speakers in his shoulder pads," May gasps.

He looks like the result of a *Project Runway* avant-garde challenge with a Prince theme. His torso is an inverted triangle winched to a corsetted waist with a fountain of lavender tulle spilling down to the floor.

"Purple train, purple train," I sing to myself.

"He does know this isn't *his* big day, right?" Gareth ponders.

May clunks her head. "I knew there was something I was supposed to tell him!" And with that she's off.

*

To understand May and Jay, you have to first be introduced to their parents. Mother Saffron was an eighties supermodel turned psychologist; father Vince was a rag trade geezer from the East End. They actually met on a photo shoot in Petticoat Lane, which always makes me picture him in a tweedy hat and waistcoat and her in voluminous lacy underskirts. She loved that he was a bit rough around the edges; he loved that she was smooth as silk. They married swiftly and, when they learned they couldn't have their own children, adopted May and Jay from an orphanage in Malaysia. Saffron loved to dress the twins in his 'n' hers outfits. They had similar bob haircuts at the time and no one really noticed when they would switch clothes—May coveting Jay's sharp shorts and braces, Jay wanting May's ruffles and bows. Both looking outrageously cute either way.

When Saffron passed away tragically young, Vince couldn't fathom raising the twins on his own but they were also what kept him going through this darkest time, so he kept them close at hand. Their primary playroom was a fabric warehouse filled with endless off-cuts and scraps and their dolls were always the most fashion forward in town. Jay loved how each fabric texture told a different story and was always experimenting with costumes, dressing himself to the ninety-nines and demanding May take pictures, which is where she honed her photography and art director skills. She had a knack for finding unusual or contrasting backgrounds, always busily cycling around London scouting locations.

Many a time people would yell comments at Jay's pose or out-fit but May would give them as good as he got and, frankly, could scare off any mouthy fool. She seemed to have X-ray vision for people's weaknesses and would hone in on them with laser precision, leaving them to scurry away, tail between their legs. But then Jay found his tribe—and dream clientele—at Comic Con, quickly getting a name as the creator of the most outra-geous, colorful, head-turning cosplay creations. Or, as he likes to call them, everyday wear.

Meanwhile May has become known as the most badass fash-ion and portrait photographer in town. I can totally see why people are intimidated by her but none of us take offense at the things she says, no matter how much she might wish we would. I just hope she doesn't take it too far today and pipe up at a sig-nificant point in the ceremony...

For now, I return my attention to Gareth's trousers. "You know, if we used a hairdryer on the dirt it would turn to dust and we could probably brush off most of it."

"It's okay—no one's going to be looking at me anyway. Not with all you beauties at large. Not large—you know what I mean."

"I do." I smile fondly. "Do you think May ran away so she wouldn't have to get fitted for her hair vine?"

"Oh, I got a buttonhole for her," he notes. "I value my life."

My phone buzzes. "It's Charlotte. Ready to go?"

He nods and offers me his arm but I take one step and my heels sink down again.

"Darnit! How do other women do this?"

"Here," he says, scooping me up for the second time. "It's easier if I just carry you."

I wouldn't have thought that the concept of "easy" and carrying me could exist in the same sentence but somehow he makes the action seem effortless. As he lightly shifts my body to get a better grip my skirt slips away at the back so that one of his hands is now firmly gripping the bare skin on my thigh. I turn my face toward his neck so he can't see the effect that the skin-on-skin touch of a man is having on me. It's been a while.

"Oi, mate!" a voice heckles us. "I thought it was the bride that was supposed to get carried over the threshold!"

Suddenly I'm aware of all the eyes upon us.

"Oh my god, are you two together?" Shelley Lane coos, still keen to create gossip from thin air.

I roll my eyes as Gareth sets me down but she's gone before I can respond.

"If it's any consolation, they said the same about me and May twenty minutes ago."

"Really?" he laughs. "Not that I mind them thinking that."

I raise a brow.

"It might deter Joy Mellor," he clarifies.

I give a little chuckle. Joy Mellor had been the school pin-up of our year and as such, she'd never been able to accept that Gareth wanted no part of her. No matter how many times she'd offered herself to him.

"Actually, you're off the hook," I say as we head inside. "Joy cancelled this morning—burned her hand with her curling tong—it was rolling off the counter and she went to catch it."

"Noooo!" Gareth shudders.

"I know. Those things are a million degrees." My hand inadvertently goes to the tip of my ear and then my cheek, both of which have experienced the scorching. "Of course, I'm more sorry Freya couldn't make it. It feels like ages since we saw her. What conference is she at this time?"

"Um..." Gareth seems quite tortured by the effort of remembering.

"They always have such convoluted titles, don't they?" I say as we head up the stairs.

"I—I should know," he frets, "I even wrote it down..."

"It's okay," I say, not wanting to stress him further. "I know it's something that is going to help save the planet and that's all that matters."

We've only made it halfway to Charlotte's suite when Gareth suddenly seems incapable of proceeding, both physically and verbally.

"Everything okay?" I nudge him.

He looks back at me.

"Gareth?"

"Can you keep a secret?" He ushers me closer to the wood paneling.

I look around. "Well, generally, yes. But you are asking me before I am about to drink an obscene amount of alcohol with a large group of people, most of whom still have good hearing."

"You're right. It's not the time." He goes to move on.

"Not the time for what?" I reach for his arm.

"No, nothing."

"Is it Freya? Has something happened? She's not ill, is she? Or pregnant?" My voice makes a little leap but Gareth's expression is less than celebratory. "Tell me," I urge.

"We broke up."

"*What?*" I reel. "When?"

"Two months ago."

"*Two months!*" I exclaim and then try a more hushed response because I still can't believe it. "Two months?"

"I didn't want to say anything to unsettle the bride." He nods in the direction of Charlotte's suite. "No one wants to think about friends breaking up before they say I do."

"True," I nod. "But, Gareth, really? You've been going through all this heartache alone?"

"It's fine."

"No, it's not!" I protest.

"Well, today really isn't the day to go into this. I'm sorry I even mentioned it. I just felt so bad lying to you."

"Trying to lie to me," I correct him. "You didn't really land that plane."

"I guess not." He looks deflated.

"It's okay. By the time twenty more people have asked after Freya, you'll have it down."

"Maybe I shouldn't risk seeing Charlotte? You could take the hair vines in for me?"

"Are you kidding?" I hoot. "She'd be all, 'Where's Gareth? What's wrong? The centerpieces have wilted, haven't they? I've had nightmares about this and it's all coming true!'"

"Hmm." Gareth acknowledges the likelihood of this scenario.

"It'll be fine. I can cover for you if she asks. Besides, there's only half an hour to go before the ceremony and you know she always finds you a calming influence."

He concedes a nod. "Last week she said I was the next best thing to having a tree for a friend."

I chuckle. "You know she meant that as a compliment?"

"Of course," he acknowledges. "It might actually be the nicest thing anyone has ever said to me."

"Well then."

He gives a light shrug. "Okay, let's do it!"

5

The honeymoon suite is far bigger than its tucked-away entrance would suggest. We step into the cream-dream of a lounge area and find the sofas, side tables and shelves discreetly accented with lilac—a cushion here, a candle there, even the book covers coordinate.

"Look at this—they've even got crystallized violets on the chocolates…" Gareth notes.

I remember this is what sealed the deal for Charlotte—not the chocolates but the fact that the venue offered the option of switching out the room's accessories to coordinate with the color theme of the wedding. These days one's Instagram feed is as much a factor as what the guests are being fed.

We see that one door leads to the luxe bathroom, which means Charlotte must be up the spiral staircase, sequestered with her hairdresser in the turret bedroom.

"Charlotte?" I lean on the handrail. "It's me and Gareth! How's it going up there?"

"Hey, guys!" she responds with a sing-song voice. "I'll be down in just a sec."

The absence of tension is notable.

"I didn't think you were going to drink until after the ceremony," I call back, with a modicum of concern.

"I'm not. I've had some CBD drops—I keep trying to get freaked out and hysterical but I just can't seem to get there."

I notice Gareth's shoulders retreating from his ears.

"I'm slightly concerned I've numbed myself—what if I'm standing at the altar and the minister says, 'Do you take this man?' And I'm all, 'Meh!'?"

"That's not going to happen," I assure her.

"I hope you're right. Anyway, the bathroom is all yours if you want to fix your hair and then I'll check on it when I'm done."

Ah, there's the Charlotte we know and love.

Gareth and I enter the gleaming marble sanctum—big, angular his 'n' hers sinks, sleek deco fixtures, a multitude of lightbulbs around the mirror. There's even a chaise, should you need to recline while you draw your Chanel No.5–laced bubble bath.

"I might skip the wedding and stay up here," I muse.

But then Gareth presents me with a reason to attend—the most exquisite hand-crafted hair vine.

"I'm not going to outdo the bride, am I?" I worry as I inspect the delicate weave of miniature purple flowers, soft green foliage and tiny glints of amethyst quartz. "It's a total work of art!"

He looks chuffed with my reaction. "Would you like me to fit it for you?"

I nod and hand it back to him, stepping up to the mirror and placing my hands on the cool sink to keep me steady. I watch as he steps up behind me, gently positioning the vine above my loosely twisted bun, taking so much care to arrange it just so.

"When I was doing my research on how to cut the quartz I learned that the word amethyst comes from the Greek '*ame-thystos*,'" he tells me. "The '*a*' means 'not' and '*methystos*' is 'intoxicate'—so it was believed the stone would protect its owner from drunkenness."

"No way!" I gasp. Things just keep getting better.

"They even studded their drinking vessels with it."

"Do you have a matching goblet for me?" I jiggle my brows.

"Hold still!" he laughs. "I have to get it level."

"I've got pins," I tell him, about to reach for my bag.

"No need, I added little hooks as part of the design—the wires bend to intertwine with the hair so it should stay in place, even with all the dancing…"

As he leans in to finesse the fit, I feel as if we really are lord and lady of the manor, getting ready for some gala. But secretly longing for the moment when we're back in our pajamas, cleaning our teeth side by side. That's always been one of my relationship fantasies—his 'n' hers sinks. Charlotte has achieved that in her new home with Marcus and I can't deny, I am a little envious.

I look back at Gareth in the mirror and feel a pang of sadness for his heartache. I loved him and Freya as a couple. I'm sure this is just a blip. I might even give her a call tomorrow.

"All set!" Gareth says, stepping back.

I take out my compact so I can turn and see my reflection.

"It's perfect!" a voice declares from the doorway.

"Charlotte!" we exclaim as we take in the vision before us—Grace Kelly meets Mother of Dragons: her white dress is a cascade of layered chiffon with a deep V neckline and a criss-cross band accentuating her waist. Her hair is at its most platinum, lying in a glossy sheet down her back. As she turns we see why the hairdresser needed a tranquil workspace—the top layer has been woven with intricacy and symmetry to create diamond-shapes, pinched together with tiny pearls.

"I don't know whether to hug you or put you in a glass display case!" I coo.

"Somewhere between the two!" Charlotte replies, graciously accepting air kisses and squeals.

We walk around her, inspecting her like an exhibit.

"Do I look good enough for him?"

"Oh Charlotte!" I tut. "You've got to stop thinking that just because he's rich he's the catch. Money is money but there's only one you."

"You are the goddess to his mere mortal," Gareth decides.

Of all the times for him to get a compliment right, this was the moment. I see Charlotte's eyes gloss in appreciation. "Thank you! I've been taking Alexander Technique classes to help with my posture and everything!"

"As poised as a ballerina!" I commend her.

She flushes a pretty pink and turns to Gareth. "Do you have the rosebuds?"

"Of course," he nods. "White to symbolize new beginnings."

He opens the case to reveal their petite perfection, complete with gold-dipped stems.

Charlotte's chest heaves with delight. "Do you want me to sit or stand while you add them?"

"You're certain you don't want the hairdresser to do this?" Gareth hesitates.

"Well, for a start she's gone—we went an hour over schedule and now she's late for the next wedding. But in terms of flower arranging, who else could do a better job?"

"He does have the magic touch," I say, leaning back on the banquette to watch him work.

This is so much better than I was imagining. Having these precious, pre-wedding moments be so relaxed and special. I hate to say it but I'm glad May isn't here—I don't have to feel on edge waiting to deflect her next snarky remark about Marcus. I can simply lose myself to the romance of it all.

Initially Charlotte is quiet, not wanting to distract Gareth as he positions each rosebud in its fine blonde cradle, but once the set is complete she switches to friend mode and asks if there's any news on the flat next door to him. We always ask and the answer is always no—no sign of the owners retiring to the Canary Islands, no sign of it coming up for sale, thus scuppering his dream of expanding the flower shop and opening The Botanist cafe.

One day.

"As a matter of fact, there is news."

"Gareth?" I caution.

"About the flat…" He gives me a reassuring look.

"Oh, finally!" Charlotte cheers.

"But not good, I'm afraid."

"Oh noooo," we wail in unison.

"The flat came on the market last night, but the price they're asking…" He shakes his head. "I didn't realize just how much bigger it is than mine—way more square footage and twice what I could afford."

"But The Botanist," I sigh. I so liked the idea of working there at weekends. "Do you think you could maybe add a walk-up window to your place and get permission for pavement seating instead? You could still surround the tables with potted plants."

"Have you seen the forecast for the summer?"

"Oh, I just can't bear it!" I complain. "It would have been such a sanctuary."

Charlotte raises her hand. "Sorry, guys! Jay just sent a text asking if we have a spare long-stemmed rose?"

"Is he planning on clenching it between his teeth?" Gareth asks.

"I'd say there's a ninety percent chance of that."

"I could probably find him something from one of the table displays—without compromising the design in any way," he quickly adds.

"It's fine," Charlotte smiles as he prepares to leave. "Don't forget May's buttonhole!"

"I won't." He gives her a reassuring smile. "Just relax and enjoy the show." He looks back at me. "See you down there!"

I give him a little wave.

"Well?" Charlotte squeals as the door closes behind him.

"Well what?"

"Am I the only one that can see the obvious solution?"

"To what?"

"Salvaging The Botanist dream!" She reaches for my hand. "You buy the flat, Gareth pays for the shopfront portion!"

I blink back at her.

"That way it would be within both your budgets."

I go to dismiss her suggestion but instead hear myself relaying the benefits: "I'd be within walking distance of my mum, I'd get to see the cats every day, I'd be living above a cafe!"

"Yes!" she cheers. "I didn't say anything in front of Gareth because I didn't want to put you on the spot but it's kind of perfect."

"You're such a problem-solver!" I marvel. "Even on your wedding day."

"Is that a yes?"

"I'll give it some thought."

"Well, don't leave it too long—Battersea Park–adjacent real estate isn't going to linger."

She has a point. And I can't say I'd mind the company either. Many an evening I wished I lived closer to my friends. It's fun to meet up for a night out but I'd love to have an actual shoulder to cry on after a bad day and Gareth could probably do with some support right now, not in a talking-about-your-feelings way but we could play backgammon or repot some plants in companionable silence. "Anyway! Back to the more pressing business of your nuptials. Is there anything else you need before the big 'I do'?"

"There is one thing."

"What?"

"I need to know May is going to be okay."

I sigh. "You know she's just acting out because she's afraid of losing you."

Charlotte nods. "I know. I can't seem to get through to her that nothing will change."

"Well, it kind of will and it probably should but that's okay. It's going to be fine."

"She did give me this..." Charlotte reaches into the pocket of her dress and pulls out a petite vintage camera.

"It's gorgeous!" I say, carefully cradling its scaled-down perfection in the palm of my hand. "You're like a spy bride from the 1950s!"

"May says she put sepia film in it because it will be flattering no matter how drunk we get."

"We'll definitely be putting that theory to the test!" I note. "Shall we take one now—the last image of you as Charlotte Dixon?"

"I want you in it too, lean in."

And that's when things go horribly wrong.

Those clever little wire hooks Gareth fashioned for extra

security make a grab for Charlotte's hair and when we go to move apart we find we are joined at the head.

"Owwwww!"

"Oh god, no!" We clamp our heads back together.

The CBD is no match for Charlotte's horror. I can almost feel her brain overheating as we lean into the mirror, trying to see if it's an easy unhook, which it's not.

"I'm going to walk down the aisle with a big patch of hair missing!" she howls.

"Don't panic, we'll fix this."

"How?"

"I don't know but worst-case scenario I could walk to the altar with you." Though Marcus may worry he's getting more than he bargained for.

"Stop moving!" Charlotte screeches.

"I'm just getting my phone out of my bag. We have to get Gareth back."

I dial but there's no reply. No great surprise there.

"Try Jay," Charlotte barks. "He's queen of wardrobe malfunctions."

"You're right! Think of all the stitches he's unpicked!"

We decide he's actually the better call—used to hysteria, always packing his mending kit and never misses a text.

"I can't believe this is happening!" Charlotte wails as we await his response. "I wanted everything to be perfect."

"No tears!" I snap. "Think of the eye make-up!"

She tilts her chin up, which means I have to as well.

"This is just a temporary glitch," I assure her. "Look—Jay's already on his way!" I show her my phone and then place my arm around her waist. "We just need to sit tight."

"Except…"

"What?"

"*I really need a wee…*"

"Tweezers!" Jay holds out his hand in head surgeon mode.

My heart is beating wildly and Charlotte is gripping my hand so tightly my fingers have gone purple.

"Scissors!"

"Nooo!" Charlotte cries out. "This can't be happening!"

"Cut *my* hair!" I insist. "It doesn't matter if *I* have a sticky out bit!"

"If you hold still, no one will lose a single strand," Jay replies, leaning closer.

"You smell divine by the way," I note.

"Light Blue by Dolce e Gabbana," he replies. "I wore it in case this one forgot to wear something blue."

"As if," Charlotte mutters. "I just didn't think that the something borrowed was going to be another person's head."

"Okay, gently now, very gently, ease apart. STOP!" He reaches for a damp cotton bud and then leans in again.

"Why damp?"

"I don't want to leave any white fluff. Okay. You're free!" he cheers, stepping back.

"Seriously?" Charlotte double-checks.

We tentatively move apart, in awe that the only casualty is a rosebud dropping to the floor.

"Just a little early confetti," Jay observes.

"Oh, you're good," I tell him.

He gives a modest shrug. "If I had a pound for every hair extension I've freed from a belt buckle!"

"Belt buckle?"

"Don't ask."

There's a rap at the door.

"Oh my god!" Charlotte grabs at her heart. "It's time!"

"Do you have any more CBD drops?" I ask. I'm really not sure she should be facing the masses in this hopped-up state.

"No! They belonged to the hairdresser. I actually think they were meant for her dog…"

"Let me handle this," Jay asserts. He heads to the door, opens it a crack and tells the venue assistant we will be ready in two minutes and seventeen seconds.

"That seems oddly precise."

"We're going to pray the only way I know how."

And then the musical version of CBD begins wafting from his shoulder pads: Louis Armstrong's "What a Wonderful World."

Charlotte resists for a second but then the warmth of the words gets her swaying along with us. As Louis sings, I sense all the tension ebbing away.

It's going to be okay. It's all going to be okay.

As Louis gives his final, rich, throaty "*Yeah…*" we collectively exhale.

"Ready?" Jay asks.

"Ready," Charlotte confirms.

Gareth and May are waiting for us at the bottom of the stairs. This is May's first look at Charlotte in her full regalia and I can see it quite takes her breath away.

"My queen." She gives a little bow.

Charlotte smiles and then reaches for our hands. "I may be about to pledge my love to Marcus but I loved you guys first, and will do forever."

And then Gareth offers her his arm, ready to take the father-of-the-bride role.

May's eyes sheen with tears, as do mine. I'm not sure about Jay as he has lowered his gauzy birdcage veil. Since Charlotte wasn't wearing one, he felt at liberty to do so and I love Charlotte for not restricting him in any way, though I do notice he prompts more than a few gasps as we enter the room hosting the ceremony.

"Fifty quid says they Photoshop out the freak!" I catch a snigger from Marcus's beer-bellied co-worker.

I hang back for a second as the others step forward. "I heard they are planning to Photoshop your head on that dress..."

The guy's face falls.

"I think it's going to suit you," I smirk as I step forward.

The room is small but ornate with floor-to-ceiling windows overlooking the lawns. My eyes are roaming around, looking for any new kissing prospects, when I catch the eye of

Charlotte's cousin Elliot and give an involuntary shudder. I'll be steering well clear of him tonight.

"You cold?" Gareth asks as we take our seats in the front row. "Would you like my jacket?"

"No, no, I'm fine," I assure him, returning my gaze to Charlotte. She in turn is locked onto Marcus. I'm used to seeing him in a suit but I have to say today's waistcoat has him looking remarkably trim. His eyes have always been a notable cobalt but right now the sunlight is catching them and giving them a laser-glow, sending out beams of love as he watches Charlotte approach.

She's fully in the bride zone now. Even the snooty in-laws look impressed.

As they begin their vows, a smile spreads across my face. You wouldn't necessarily put these two together at first glance but the way they look at each other shows they are a perfect match. I get a warm feeling just looking at them.

Suddenly there's a whoop—it's done! Marcus and Charlotte are husband and wife and kissing with notable ardor.

While everyone else cheers and wolf-whistles, May mutters, "I need a drink."

"Well." I take her arm. "You've come to the right place."

6

There's champagne at every turn, wine awaiting us on the Lilac Room tables and two well-stocked bars set up in the corners for when the room becomes a disco. But I guide May to ye olde bar behind the main staircase. It's a dimly lit cavern, seemingly burrowed into the wall and inlaid with dark wood. The ideal place for covert activity.

With just five minutes before we have to pose for the pictures, I want to have a last shot at persuading her to be happy for Charlotte. And speaking of shots...

"Two Patrón, please."

May knocks hers back in one. "I kept telling myself she wouldn't go through with it. I never thought she'd be the type to marry for money."

"May, sshhhhh! Someone might hear and get the wrong impression."

"I'm just telling it as I see it."

"No you're not, you're distorting the facts and that's not fair. They love each other. You've got to at least grant them their wedding day. Surely you don't want to spoil it for her?"

"It's just…"

"Yes?"

"We're not going to be able to keep up now. He's so megabucks she's going to be in a different league with a whole different lifestyle. She might even give up work!"

"Do you really begrudge her a bit of financial ease knowing where she came from?"

May looks sheepish.

"Let her have her fun," I implore.

She huffs and then summons the barman. "Can we get two more, please?"

"Will you at least smile for the pictures?"

"You know there's one thing I don't do in life and that's mess up photography."

I soften my tone. "I saw the vintage camera you gave her."

May flushes pink, embarrassed to be caught in an act of kindness.

"I thought that was a lovely gift," I tell her. "We want to be able to look back on today's memories with fondness, don't we?"

She concedes a nod. And then her face transforms with mischief. "I tell you what—I'll behave myself on one condition…"

"What's that?"

"You *mis*behave. With at least three men."

"What?" I hoot.

"Come on, we spoke about it earlier. I'm serious about not letting this opportunity pass." She then clasps her hands either side of my head, eyes boring into mine.

"What are you doing?"

"I'm using a Jedi mind trick to convince you to be open to offers."

"You're denting my hair vine."

She releases me testily. "Do we have a deal or not?"

I weigh my options. What is worse, May spoiling Charlotte's wedding or me having to endure three more awful premonitions? I suppose if I drink enough, I won't remember them anyway.

I reach for our refilled glasses.

"Deal!"

We clink, slug them back and slam them down.

I have quite the buzz going for the pictures. May is completely in her element—having originally said she wanted to step down from the day's photography duties, she takes to bossing the unsuspecting replacement snapper around like she's art-directing the annual Hollywood cover for *Vanity Fair* magazine. She bids some guests sit, some stand, some cluster while others are wistful and set apart.

Charlotte is thrilled. Her mother-in-law is less convinced, until May says she needs a solo portrait of her because she looks exactly like Catherine Deneuve.

"You aced it!" I high five her as we head through for dinner. And then I stop in my tracks.

Charlotte said Gareth had gone above and beyond with his floral arrangements but I didn't know she meant literally—we stare wide-eyed at the clusters of purple blooms seemingly cascading down from the ceiling. A slight breeze moves their confetti-light strands and creates a feminine wonderland of fragrance.

"It's so beautiful!" I gasp, looking around for Gareth to congratulate him but Jay tells me he's gone on ahead, in search of a bread roll. "It reminds me of the pictures of Marcus proposing in that tunnel of wisteria in Florence."

"That was the inspiration," Jay confirms. "Oh, for f-oxgloves' sake!" He quickly adapts his swearing as a child passes by, switching between rapture and frustration as he tries to solve the conundrum of wanting to photograph his face from above but needing to hold the camera low to showcase the ceiling.

"How sturdy do you think that chandelier is?"

"No," I tell him firmly.

En route to our table I notice that no one is having to decipher tiny calligraphy name cards because each place setting has a Polaroid-sized photograph of the invitee—in uniform black and white with a subtle lavender tint.

"Who thought of this genius idea?" I ask as we take our places.

"You didn't really think I'd let our girl down, did you?" May smirks.

My heart plumps in delight. "I love it!"

"Good. I've done my bit. Now it's your turn."

She motions to the ridiculously handsome man sat three

place settings to the left of me—honey blond with a golden complexion and a defined chin dimple.

"Talk about a wedding gift."

"May!" I hush her. "Don't make it so obvious. He's way out of my league."

"Nonsense!" she tuts. "Who else is he going to go for—Miss Moneypenny from Marcus's office or the flower fairy that's all but got Gareth's name embroidered on her cape?"

"Who *is* that?" I ask, taking in the auburn-haired vision perched beside him.

"I believe her name is Peony. I saw her eyeing him during the photos. I'm just trying to pick my moment to tell her he's out of bounds because of course Gareth won't even notice that she's into him. I mean, look at her body language!"

She's touching her hair a lot, studying him when he glances away, reigniting the conversation when he lets it subside.

"Apparently she's some kind of Ayurvedic masseuse," May adds.

"Really?" I say, glancing at her dainty hands, each finger adorned with raw crystal in a pastel hue. There's some potential healing right there.

"I'm going to go over there now, before they start serving the food."

"No, no, no." I yank her back down.

"No? Why not?"

"I'd just leave it."

She cocks her head. "I'm not just looking out for Freya; better she knows now that he's not available."

"You don't know the full story."

"What story?"

"I can't say."

"What are you talking about?"

"I can't say because if I do, your face will give the game away."

"No it won't."

"Yes it will."

"Meet me under the table."

"What?"

"No one can see my face under the table."

I hesitate for a second and then knock my fork onto the floor. "Oops!"

"Here, I'll get it!"

"No, I will!" I say, and we both disappear under the folds of fabric.

"Oohh, look at the hand-stitching on Mr. Chin Dimple's Italian leather."

"You and your shoe fixation!"

"You can tell a lot about a person from their shoes. And which way their shoes are pointing," she says, looking accusingly at Peony's laced sandals.

"This is not a bad thing," I begin.

"What do you know that I don't?"

I shuffle closer. Gareth told me in confidence but really only with a view to keeping this from Charlotte. May is already disillusioned about love so it can't hurt, can it?

"Gareth and Freya split up."

"What?" she squeaks.

"And this is why I shouldn't have told you."

"This can't be right!" She bombards me with questions, none of which I have an answer for.

"Well, that's it. The world has gone crazy—Gareth and Freya split up, Marcus and Charlotte marry."

"Sshhhhh!" I despair.

"I might just stay down here until Cupid comes to his senses. I mean, who would ever put a man in charge of love?"

"Come on!" I say, dragging her out from under the table. "What about you and Jay? Have you seen anyone you like?"

"There's nothing here for me and you know Jay, he'll just sit back and let them come to him—moths to a flame."

"Okay, well, let's just try and have some fun."

As I settle into my chair I catch sight of the photo of the man due to sit between us and gulp. It's the guy who called Jay a freak as we were headed up the aisle.

"What?" May frowns at his card. "You've had worse."

"Have I?" I take a look around the room, wondering what's holding him up, only to spy the man in question wedging himself onto the main bankers' table. Ha! He obviously couldn't face sitting next to me. I feel oddly satisfied as I reach for my glass of iced water. I may not be able to attract men on a whim but it's good to know I can repel them when needed.

I go to tell May he got a better offer but instead almost clink my tooth on a proffered bottle of wine.

"Oh, sorry!" The waiter jumps back. "I was just going to ask whether you wanted red or white?"

"Red, please." May moves her wine glass toward him.

"And you?"

For a second I'm thrown by how much he looks like Timothée Chalamet.

"Red or white?" His dark eyes hold my gaze.

"Um, sorry, is it at all possible to order something from the bar? If not, I can go myself but—"

"I can get whatever you like."

Something about his tone sounds so wish-granting, my heart gives a little pang.

"Kraken and ginger ale?" I venture.

"A woman after my own heart," he beams broadly.

I watch him as he moves away. He's so tall, I wonder if he gets a bad back stooping to serve everyone.

"Are we looking at number two?" May raises an eyebrow.

"I wouldn't mind…" I say, surprised to find hope creeping back so soon after swearing off men for all eternity. But that's all it takes, isn't it? A tingle of desire with someone your body responds to…I'm just reaching for my compact to check my reflection when I see one of the other female guests beckoning him over. She's younger and prettier than me with long black hair and the densest of lashes. I watch as she places her hand on his arm and, as he leans down to speak to her, my stomach does a sickening swoop. What am I doing? Could I be any more of a cliché—tipsy girl at wedding flirting with the waiter! I look around at all my paired-up schoolfriends. They've been with their people for years. Clancy just celebrated her tenth wedding anniversary and they were together five years before that. I feel my eyes prickle and suddenly feel in urgent need of some air.

"Where are you going?" May halts me as I get to my feet.

"Just running to the loo!" I say, picking up the pace as I weave through the tables.

"Look! A runaway bridesmaid!" Charlotte's cousin Elliot quips as I pass.

The rain prevents me from running outside and I swerve away from the ladies', seeing how busy it is—I can't do peppy small talk with former schoolmates right now.

Out of desperation, I tuck myself into the nook under the stairs, knowing no one will find me there.

It smells woodsy and a tiny bit musty. I take in the low wooden bench, an empty tweed dog bed and a pair of Wellington boots. How I'd like to slip them on and go striding across the grounds, my trusty pal by my side. I kneel beside the plush cushion to see if I can deduce the breed from the traces of dog hair—I'm picturing a wire fox terrier; they go so well with tweed. And then I see a decidedly modern pair of shoes beside me—black, embellished with a fan of playing cards.

"Your rum."

I bump my head on the low slant of the alcove as I rise up to greet the waiter.

"Ouch!" His hand instinctively goes to my head. "Are you okay?"

The sensation of his touch is so welcome I forget to speak for a second. But then I remember I'm just one of many admirers and focus on the booze. "Gosh, that's good service! How did you know I was here?"

"I saw you as I came out of the bar—lucky I caught you before you curled up for the night."

I give a little snuffle as I look back at the dog bed. "It does look tempting…"

He glances around then asks, "Are you trying to avoid someone?"

I sigh. "Someone, something, maybe even myself…"

"How cryptic…"

I give a shrug. "Nothing more mysterious than heartache and bad choices. Or the other way around—bad choices and heartache."

Did I really say that out loud? Apparently booze acts like truth serum when combined with his soulful eyes.

He goes to speak but a whistle from a fellow waiter calls him away.

"To be continued…" he smiles.

"Keep 'em coming!" I say, raising my glass.

Well. That's interesting. I thought I was on a non-stop train to Tear Town but I seem to have changed track. I take a sip of my drink, getting an extra kick knowing that this is his beverage of choice. It's funny—I've been wanting to feel noticed and this guy saw me even when I was hiding. Maybe tonight *will* be different. I mean, the odds seem to be greater at a wedding, even with so many couples present. Why not go all in?

7

When I return to the dining table I find May has switched seats, placing me next to the out-of-my-league blond with the chin dimple.

"Your first course..." she says, motioning somewhere between the salad plate and his lap.

I push through my embarrassment to greet him. "Apparently we're playing musical chairs!"

He looks bemused then distracted as I lower into my chair, bringing my cleavage into his full view. I knew this neckline was too provocative—the silk drape has a way of falling off to the side, giving the impression that the whole dress might peel away of its own accord. Of course, I know there's no danger of that, but he looks optimistic.

"I'm Tristan," he says. He reminds me of an aftershave model, not just because of the polish of his jawline but because he's been a little heavy-handed with the cologne. It's a clean, almost metallic scent—very banker by day, Bond by night.

"Amy," I smile politely. "You work with Marcus?"

"I do now, but I've known him for years—we did Ten Tors together as teenagers."

I nod as if I know what this means—I think it's something rigorous and outdoorsy designed to help budding alpha males expend energy.

"I'm Charlotte's friend from school." I go to make a joke about how "We did Maroon 5 together as teenagers!" but I don't think he'd find it funny.

"More Sancerre, sir?"

I feel a little self-conscious as my waiter steps between us to top up Tristan's glass.

"And this one." Tristan moves an empty glass into the line of pour. "You seem to have lost yours in the move."

"Oh no, not for me!" I protest.

"Not drinking?"

"I'm just not a big fan of wine."

"That's because you're drinking the wrong wine."

"Is it?" I say, mildly offended.

Tristan leans back in his chair, addressing the waiter. "Do you have a Château Canon 2016? Obviously I'll pay separately."

"I can check."

"I hope you're not doing this on my account."

"My grandparents have a vineyard in Saint-Émilion," he responds. "I can please anyone's palate."

I find myself squirming slightly and turn back to May to see if she'll let me off the hook with this one but she's head down in a whisper with Jay. I never thought I'd say this but it's a blessing when the best man's speech begins.

I fix an amused expression on my face to cover all eventualities and then let my gaze wander. I see that Peony is taking the opportunity to lean into Gareth on the pretext of trying to hear better. He looks as oblivious as ever. She'd better be as nice as she looks. I sneak another peek at Tristan. He's a lot more attractive when he's not speaking. I wonder what it would be like to have a boyfriend that model-handsome. I'd probably want to start an Instagram account just with pictures of him, like people do with their dogs.

"Your wine, sir."

Before Tristan can redirect the bulbous glass of liquid garnet to me, the waiter leans in low and adds, "And your ginger ale, miss."

I smile delightedly. He's trying to stop me making a bad decision, I know it.

"Thank you!" I beam back at him.

"What are you doing?" May hisses at me.

"What?"

"There'd better be booze in that ginger ale."

"You're the worst kind of pimp," I groan.

"Ooh—dimple chin is trying to get your attention," she nudges me.

I turn and find Tristan holding the glass out to me like a villain offering a poisoned chalice.

"Not just yet," I tell him, pretending to be rapt with the speech.

I don't want him to think he can snap his fingers and make a decision for me. I hate to feel steamrollered. Coincidentally, that's exactly how Charlotte felt when she first met Marcus… I listen as the best man relays how Marcus whisked her first class on Eurostar to Bruges on their first date. He'd read about the beautiful swans on the Lake of Love and the folkloric promise that if you kissed your beloved while crossing Lover's Bridge, your romance would be eternal.

I remember her telling us how uncomfortable she felt by him making such an over-the-top gesture when she wasn't even sure if she was attracted to him. She actually refused to kiss him on the bridge. "I mean, I'm not overly superstitious but doesn't that strike you as a little presumptuous?"

She became further frustrated throughout the day as he insisted on the best-of-the-best of everything—she felt she couldn't really get a handle on his personal tastes.

"Do you actually like caviar?" she asked.

"It's Royal Belgian Caviar."

"But do you like the taste?"

It was only when he had a mild panic attack at the top of the Belfry of Bruges tower (having ascended 366 steps at her challenge) that she saw the human being so keen to impress her. And then she kissed him to distract him from his palpitations. It worked.

Look at them now! Mr. & Mrs. Besotted of Pimlico.

I look back at Tristan. I suppose he doesn't have any dastardly motive with the wine. Perhaps I should be flattered by the gesture? Tentatively I slide the glass toward me. He's too busy heckling the best man to notice me taking a sip.

Oh.

Well, that's annoying.

I had prepared a scrunched nose response along the lines of, "I'm sure it's a very fine wine but it's just not for me," but it is actually delicious—silky smooth and reminiscent of violets and blackberries, with none of that acidic aftertaste. When it comes to raising our glasses, only the dregs remain.

"Ha! I knew you'd like it!" He gives a satisfied smile.

"I hate to admit it but I do."

"It's fun trying new things, isn't it?"

He holds my gaze long enough to give it a sexual undertone. For a second I think he's going to lean in and kiss me but he's just reaching for the salt for his chicken dish. Disappointing. Perhaps it's the tequila shots, rum and red wine but I suddenly find myself warming to the guy.

The rest of the speeches prompt a mix of forced laughter and teary-eyed affection—married couples wish they were single, singles wish they were married, and (nearly) everyone wishes the couple the very best, because though it may all be cake and confetti today, we all know how much work wedded bliss can be.

I give Tristan an assessing look. I bet he'd opt for some

week-long bacchanal at his grandparents' vineyard. I have to admit, the chateau sounds idyllic. He's been there every summer since he was a child and shares assorted anecdotes over frangelico coffee and petit fours, breaking in and out of French as he does so. I want to be all chic and knowing but instead find myself asking, "Have you ever trampled grapes with your bare feet?" and "What's the French for hangover?"

Apparently it's "gueule de bois," which translates as wooden mouth. I like this so much that when he heads off to congratulate Marcus, I track down my waiter pal at his new position at the mobile bar near the DJ box.

"You say it 'gool de bwa,'" I tell him.

"Are you working on yours right now?"

"My hangover?" I say, swaying slightly. "Yes, I sense it's coming along marvelously."

He sets a San Pellegrino before me. "You'll thank me tomorrow."

"Oh, will I?" I ask with what I hope is a cheeky glint, conveying my fantasy of waking up beside him. But then I turn away so he can't see me blush.

"So, who would you say is the most drunk person here?" I ask, making a sweeping gesture across the room.

"Besides you?"

"Hey!" I complain.

He smiles. "I'd say that girl who's having trouble standing upright."

We watch for a moment as one of the bankers' wives tries in

vain to straighten her spine—she has to keep reaching for the table, which you'd think was on a tilting fairground ride, the way she's staggering to and fro.

"She's also most likely to throw up."

I grimace. The scene is all too horribly familiar. "What about the man most likely to get a drink thrown in his face?"

"Good one!" he muses. "There was one chap I saw earlier with a super creepy vibe but I don't see him now."

"Ah, shame." I'd like to have seen his choice. "What about most likely to fall over?"

"Easy—the guy doing the Russian Cossack dance."

He lasts three more squatting kicks then falls back and knocks into a table, pulling the cloth and assorted cutlery onto his head.

"Oh, you're good."

"I look upon all this as character research for my work."

"You work at a rehab facility?" I frown.

He chuckles as he shakes his head. "I'm actually working on a screenplay."

"Really?" My eyes widen.

He nods. "And it's impossible to say you're writing a screenplay without sounding like a dick but I can tell you because you'll have forgotten by the morning."

"I will not!"

"Yes you will."

I look back at him. I like that he has his own kind of premonitions and predictions, though his are based on body language and psychology. If his boss wasn't lurking, I'd kiss him now, just out of curiosity.

"I bet you get a lot of women throwing themselves at you at weddings." I test the water.

"Not with a crowd like this."

"Why not?"

"They're more interested in bagging a banker than a waiter."

"You're not a waiter, you're a writer."

He smiles. "I'm both."

"Three beers, mate." One of Marcus's uncles steps up to the bar.

I was planning on continuing our conversation but the DJ has announced the school disco playlist and there's a sudden rush to the dance floor to "Pump It" with the Black Eyed Peas.

"See you later!" I wave at him before I pogo onwards.

"Pump it!" The DJ throbs the sound system.

"Louder!" we all holler back.

Next up is the laid-back beat of Gnarls Barkley's "Crazy," bringing with it a chorus of, "Oh, I love this song!" and "Do you remember when we…?" Suddenly it feels more like a reunion than a wedding. But then I spy Tristan heading my way claiming Justin Timberlake's "SexyBack" as his theme song. He's quite the mover and we seem strangely in sync with the pulsing, synthy beat. He places his hands on my hips, drawing me closer as the lyrics get naughtier. The music is loud, the room is hot and I feel myself surrendering to a drunken haze. I haven't felt this happily hedonistic in a while.

He leans close to my ear. "Are you staying here tonight?"

I feel a shudder rush through my body then nod a little nervously.

"Maybe I can visit you later?" His voice lowers.

I hate to spoil any vision he might have of chasing me around a four-poster bed but I feel obliged to share the reality: "I'm in some kind of children's nursery type room—with two tiny single beds."

"Well, we only need one of them…"

I wag my finger at him. "May is in the other bed and we wouldn't be able to do anything anyway cos the ceiling is so low you'd crack your head." I pause. "Or I would. Either way!" Suddenly I feel very flustered and tell him I need to get some water. "You want some?"

"Sure," he shrugs.

My waiter's bar is too crowded so I hit up the one on the other side of the room. This barman has no qualms about my boozing so I down a double Kraken to make up for the earlier Pellegrino. And then I order a glass of red, seeing as I'm now a sophisticated wine connoisseur. Oh. This one isn't nearly as good as Tristan's fancy one. What was its name? They'd probably know at the proper bar…

"Amy! Come and get in the picture!"

A bunch of schoolfriends are positioning themselves on the main staircase like a family dynasty portrait.

"Cheers!" We all raise our glasses.

"Now, everyone do their sexy pose!"

We couldn't look any more ridiculous. There's a blur of laughter and hugging and spilled drinks. I'm starting to feel dizzy and overwhelmed. I need my friend-friends! Where's May? Where's Gareth? And then someone starts a conga that leads us back to the seething mass of the dance floor. I try to make my way back to Tristan but find myself in the arms of Marcus's grandfather Ernie. He dances in a ballroom hold which feels nice and secure and gives my head a chance to spin freely. So I stay awhile.

"Amy?"

"Hmm?" Did I fall asleep while dancing?

Ernie passes me on to Jay, who has changed into a "casual" purple sequin jumpsuit, allowing him to dance without people stepping on his train. At some point he starts a big salsa circle and we switch from partner to partner. My body tells me I'm back in Tristan's arms before I even see his face. He says something to me which I don't catch, holds me extra tight and then leads me away from the dance floor. I hope we're going outside, the rain would feel so good right now. I've had too many people's hands on me, too much sweat. I just want to wash it all off and clear my head.

"Charlotte!" I reach out for her as we pass and then the next thing I know I've lost Tristan and us two girls are in the nook under the stairs.

"I'm having the time of my life!" Charlotte confides. "I've finally bonded with my mother-in-law—she loves cleaning mirrors just as much as me!"

"I don't know what to say to that but I'm very happy for you!"

"Have you kissed Tristan yet?" She leans in. "May said it was in the cards."

I go to answer but nothing comes out. Have I? You'd think I'd know but my brain seems so jumbled.

"Well, your lipstick is all off," Charlotte notes, applying a smudge of her lip gloss.

"Mmm, tastes like mango. Hey! I meant to ask," I say, grabbing her in a heavy-handed way. "Why did you sit me next to that awful banker at dinner? Not that he ended up at our table but…"

She grimaces. "He was the one who liked the look of you."

"What?"

"The one who was over the night Marcus and I were doing the seating plans…"

For a millisecond I feel bad but, of course, it wouldn't have panned out—love me, love my friends and all that. Speaking of which. "I need to find Gareth!" I try to get to my feet in a hurry.

"To get him away from Peony? She's all over him like a rash!"

I blink back at her. "Yes. Because he's still with Freya."

"Of course he's still with Freya." Charlotte looks confused.

"Oh my god!" I exclaim. "They're playing our song! We have to dance!" Charlotte looks slightly bemused to hear Flo Rida's "Club Can't Handle Me" referred to as our song, but goes along with it anyway.

8

I wake up with a start, banging my head on the low slanting ceiling as I sit upright.

"Owww!" I cry out.

"What is it?" May startles and does the exact same thing. "Jesus!" She grimaces, rubbing her skull. "Why don't they cushion this area?"

"Or just put bunk beds in the middle of the room."

"Right?"

We both lie back down.

"What a night!"

"Was it?" I groan. My brain feels like a porcupine turned inside out and twisted in two. I attempt to turn onto my side. Oh no. There's certain muscles that only hurt after I've been twerking. I peer under the covers. I'm still in my dress. Which I suppose is better than a number of alternatives.

I sense May staring at me. "What?"

"You don't remember?" she gasps.

"Remember what?"

"*You met Him!*"

"Him who?"

"Him-Him!" she urges. "You, Amy Daniels, had a kiss with a good premonition—for the first time in your life you got the happy ending!"

I feel a sudden wave of warmth engulf me—as if the sun itself is shining out from my heart. A sense of wonder and delight flares within me. I have never felt so adored, or such a keen sense of belonging. He knows me, really knows me. And he loves me anyway.

"This is incredible!" I marvel, waiting for his face to come into focus.

But instead, darker images begin layering on top, stifling the beautiful, grateful feelings—there's a tussle, a struggle, a splash of red wine on a white shirt.

"Oh no," I bleat as the anxiety increases.

I'm outside on a street now, it's somewhere I know well yet can't place; voices are raised, angry words exchanged. I feel a mix of outrage and disgust—someone is being accused of cheating, a phone is being commandeered as evidence, there's a screeching sound as a taxi swerves and then a shattering crunch.

"My phone!"

"It's right here," May soothes me, kneeling beside me, looking concerned. "Are you okay?"

"That was the weirdest thing," I say, waiting for my heart to stop yammering. "It all started so well then it took a turn. And then another. It was like three different premonitions, one after the other."

"Well, that makes sense."

"Does it?" I look confused. "What does it mean?"

"It means you kissed three men last night."

"Noooo!"

"Don't sound so scandalized, that was our plan."

"I was only humoring you!" I protest. "I didn't think I'd actually do it."

"Oh, but you did and I have the proof."

She gets up and starts padding around the room, lifting up cushions and moving my suitcase.

"Are you looking for underwear or actual bodies?" Surely she doesn't think I brought all three of them back to the room?

"Tokens," she calls to me from the bathroom. "I'm looking for the tokens."

"If you mean paracetamol, I'll take one."

"Don't you remember?" She stands in the doorway. "You gave me a bottle top for every man you kissed. Aha!" She locates her jacket under the bed and digs out three from the inside pocket, each representing a very different experience for me: one blissful, one vexing, one alarming.

I twirl the crimped metal around my fingers. "I think one is Tristan."

"He was my first bet," May concurs. "But what about the other two?"

My head hurts just attempting to use it.

"Try and give me a visual," she encourages. "I could do a suspect sketch if you can describe their features…"

While May gets poised with the bedside pen and notepad, I prop myself up with a pillow and try to pick out a face from the blurry images in my mind. I can barely differentiate between them, or the associated sensations. It's like when we were dancing our chaotic version of a Cuban rueda—salsa-ing in a circle, switching partners at every call. I feel dizzy just thinking about it: the steps, the turns, passing from body to body. Some partners were masterful, some grabby, some timid. Some smelled divine, others not so much. But of all the men I danced with, one face is clearer than the rest.

"You know, I did spend a lot of time dancing with Ernie."

"Marcus's grandad?"

I nod. "He was serenading me."

I recall resting my head on his shoulder, closing my eyes and listening to his warbling. "It was so romantic."

"Please tell me you didn't kiss him?" May gasps.

"No, of course not," I tut. Though I can't be 100 percent sure.

"I do remember that baklava routine got pretty steamy."

"Bachata," I correct her. "Who was that guy? He looked like Bruno Mars."

"He really did, so no need to sketch him." May reaches for her phone. "I wonder if Charlotte has a guest list we could check through?"

"We can't bother her on her honeymoon!"

"It hasn't started yet, she won't mind." May is already texting her. "Besides, you know she's our best bet for solving the mystery—she's always the first to get the clues at the escape rooms."

This I can't deny.

"You want some water?"

May nods without looking up from her texting.

I get up and shuffle over to the bathroom, leaning against the wall as I set the tap running. Something about the sound of the water triggers another swoop of emotions—a longing, a tenderness. As I hold the glass under the tap I see my hand is shaking. I let the water overflow and trickle over my fingers. It was raining last night. Did I go outside? I peer into the mirror. Nope. I know what my hair looks like when it's exposed to the merest hint of moisture. My "do" is no longer up but the strands are fuzz-free.

"Did you remove my hair vine last night?" I call to May.

"Yes, and what a bastard that was—all those little claws."

So much for amethyst preventing drunkenness. I check my chin for stubble burn. Nothing. Apparently I didn't kiss anyone for very long or with any great vigor.

This is weird. I should be feeling ecstatic—I met Him! Kissed Him! But instead, I feel confused and slightly ashamed.

"Did I make a complete fool of myself?" I ask as I set down May's glass on the bedside table.

"Not to my knowledge but I think we need to pool our resources to get the complete picture. Speaking of which. We need to check your phone for photos."

"What about yours?" I ask.

"I didn't take any pics."

"*What?*"

"Well, I knew Charlotte's photographer was capturing all the special moments and I was saving my battery in case I found Marcus in the coat room with one of the bridesmaids."

"We were the bridesmaids," I despair.

"You know what I mean."

I heave a sigh and start thumbing through my pictures. All of them were taken early on when everyone was still with their make-up and dignity intact, posing in deliberate, self-conscious ways to show off their best angles.

"Well, that was no help."

"Check your contacts," May suggests. "See if you added anyone new."

"How would I know if they were new?" I ask, scrolling through the all-too-familiar names.

"Look at recents—people often call to save entering the number."

"Oh my god!" I grab her arm. "Tristan Wedding."

"Why are you looking so stricken?"

"He's an outgoing call—at three a.m.!!!"

May huddles up. "Ooooh! Booty call. I guess that puts him at the top of the Most Wanted list."

I scrabble around the debris in my mind, trying to remember what was said but finding no trace. "This can't be good," I fret.

"Why don't you text him, see what he says?"

"No way. Can you imagine if I called and said, 'I had a premonition that you're The One! We're going to get married and have kids and grow old together and you're going to love me forever and ever'?"

"Well, if you said all that, he would have changed his number by now so you've got nothing to lose."

"You're not helping," I tsk.

"Yes, I am. Text him."

I gnaw at my thumbnail.

May gets to her feet. "Knowing how long you take to compose a text message, I'm going to jump in the shower. Be ready to press send by the time I come out."

"Bossypants."

"You say that like it's a bad thing when it only makes me *more* like Tina Fey."

It takes me her full shampoo, soap and towel dry to come up with the wording.

> *Hi Tristan. I am one of the many drunken women at Charlotte's wedding but more specifically the one who called you at 3 a.m. As I have no recollection of what was said, I wondered if I should be apologizing or blushing, or both. Then again, perhaps you too have no idea...*

I add a little fingers-crossed emoji.

"Now, which face emoji should I add?"

May reaches over me and presses send.

"*What did you do?*" I squeal.

"Firstly, we don't have time to assess every possible implication of every eyebrow slant and O-shaped mouth. Secondly, Tristan doesn't strike me as an emoji kind of guy."

"You have a point there," I concede.

"Wahhhh!" I leap up as the phone buzzes in my hand. "He's replied. Oh god, he's replied. I can't stand it!" I grab the pillow and put it over the screen.

May tuts and reaches for it, cocking her eyebrow and adopting a seductive tone as she reads his words:

Oh, I remember everything…

My stomach dips as the rest of me swirls with lust.

"What do I say to that?" I panic.

"He's typing…" May alerts me.

I peer at the phone over her shoulder, clutching at her petite frame.

"Amy, you're hurting me."

"Sorry, sorry." I release her and pace across to the other side of the room, trying to get a grip. "What's he saying?"

Dinner. Saturday. My treat.

I give a little squeal of excitement. Whatever I said at three a.m., it's got me a date. Not coffee, not a drink or a quick bite — actual dinner. With a man that could be my warm feeling. I twirl around and then hurry back to May's side. I should probably reply.

"Just keep it short and sweet," she advises.

Lovely! I type. A model of restraint.

There's a short pause where I fear he's changed his mind and then:

Milo's of Mayfair. 7 p.m.

"He's out to impress," May notes.

I tell him I'm looking forward to it but he doesn't respond further. Which is fine. He's obviously a grown-up, talk-in-person person which is something I am hoping to become.

"Well, do you think he's The One?"

"I don't know!" I tap my lip. "I don't know anything anymore. I always get it wrong. I would have said he wasn't my type; he's too good-looking for a start."

"Talk about first world problems."

"It's just all so weird," I sigh. "One dream option but two horrible ones. How am I going to know if I'm making the right choice?"

"Well, I guess the only way is to date all three of them."

"I'm not some reality show contestant!" I protest. "I honestly don't think I'd have the emotional bandwidth to juggle three men. Even one is pushing it."

"You really are going to have to get over yourself," May tuts. "And learn to trust your instincts. On some level you'll know if it's right when you're with him."

I nod, wanting to believe her.

"Of course, there's the small matter of identifying the other contenders in this love triangle."

"I think technically it's a love square," May notes, but then her phone bleeps and she punches the air. "Yes! Charlotte says to meet her downstairs in the Lilac Room in twenty minutes. I knew she'd be into this!"

"Isn't she supposed to be leaving for her flight?"

"She says Marcus will take care of the packing so she's got nearly an hour free. And she wanted to see us all before she leaves anyway." May reaches for the guest phone and dials the kitchen. "Hello? Yes, I was wondering if we could get coffee and some breakfast items for five in the Lilac Room?"

I'm just staggering over to the bathroom when May puts her hand over the receiver and hisses, "Amy! Wait!"

"What?" I jump.

"Before you wash off all the evidence, do you think we should cover you in talc and dust you for fingerprints?"

I hate to spoil her fun as she falls about giggling but I'm genuinely worried about making the wrong choice here—I have a horrible feeling there might have been more than a phone crunching under the wheels of that taxi.

9

Charlotte is already waiting for us in the Lilac Room, stood beside a table loaded with every place card. Correction—every *male* place card.

"We haven't got much time before I leave for the airport—we need to establish a list of suspects." She addresses us like she's the head of MI5. "I've divided up the photos into groups: single men, married men and married men that would cross the line."

I can't help but notice that Ernie is in that section.

"His wife is just as bad," she tells me when I voice my dismay.

"I did dance with him rather a lot," I worry.

"It's okay, I already asked him and he told me no."

"You asked Marcus's grandfather if he kissed me?"

"We're looking for answers here, Amy. I've been waiting twenty years for you to have a good premonition, I'm not going to let this man slip through our fingers now. Whoever he is."

"Okay," I gulp.

"So. Starting with the single men."

"Tristan," says May with a mouthful of chocolate croissant. "She's already bagged a date with him."

"Nice going," Charlotte says as she clears a space for likely candidates.

"We can rule out cousin Elliot," I say with a shudder. "I know you're related but he creeps me out."

"That's okay, he creeps me out too," Charlotte admits.

"I remember this cutie." I point to a man with mini dreadlocks. "I think I had a conversation with him near the toilets."

"He's nineteen."

"Well, booze doesn't discriminate on the basis of age."

"Do you want me to put Ernie back in the running?" Charlotte raises a brow.

"No," I pout.

"What's Jay doing in the possible group?" May snorts.

"You know how carried away they get with their dance routines," Charlotte explains. "I thought Jay might be a red herring kiss."

"Where is he anyway?"

On cue the door is flung open and in wafts a figure in a gold turban, black sunglasses and a lurid kaftan.

"Ah, here's Gloria Swanson now."

Jay quickly assesses the situation and then moves his place card over. "I was drunk but I wasn't that drunk."

"Charming!" I mutter as he heads for the coffee.

"No offense. Besides, it was take a ticket and get in line with you last night."

"What did you see?" we clamor. "We need details!"

He sets down his coffee cup. "You mean, aside from Amy dance-flirting with every man in the place? Honestly, it was like watching J-Lo in *Hustlers*."

"Oh god!" I groan.

"But did you see her *kiss* anyone?" May demands.

"Well, there was this guy." He points to Tristan. "But I'm guessing you already knew that. I did walk in on you in the kitchen at one point. That must have been near the end of the night because I wanted a snack to take up to my room. And apparently you did too…"

"The waiter!" I exclaim. "I'd forgotten about him! Oh, he was lovely!"

"What was his name?" Charlotte gets out her pen. "I'll call the catering agency."

"No idea." I bite my lip.

"Well, can you describe him?"

"He had a sort of Timothée Chalamet vibe—tall, floppy dark hair, wistful…"

"And cool shoes," May chimes in. "I remember they had playing cards on them—like poker or blackjack."

"Yes!" I confirm. "I saw that too. The design looked like something you'd find in a tattoo parlor."

"Blackjack tattoo shoes," Charlotte adds to her notes.

"There was this one other guy..." Jay squints into the distance like a fairground psychic.

"Yes?"

"I think you were having some kind of argument with him."

May and I exchange a look.

"Can you remember who?" Charlotte encourages him to study the faces in the photos.

"I only saw the back of his head—I was on my way over to see if Amy was okay but then Beyoncé came on so..." He gives a little shrug.

"Wait, do you mean 'Crazy in Love'?" I ask.

He nods.

"I was definitely there for the Jay-Z break." That's my party trick, doing the "crazy and deranged" rap while Jay prowls around me.

"Oh yes," Jay confirms. "I guess it wasn't a long argument."

"Hmmm." My brow furrows. "You didn't happen to see me throwing red wine on him?"

"Are we going to have to get a bodycam for you?"

"If only I was wearing one last night," I sigh.

"You know, I did video you at one point." Jay reaches into the folds of his kaftan and pulls out his phone. We huddle around him but all he has to show are a million artful selfies. "That's so weird, I could've sworn I filmed you and Gareth on the dance floor."

" 'Hey Ya!' " I gasp, feeling a rush of joy—finally something I remember! Gareth was resisting joining us on the dance floor so Charlotte got the DJ to play the one tune he can never resist—"Hey Ya!" by Outkast.

We created a routine for it one lunch break in our last year of school, figuring even Gareth could manage the three hand claps, gradually building up to outstretched arms and wiggly fingers. It always cracked us up because the rest of us were giving it full-body sixties swing and he was so stoic and upright. But last night he broke free and was really shaking it like a Polaroid picture. Everyone was screaming in delight. Except maybe Peony.

"You know, I don't remember seeing Gareth again after that," May muses.

"Has anyone seen him since?" I ask, feeling a little uneasy.

We look between each other but draw a blank.

"You don't think he went home with Peony?"

"He would never be unfaithful to Freya!" Charlotte splutters.

May and I exchange a look.

"What?"

"Nothing."

"That wasn't a nothing look," she accuses.

"Just tell her!" Jay huffs.

"You told Jay?" I turn on May.

"You know how much he loves Freya, I didn't want him hearing through the grapevine."

"Hearing what?" Charlotte demands.

"Look, we didn't want to say anything to spoil your day but they split up, two months ago."

"Who did?"

"Gareth and Freya."

"They didn't!" She's aghast.

"I'm sure it's just a temporary thing, they'll totally sort it out," I try to back-pedal.

"Of course they will!" Charlotte instantly latches on to the hope.

"It's just a seven-year itch."

"Of course! It has been seven years, hasn't it?" Jay confirms.

"Well, that explains it."

"Nothing to worry about."

"Nothing at all. I'll just text him again. Make sure he's okay."

"In the meantime, Jay—gaydar. Anyone else we can rule out?"

He dutifully studies the place card photos and then moves a number of them like he's playing a game of chess. "Though two of these may not know it yet," he concedes.

And then the door swings open and in walks what is left of Gareth.

Gone is the pristine man we were admiring yesterday—his hair is a mess, his eyes are shadowy and I'd say he might have cut his lip shaving were it not for the uneven stubble.

"You look like you fell down the laundry shoot," Jay observes.

"And then got roughed up by a bear," May adds.

"Are you okay?" I ask, stepping closer.

He nods but even that seems to hurt his head.

"You look really fragile."

"I'm fine. I just didn't get much sleep."

"Miss Peony keep you up all night?" May teases.

"Nothing happened there. We just exchanged numbers."

"I thought you two would have a lot in common," Charlotte acknowledges. "Not that I was trying to fix you up because I didn't know then…" She trails off, flushing pink.

"But you do now?" He looks at me.

"I'm sorry!" I wince. "It came out by accident. Just a few minutes ago."

He holds up his hands. "Okay, we're not getting into this now. This looks a lot more interesting, like you're playing a real-life game of Clue."

"That's right," Jay titters. "We're trying to track down Professor Plum and his lead pipe."

I roll my eyes.

"Amy kissed three guys but she can't remember who," Charlotte clarifies.

"Really?" Gareth rubs his face wearily. "Does it matter who if they were just more bad premonitions?"

"As a matter of fact it does, because one of them was a good premonition!" May asserts.

This stops him in his tracks. "Are you serious?"

I nod.

"Wow. That's major. Congratulations."

"Thank you," I say, not feeling remotely celebratory.

"We know one of them was Tristan." Charlotte brings him up to speed. "But as for the other two…" She directs his attention to the cluster of "possibles." "Do any of these faces prompt a memory?"

"You really don't recall anything?" Gareth turns back to me.

"I know it sounds bad, but the whole night is a blur—I recall glimpses of faces, snippets of conversation, flashbacks to dance moves…"

"Your phone!" Jay grabs Gareth's arm. "I was videoing Amy with *your* phone!"

"What?"

"Remember you were videoing us and then 'Hey Ya!' came on so we switched!"

Well, that's one mystery solved. We cluster around Gareth and eagerly wait for him to press play.

The first few minutes show the tail end of our "Crazy in Love" routine. It's a little disappointing to see the gap between how I think I look in my head and how I actually look on screen. Though I have to say Jay is fully channeling Queen Bey.

And then we hear the opening bars to "Hey Ya!," seamlessly blended by the DJ. I respond by squealing and lunging at Gareth. The phone records the floor for a second or two and then we hear Jay telling us divas to show him what we've got.

Apparently we have a lot to show.

Suddenly the video is interrupted by a phone call, from Freya.

We all tense and look expectantly at Gareth.

"Just ignore it." He reaches over and presses decline.

"Are you sure you don't want to get it?" Charlotte tries in vain to keep her voice light.

Gareth shakes his head in an emphatic no.

We go to press play but the phone rings again. It's Freya, again.

"It seems like it might be urgent…" I venture.

"I already know what she's going to say."

"Do you?" May challenges.

Gareth sighs and rubs his brow. "She's getting married."

"*What?*" We gasp and look between each other as if seeing our own shock mirrored back might somehow make it easier to process.

"And before you ask, I don't know any of the details, I just found out last night."

Well, that explains his disarray. Obviously we were all too drunkenly oblivious to console him, whenever it was that he found out.

Charlotte looks serious. "I think we need to address this, while we're all together."

"We really don't. Let's get back to the video."

"Don't you want to talk about it at all?" Jay looks forlorn.

"Not at all," Gareth confirms.

"I'm so sorry," I say.

"Me too," May agrees.

"We all are," Charlotte confirms.

He gives an awkward shrug and rewinds ten seconds in the video, forcing us to shift our focus back to last night. "Let's get this mystery solved, shall we?"

Reluctantly we scan the faces, searching for clues—Peony is looking a bit peeved, as I guess I would if I was in her vegan leather shoes. Elliot is as sulky as ever, no sign of Tristan but the waiter is cheering us on.

"Arghhh!" We reel back in unison.

In an overzealous burst of enthusiasm I appear to have thrown my arm back and thwacked Gareth in the face with my braceletted wrist.

We replay the shock on his face, followed by the realization that his lip is bleeding.

"Damn! That's straight on *You've Been Framed!*"

"Oh my god, I did that?" I go to touch his face but he flinches, head instinctively jerking away.

"That's gotta hurt," Jay winces.

How did I not remember this?

"Well, I guess that's you ruled out." May promptly moves his card across.

"Unless…?" Charlotte turns back to him to double-check.

He gives a terse snort. "I can assure you that I'm not The One."

"All right!" I huff.

"I don't mean it like that." He looks rueful.

Just when I think things couldn't get any more jangled, Marcus bursts into the room telling Charlotte she needs to stay calm.

Which can't be good.

"The taxi company have just cancelled our ride and they don't have any other available drivers. We need to find someone with a car that can take us to the airport."

We all turn to Gareth. The only one of us with wheels.

Marcus isn't convinced. "You look like you might still be over the limit…"

"This isn't booze-related." Gareth addresses his own face. "I'd be happy to take you."

"I don't want to cut short your time here," Charlotte protests. "You haven't even had breakfast."

"I'm not hungry, honestly. I'll just grab my bag."

"At least have a coffee..." Marcus offers, keen to show his appreciation. "No great rush now you're saving the day."

"Actually, I think the sooner we leave, the better." Gareth heads for the door but pauses beside one of the flower chandeliers, now lowered to shoulder-height. "Amy, are you seeing your mum today?"

I nod.

"Take these for her," he says, deftly pulling together a mix of blooms and offsetting them with wispy greenery.

"That's beautiful," I say, hurrying over to accept them and then whispering, "I'm just so sorry about Freya, that must have been such a shock."

"It was quite a night all round, wasn't it?" He raises a brow.

I smile. "It was indeed. I just hope me busting your lip didn't mess things up with Peony."

"It's fine. We'll meet up when the surgeon has stitched me back together."

"Oh, don't say that!"

He laughs but then his hand goes to his mouth. "I think I'd better keep my serious face on for a few days."

"You do that." I want to give him a hug but fear I'd have his eye out with a poky bit of foliage. "Drive safe!"

"You too, well, not drive but you know."

"I know."

As he leaves Charlotte sidles up behind me. "I can't believe Freya is getting married. Who could be better than Gareth?"

"I bet it's her childhood sweetheart," I say. "Do you remember seeing them at that party in Sweden, there was a vibe." He'd spoken to her a few times in Swedish, which of course we didn't understand, and the tone had felt a little too intimate...

Charlotte nods. "I do, but I never thought it would come to this. I thought he'd moved to Iceland?"

"I guess there's a lot we don't know."

"I'll see if I can fill in the blanks on the way to the airport."

"Or we could respect his wishes and leave him in peace?"

Charlotte gives a little snort. "Like any of us have ever managed to do that!"

"Guys!" May beckons us back to the breakfast table. "We're packing a little breakfast picnic for Gareth. Which flavor croissant do you think he'd like?"

"Almond," I say. "And switch the strawberries for figs. He loves figs."

Jay meanwhile focuses on scribbling plant-themed jokes on the paper napkins.

"How do succulents express their feelings?"

"Tell us!"

"Aloe you so much!"

We heave a collective sigh, wishing we could do more.

"I guess it's time to go." Marcus looks at his watch.

"It is indeed."

"It never rains but it pours," May mutters as we follow the newlyweds out onto the driveway.

I put my arm around her, remembering that she too is going through the emotional ringer. She in turn reaches for Jay, who is twisting the ring that Freya gave him last Christmas. Bang goes one of his favorite friendships. But he puts on a brave face, as ever.

"Can't believe they're going to South Africa. Lucky buggers."

"Twelve-hour flight?" May scoffs. "Personally, I think we've got the better deal going home to bed for the rest of the day."

"Wish her well, May," I plead.

She looks up at me with teary eyes and then blows a kiss in Charlotte's direction. "I hope you get to see the penguins."

"What?"

"She said she wanted to see the African penguins that live on the beach near Cape Town."

I sigh. "That's not really what I meant."

"I know, but it's the best I can do."

"Everyone ready?" The stately home owner is keen to drop the last lot of stragglers at the train station.

"My mum's flowers!" I exclaim. "I'll be two seconds!"

Darting back to the event room, I can't help but give the place cards one last look. I even take a few quick snaps as reminders, grouping the guys I hope are on the shortlist. And that's when I see Gareth's phone, forgotten on the table.

"Nooo!" I cry but then acknowledge that it's not the end of the world—I can drop it round to his after I've seen my mum. He'll easily be home by then. And that way I can check to see how he's doing without feeling intrusive.

The phone rings again. I am so tempted to hear what Freya has to say. Maybe she's come to her senses. My thumb hovers over the green button. Would it be so wrong to answer?

"*AMY!!!*"

Jeez. For a small person May can sure bellow.

"Coming!" I yell back, placing the phone in my bag, unanswered.

10

It happens every Sunday on the way to visit my mum. As I cross the Thames from Chelsea to Battersea, I get a bout of mid-bridge queasiness, wondering whether her face will light up at the sight of me, or whether she will have a distant look in her eyes, busily fretting about something that happened over thirty years ago.

Early onset Alzheimer's. I remember my bewilderment when the doctor first broached the subject. In my mind the word dementia was reserved for the elderly and frail. The same term couldn't possibly apply to my sharp-as-a-tack, Pilates-trim mama. She was in her mid-fifties when they diagnosed her—all the memory loss, disorientation and anxiety, now available for under sixty-fives. I was shocked to hear that people as young as thirty could get it. By their standard she was lucky but three years on I still can't wrap my head around it—she's the same age as Lisa Kudrow and younger than Jane Leeves aka Daphne from *Frasier*. That's her favorite sitcom and the first thing I put in the DVD player when she is in her worried, searching phases. I've grown rather fond of it myself—the perfect blend of wit and farce. Plus, when my mother laughs everything is all right with the world. Everything.

The high I get from her being her "normal self" can get me in trouble because I start telling myself that it's going to be all right—that the diagnosis was wrong and that she's coming back to me for good. But when the "muddle" takes over, despite being physically healthy, she can't be left alone—too many times she's wandered out into the night, which is just terrifying. Hence the nursing home.

I am still trying to come to terms with it, attempting to accept the new normal. But it's hard to make peace with something so maddening, so cruel. I wish there was some court I could complain to, that she has been swindled out of the last twenty or thirty years of her life. Selfishly I'd also want to protest feeling like another person has infiltrated our mother–daughter bond. I want to have nothing but compassion for the person she morphs into but my heart sinks and the loneliness I feel in those moments makes my whole body wilt with sadness. It's like getting a preview of how it will feel when she's gone for good, while she's still standing in front of me.

Still, whatever state she's in, she'll love these flowers from Gareth. She's always had a soft spot for him and he's at his most chatty in her presence. Conversely, Jay becomes his most quiet—his favorite thing is to curl up beside her like he's a cat and have her smooth his hair, offering him the motherly comfort he lost too young. Personally, I could do with a little motherly advice today. Then again, my mum doesn't exactly have a broad spectrum of romantic experience to draw from—since the age of twenty her world revolved around the man that would become my father. He's long gone now—a swift and unceremonious bolt when I was seven—but my mum often returns in her mind to the days prior.

"Where's your father?" she asks me on her bad days. "He should be back by now…"

This mental time travel is something of a theme at the nursing home. Jean in the room next door is always wandering around looking for her boys, age five and seven. She's eighty now but that's the pre-trauma place her mind takes her to when the sun goes down. I suppose we're all searching for that feeling of being reunited with a source of love.

Here she is now—jabbing at the ceiling panels with her walking stick when I arrive.

"They're up in the loft playing again," she tells me. "I've got their tea on and it's all going to spoil."

"Oh, they'll be back down soon enough," I say. "You know they love your bread and butter pudding."

"Well, I know but—"

"Come on, Jean," nurse Lidia steps in. "Shall we have a nice cuppa while we wait for them?"

She heaves a resigned sigh. "All right. But they are naughty, they know they should be down by now."

Lidia eyes the bouquet I'm carrying. "Did you catch that at the wedding?"

"No!" I laugh as I walk alongside them. "Gareth put them together for Mum."

"He does have a gift. My friend just ordered a rainbow arrangement from him and was so impressed. So, how was it?"

"Eventful," I reply, glancing at Jean. "I'll have to tell you later, drop by Mum's room if you can?"

"I will," Lidia confirms as she prepares to take a left as I head right. "Come on, Jean, let's get that kettle on."

"Lidia?"

"Yes?" She turns back.

"How's she doing?" I feel compelled to ask, though I'm always a little afraid to hear the answer.

"Good today," she assures me.

"Really?" I smile.

She nods and my chest inflates with gratitude.

I always feel better for seeing Lidia. Eternally patient, she manages to flit between the residents making each one feel like her main squeeze. A few were thrown initially by her peroxide crop and tongue piercing but then they looked into her clear, trustworthy eyes and felt instantly soothed. She never tires of their chatter and my mum has even adopted some of her native Polish sayings, so now instead of "Let sleeping dogs lie," she says, "Don't call a wolf out of the woods." There's also something to do with gingerbread and windmills that I can never quite remember.

Personally, I'm most grateful for Lidia's dementia insights. In the beginning I used to get so upset by how quickly my mum would forget that I had visited her, but Lidia assured me that the positive feelings from our time together would linger way longer than the memory itself. She even gave me a little card with a Maya Angelou quote: "People will forget what you said, people will forget what you did, but people will never forget how you made them feel."

It's comforting and true. I mean, when you think of your friends you don't have a transcript in your brain of every single thing you ever said to each other, but you do know whether you get an "Ooh, she's just the best!" feeling versus a sense of irritation or wariness. And you never forget someone being kind to you when you were blue.

Early on Lidia told me that I'm allowed to feel impatient or exasperated sometimes—because that's just human. You know logically they're not behaving this way on purpose but sometimes it's wearing, sometimes you won't be in the mood to answer the same question ten times in a row. Just like a mum would get annoyed being asked "Are we there yet?" by a six-year-old on a car ride, so a thirty-something daughter can get annoyed by being asked where her father is over and over again. Especially when she'd rather not think about him at all.

Lidia has also taught me the value of a manicure. Sometimes conversation can be a little awkward or faltering and I can't bear to see my mother berating herself, thinking, *I should know this! Why can't I answer this simple question?* So we put on some nice music and set up a mini salon with a bowl of soapy warm water, cuticle remover, nail files and an ever-expanding range of nail polishes. Picking out a new one gives me a whole new sense of purpose at Boots, plus I get to hold her hand without feeling the need to squeeze too tight and plead, "Don't leave me, please don't leave me!" Instead, I'm able to say, "Ballet Slipper Pink or Scarlett Woman?"

I take a breath as I come to her door. It's open but I give a little knock out of courtesy.

"Amy!"

"Mum!" I cheer.

It's her! She's here!

"You sound surprised to see me—who were you expecting?"

I don't know quite how to answer that so just move in for a hug.

"Oh darling, you don't look well…"

"It's just hangover dishevelment," I explain. "From Charlotte's wedding…"

I quickly take out my phone to show her a photo so she doesn't have to struggle to picture my friends.

"Look how smart Gareth looks in his suit—these are from him, by the way." I hand her the flowers.

"Ooh, lovely!" She buries her nose in the silky petals as she continues to look at the pictures. "He does look handsome. But what's that on his knees?"

"Funny you should ask…" And so, as she places the flowers in a vase, I begin telling her all about how he saved me from falling, the beautiful hair vines he created, the tangle with Charlotte's hair, the ceremony…

"Is that your phone?"

I frown. I hear the ringing too but the tone isn't familiar.

"I think it's coming from your bag."

I rummage through. "Ahh! It's Gareth's phone!" The number hasn't been assigned a name—it could be him calling from the airport. "Hello?" I blurt eagerly.

"Oh!" the female voice falters. "Sorry, I think I've got the wrong number, I was trying to reach Gareth?"

"Yes, yes, this is his phone. Is that—"

"Peony," she states.

"Peony!" I cheer. "It's Amy! From the wedding!"

"Oh." She sounds dismayed.

"I've just got Gareth's phone because he left it behind and now he's driving Charlotte and Marcus to the airport. He'll have it back tonight. Shall I let him know you called?"

"Don't worry, I'll send him a text. Do you know roughly what time…?"

"Around six p.m.?" I estimate.

"Okay. Thank you."

"No, thank you! Thank you for calling him."

So. All is not lost there. That's something.

"Where were we?" I huddle up.

"Have I missed the photos?" We look up to see Lidia peeking around the door.

"No, come on in," I smile.

"Show her the one with you all lined up." Mum taps my arm.

"Oh, I love it!" Lidia coos, using her fingers to zoom in on the faces. "You want me to print it out for your wall, Sophie?"

"You're so sweet, yes please!"

I swiftly text it to Lidia, as we do from time to time. My mum takes a shine to the strangest pictures. She's got a whole bunch of my co-worker Becky's Jack Russell because he has the same wiry coat and tan eye patches as Eddie from *Frasier*. She never tires of hearing how the real-life dog ended up with dementia but spent his retirement living with the Brussels Griffon who played Jack Nicholson's dog in *As Good As It Gets*. You know these celebrity couples...

But back to *my* coupling situation. I am about to begin with "It's a tale of three kisses...," as if reading from a book I dusted off from the attic, but Lidia throws in a new tangent.

"You should invite your friends to our fancy dress party. It's been a while since they've been in as a group."

"When is it?" I ask.

"Three weeks from now. We just decided last night. We're asking people to dress as their favorite sitcom character."

"Really?" I like the sound of that. Though I suspect there will be an inordinate number of *Golden Girls*, with even the sharp-as-a-tack Dorothys experiencing rambling Rose moments.

"Guests are encouraged," Lidia continues. "We want to try and get everyone up dancing and it helps if at least one half of the partnership is stable on their feet."

As Lidia and my mum start casting the residents—flirty

Nyreen as Dorien from *Birds of a Feather,* well-meaning Morris as Baldrick from *Blackadder*—I consider who my date might be. The waiter is lanky enough to be Basil Fawlty but would a mustache and cravat project *Fawlty Towers* when he's so chilled and smiley? What if I came with Tristan? Hmm, I can't say a nursing home would really be his scene.

Suddenly I get a weird, disorientating feeling, like a memory is trying to force through a sheet of rubber. I can't make out the details but I feel like he's here, at the nursing home.

I walk to the window and try to catch my breath.

"What do you think?" Lidia asks me.

"What's that?" I'm still trying to bring the memory into focus but already it's dissipating.

"I was just saying I could go to the army surplus shop and kit out all the old fellas as the cast of *Dad's Army*?"

"Oh, they would love it!" I reply.

"I'm going to go and get some measurements now!"

"Better have your slapping hand ready!" I call after Lidia, knowing she's going to make several chaps' night.

And then I pull my chair closer to my mum and cut to the chase. "Mum. I've got news. It's happened, I kissed The One!"

Her eyes widen. "What?"

"It's true! I felt this amazing flood of contentment and joy, like I couldn't believe my luck. And I got the sense that we were old in the premonition, so I think it's for life."

"Oh darling." She takes my hand in hers, her eyes glossing with tears. "Then it is real."

I nod back at her. "After all these years of disappointment, I can't believe it!"

"I don't know what to say...except, *who is he*?"

"Well, funny you should ask!" I take a breath. "It happened at the wedding so there are actually three candidates: a waiter, a man called Tristan who works with Marcus and, well, I don't know the identity of the third man but I'm working on it."

She raises an eyebrow.

"My biggest concern is making the wrong choice."

"Maybe I can help—my mum always said she knew I was meant to be with Pete."

"Pete? Who's Pete?"

"It doesn't matter now. I didn't choose him, I chose your father."

"I didn't realize there was an alternative..."

"Well, I don't like to dwell on that."

"But—"

"Could you bring them here, so I can meet them?"

"The three guys?"

"Yes, bring them to the fancy dress party!"

"All of them, at the same time?" I balk.

"You're right, it's too much. At least bring one?"

Considering I don't actually have any contact info for the waiter and I still don't know who number three is, I guess Tristan is now the prime candidate. Which would also tally with my flash-forward to him being here.

Suddenly I feel really nervous. What if my mum and I favor a different man? Would I go with her judgment or mine?

"Whatever choice you make, I'll support it." My mum reads my mind. "I just want you to be happy."

"Thanks, Mum. It means a lot."

"You know I'll always be here for you."

My heart sinks. If only that were true.

"Ah, there's the love of my life!" A male voice interrupts our flow. It's Scottish Malcolm, burly, bewhiskered and clearly the jealous type. "Who gave you those flowers, Sophie? Was it Derek? I can't believe it. I've made it quite clear you're mine."

"She's not yours, Malcolm."

"They're from Jimmy, of course," my mum scolds. "He'll be back soon and he'll fly into such a rage if he finds you here."

"Jimmy?" Malcolm frowns.

"My husband!" my mum announces.

"But—"

"Come on, Malcolm. Today's not the day." I walk toward him. "And next time, try putting on some trousers. Oh god, and underwear!" I blanche as his shirt rises.

I make sure he's puttering in the right direction down the corridor then turn back to my mother.

She's staring out the window. "He should've been back by now. I always worry so much when he's late. Anything could have happened to him."

I try not to be too disappointed. I've had a good time with her today and she's given me a lot of food for thought. I just can't bear that she returns to this anxiety-ridden state. Though it must be so familiar—every day of her married life thinking this could be the day he leaves. I do remember her crying a lot when I was young. Or not so much the crying itself because she tried to hide that from me, but the puffy, pink eyes the following day.

My heart feels heavy again.

"Mum?"

"Oh, hello, dear. When did you get here? Did you see the flowers your father bought me?"

I sigh. "Yes, they're beautiful. He obviously loves you very much."

"He does. He would never leave me."

For a second I stand motionless. But then I jolt myself into a faux-cheery state, asking, "Do you want to watch an episode of *Frasier*?"

"Hmm?"

"Here, I'll just put it on."

As I reach for the remote control I go to remind her where we left Niles and Daphne's romance, but of course, it's all by the by.

Within minutes, she's absorbed and chuckling. I'm glad for the distraction myself and titter along. We continue to click "play next episode" until the dinner gong rings.

"Right! I'll leave you to it, I'm off to return Gareth's phone." I bend down to kiss her. "I love you, Mum." I press her close, layering the sensation of her warmth and affection atop all the love that has gone before.

"I love you too, darling," she whispers into my hair. "To the moon and back."

"To the moon and back," I echo.

My eyes well up as I leave. I hold it together long enough to wave to Lidia, who is helping Malcolm to the dining room, now sporting a kilt. That man obviously wanted to feel a breeze in his nether regions today.

There's no one around as I step back onto the street so I let my tears stream unchecked. I've learned to just ride out these swells of emotion—to let it all out, even though I sometimes fear the pain might engulf me—and then wait for a sense of calm to return.

By the time I reach the top of Gareth's road my face is wiped clean. I just hope his face is now angst-free. It must have been such a shock hearing about Freya's wedding. As for his poor lip, I feel so bad about assaulting him. I must think of a nice way to make it up to him.

Like maybe buying the flat next door...

11

The green shutters are closed but I can see the light on inside. I get a warm feeling knowing Gareth's old leather chair and a glass of homemade rosemary ale awaits. If I'm lucky, he'll ask me to stay for dinner and then we can watch some documentary I have no interest in but then find utterly compelling, all the while snuggled up in one of his big gardening jumpers and outsize Tibetan knit socks. He's offered for me to take a set home since I always express my contentment at wearing them, but part of the pleasure is knowing they are exclusive to his pad. His cats, however, I'd snap up in a second.

Gareth first encountered the duo as abandoned, flea-bitten kittens. No cute wisps chasing pink yarn here–they resembled threadbare cat toys that had been swept out from under the sofa covered in dust bunnies. Too weak to stand on their own teeny paws, the vet decided their inner organs were so depleted it would be kinder to cut short their malnourished misery. But

Gareth had revived many a withered plant in his time and ever since he looked into their tiny glass-bead eyes, he knew he was their last and only hope. He took them home, cradled them in feather-soft warmth and set alarms throughout the night so he could feed them with a pipette, even taking time off work to monitor their progress. I think the kittens must have found the smell of Gareth reassuring—a combination of dewy grass, damp earth and every plant he had encountered that day. Perhaps that's what gave them the will to live—the promise of one day leaving their blanketed box beside the radiator and tiptoeing around the garden discovering all those fragrances first hand.

When that day came, it was such a beautiful sight to watch them exploring the kitty Shangri-La that Gareth had created for them, complete with sun trap terrace, mini bamboo jungle and trees dangling baubles they love to bat in the breeze. It was only after several days' watching them pounce and roll and leap and tumble that Gareth named them.

"I wanted to see their personalities first," he reasoned.

The girl he named Zazel, after the first human cannonball, on account of her high-flying acrobatic qualities. Zazel's brother was also a natural circus performer: he would squat solidly on his back haunches, rise up like a gopher and then do the begging paw motion more affiliated with dogs or performing bears.

"How on earth did you teach him that?" I gawped the first time I saw it.

"I didn't," Gareth shrugged. "He did it spontaneously and seemed pleased with the response so now he does it all the time!"

But not just for food or attention, he does his little begging prayer at the wicker toy basket like a snake charmer or before snuggling on one of Gareth's fleecy throws—anything that pleases him, he performs this ritual.

For this he earned the name Frankie—as in Frankie Valli and the Four Seasons, specifically for their song "Beggin'."

I think of how different I would feel coming home after work if I knew I'd get some silky-furred playtime with them. The only possible downside to my neighborly visit would be having to turn up the TV a few notches to drown out Zazel's purrs.

Suddenly I find myself smiling, eagerly knocking on the door and ringing the bell, excited to propose the idea of a joint purchase.

"Cooee! It's just me!" I call through the letter box.

While I wait for him to respond I eye the property next door. I never used to like those doors with the stained-glass panels but now I'm looking with "potential owner" eyes, I can see a certain appeal to this cornflower-blue fleur-de-lys design. Imagine if I painted the wood panels the same hue…

I'm just stepping up for a closer look when Gareth's door opens a cautious crack and an unfamiliar voice calls, "Hello?"

"Oh, hello." I hop back into view, surprised to see a young man in an Embrace Science T-shirt. "Is Gareth in?"

"No, sorry. Can I take a message?"

"Um." I feel decidedly wrong-footed. "I was just with him earlier today—he left, er, something behind so I was just returning it. I'm Amy?"

"Oh right," he nods. "I'm Dharmesh. His new assistant? He asked me to feed the cats while he's away."

"Away?" I repeat.

"Apparently he was dropping some friends at the airport and he made a last-minute decision to hop on a flight himself." He gives a light shrug.

My jaw drops. Has he decided to try and stop Freya's wedding? "To Sweden? Did he say he was going to Sweden?"

"He didn't say."

"I know he had an overnight bag but did he have his passport? I know he doesn't have his phone."

"Well, you know he's not as attached to it as the rest of us." Dharmesh offers a smile.

"True...Do you know how long he's gone for?"

Dharmesh shakes his head.

"But you're okay with running the shop?"

"Yeah, we've got a pretty quiet week. Anyway, I'll let him know you came round."

"Right." I note the cue to wrap things up. "If he calls, can you let him know I have his mobile?"

"Will do." He loiters awkwardly for a second before adding, "Goodnight then."

"Goodnight."

I take a few steps and then stop. This seems really odd. I go to call Charlotte to see if she has any intel but realize she'll still be in the air. And even when she lands she will be on her honeymoon so I should respect the Do Not Disturb sign on that particular doorknob. Still, an email wouldn't hurt, she can answer that at her leisure.

In the meantime, I text May.

Gareth has left the country. Possibly. At the very least he got on a plane at Heathrow. Should we worry?

There's a few seconds' pause then she replies:

Unless he's joined Marcus and Charlotte for a ménage à trois, I think we can refrain from alerting the authorities.

Okay. I'm overreacting. He's a grown man, free to go where he pleases, when he pleases. And halt the wedding of an ex-girlfriend if he sees fit.

The phone buzzes. It's May again.

BTW are you free Thursday night?

Short of one of my mystery suitors making me a better offer, yes, I tap back.

Good. I need you to come to a photography exhibition with me. Teagan will be there.

Wow.

I can't keep avoiding her, May adds.

No. It'll be good, I encourage her. *Well, maybe not good but a step forward.*

Right.

Okay. In the diary.

Thanks. And don't worry about Gareth. He'll be fine—maybe he eloped with Peony.

I'm about to bring May up to speed on Peony's call when I hear a voice behind me.

"Julianne?"

I turn to find an elderly man peering out of the stained-glass door.

"No, sorry—I'm Amy."

"Oh, I thought you were here to view the flat."

I hesitate. "Could I?"

"Are you in the market for one?" He gives me an assessing look.

"As a matter of fact, I am—I'm actually friends with your next-door neighbor, Gareth…"

He looks at his watch. "Come on then, if you're quick."

Whereas Gareth's side of the building has a big shopfront and a modest living space out the back, this side has two bedrooms, a balcony and the lion's share of the garden.

"I never realized how much bigger this side is…" I say, gazing down from the back bedroom and imagining how amazing the garden area could be if you took down the dividing fence. Gareth could transform this tumbledown, weed-tangled sprawl into a dining terrace, reading nook, fire pit—the works!

"It's a sun trap here in the afternoons and in the evenings you can sit out on the balcony and watch the sun go down."

I sigh, imagining being able to bring my mum here on a Sunday to give her a proper break from the home. I'd set out the garden table with a pretty tablecloth and a sprig of wildflowers, use a cut-glass decanter for the water, complete with slices of strawberry bobbing alongside the ice…We'd chat away as I rustled up my latest HelloFresh taste sensation and, after her favorite dessert of sticky toffee pudding, she would take a little snooze in a sun lounger while I did the washing-up. If it was raining, as it so often is, we'd just set up within the patio doors and rustle up a fire.

"Does the fireplace actually work?" I ask.

"Oh yes, you can get nice and toasty in front of it."

The bathroom is charming—vintage fixtures and tiling but the shower jet blasts out with enough vigor to loosen the knots at the back of your neck.

"Impressive," I note.

As he chats away, pointing out other features and foibles, I notice I'm getting a light-headed, happy but assured feeling— *This is my place, I have to live here, can I move in tomorrow?*

"I had no idea how beautiful it was in here…"

"Well, it doesn't look like too much from the outside," the old chap concedes.

"Do you know much about this Julianne person?"

"Not a lot. Apparently she'd want to gut it and modernize it—"

"Noooo!" I protest. "Wouldn't you rather know that it was being preserved and enhanced? You know Gareth would do an incredible job with the garden, no one could do it better."

"That might be true but it's the wife that makes the money decisions and she wants to retire to Lanzarote, so it's basically going to the highest bidder."

"But…" I begin. There has to be a way around this. "What if…What if you had a cut of the new cafe business?"

"The Botanist?" His face brightens.

"Yes!" I smile, glad to hear that Gareth has broached the topic with his neighbor. "So you'd have the lump sum from the sale of the house but then every month you'd get a check for your share of the profits?"

"Are you Gareth's business partner?"

"Well, no, not technically, not yet. But I could be."

"Does he know about any of this?"

I puff in frustration. "We've half talked about it." As in I've always been very enthusiastic about his cafe idea.

"Well, get back to me when you've whole talked about it."

My shoulders slump. "He's gone away, without his phone."

"Then I guess we're at an impasse."

"I guess we are."

The doorbell rings.

We look at each other. "*Julianne.*"

*

133

I walk out into the street in a daze. I feel a mix of fired up and fatigued. Perhaps I should sleep on this scenario? I mean, a lot has happened this weekend, it's probably not the best time to make a massive life decision. Especially when Gareth could announce tomorrow that he's relocating to Sweden.

But it just feels so right!

I turn back to look at the building. I could totally see myself living there. To be this close to my mum and live next door to one of my best friends! Even if my dream guy moved in with me and Gareth shacked up with Freya or Peony, we'd progress to couple friends and have the best of both worlds—bickering away with our partners but always on good terms with each other.

I take out my phone and plot my route to work. Not exactly a hop, skip and a jump but doable. Especially with a bazillion podcasts to listen to en route. And if I get the four-day week I'm angling for…

I wonder if I should propose this to Gareth via email. Even without a phone he could still get access to his account, right? I start typing to him on the bus home but then decide I'd rather wait and do it in person so we can really hash out all the details. For once, scrolling Instagram has little appeal. I put my phone in my bag and look around at my fellow passengers. Normally I'd be just as glazed and dazed as them but tonight I feel weirdly alive, like my life is about to get some momentum after so many false starts. I take a tremulous breath as I wonder how many changes the week ahead could bring.

12

Monday, Tuesday and Wednesday I stick to a strict schedule: daydream all the way to work, spend half my day googling *How to Tell If He's the One* (because heaven knows, I don't want to make the wrong choice) and the other half researching wigs and outfits for my mum's fancy dress party. So, you know, productive.

Come the evening, I order a takeaway and binge-watch Netflix to the point that I become so merged with the lives of the people in the shows I now think that I live in a beach house in San Diego with a couple of eighty-somethings named Grace and Frankie.

Occasionally I check in with my real friends. Charlotte messages me from her safari tent to say she hasn't had any joy from the wedding caterers due to annoying privacy issues, and it will be Monday next week before I can get my mitts on the professional photographer's wedding pics. I'm hopeful they will offer some clue to the identity of Kiss Number Three.

In my impatience, I briefly consider visiting a hypnotherapist, wondering if they could extract the memories I can't access due to booze-fogging, but ultimately feel too nervous about revealing my premonition quirk, so I give it a miss.

Come Thursday night, with no word from Gareth, I realize there's really nothing I can do to challenge Julianne's bid on the flat. I don't call Mr. Atkins because if he tells me the deal is done, I'll have to stop mentally decorating the whole place. At least today I get to meet up with May and chew things over with her. I do worry that seeing Teagan is not going to be the cathartic experience she's hoping for but I hope I'm wrong.

As the escalator wields me up to ground level at Highbury & Islington station I spy her by the ticket machine and wave wildly. She looks the very hottest version of cool—skin-tight waistcoat reminding me what a toned arm looks like, black leather trousers with strategic slashes and blue tips added to her hair.

"Well, you don't want to look the same as you always did when you run into an ex," she shrugs when I compliment her.

She does, however, look uncharacteristically nervous.

"Are you absolutely sure you want to see Teagan?" I check.

She nods. "I'm sick of living with this dread of bumping into her. I need to get it over with."

"Okay," I say, sidestepping a businessman who seems intent on walking directly through me. "Let's see if karma has begun catching up with its enormous backlog."

"I think I have to stop caring either way," May decides as we wait at the crossing. "It really shouldn't matter to me what is going on in her life."

"Well, it's only human to be miffed when your ex seems to get rewarded for her bad behavior, while you get punished for doing nothing wrong."

"Well, I wouldn't say I was *all* sweetness and light."

"No one would ever think that," I assure her.

She smiles. "Anyway. It feels like time. Things are changing for all of us. I want to be able to move forward too."

"Atta girl!" I say as we burrow down into the subterranean space. "We might even have fun!"

Ah. I spoke too soon.

The place is full of late teens in mom jeans and Billie Eilish wannabes. I'm not sure my attempt at beatnik is translating—black cropped trousers and a boat-neck top teamed with a cerise scarf showing assorted scenes of Capri. I'm tempted to ask to switch shoes with May so I'm not so matchy-matchy but I can't see her wearing any form of pink outside of a breast cancer ribbon. Even my make-up feels dated.

"Where do you want to start?" I ask, trying to suss out the layout of the room. It seems as if the exhibits are divided into booth-like sections, a few of which are interactive.

"Let's go clockwise," May says. "That raised platform will give me a chance to scout the room."

I learn from the brochure that the theme for the night is "Disruptive Beauty" but the series of botched facial surgery portraits are a step too far for my delicate constitution so we hurry on to the "Cry Your Heart Out" collection, featuring a dozen tear-stained faces. It's actually quite jarring to view, possibly because it's such an unusual time to pose for a camera—liquid pain pouring from your eyes, face all blotchy and snotty.

The information panel (which itself is streaming behind a sheet of plastic) talks about how we are increasingly photographing little more than a mask while true beauty comes from being vulnerable and sharing our souls. They say that one of our most honest states is when we are crying. Some of the faces look angry, some broken, some exhausted, others haunted or lost.

"Well, it's a laugh a minute so far," I note, only to see that May has moved up onto the platform and is busily scanning the room for Teagan.

"She's not here," she asserts, as she steps back down.

"Are you sure?"

"You don't think I'd recognize my own ex-wife?"

Ohh, she is tense.

"Shall we move on?"

At the next booth guests are photographed on arrival then invited to answer a series of questions on a computer screen, calculating how many hours we spend feeling bad about how we look, or trying to alter and/or disguise our physical attributes. I'm almost scared to input my figures, though my one consolation is that I've never fallen foul to beauty's biggest time-suck: contouring.

At the end, the computer calculates the number of far more constructive things we could have done with our time that would have resulted in us a) stepping out with more confidence, b) making a greater contribution to the world and c) putting a higher value on being a good person than being good-looking.

All the books we could have read, the languages we could speak, the hours we could have volunteered and lives we could have impacted in the collective time it took to align our false lashes, reapply lip gloss or whiten our teeth in an Instagram pic.

It's quite the humbling mind-bender. Suddenly I feel as if I've been on a beauty treadmill and I'm now looking around at this incredible world I could be enjoying—if I could just accept my face for what it is.

"Imagine if we could all be invisible for a year," I say to May. "So everyone reacted to each other in terms of what we said and did and looks simply weren't part of the equation."

"We'd probably just get really fixated on a person's voice," she decides.

My brow rucks. I've been trying to picture the face of Kiss Number Three but as she says this, I hear myself saying, "It was someone I knew."

"What was?"

"The kiss with the third man, I knew him. I knew his voice."

I feel as if I'm turning a dial in my head, trying to find a radio frequency and match it to one of the "suspects" from the wedding. "I can hear him saying my name…"

May watches me for a second then loses interest and moves on.

Who is it? I tap my head impatiently. It's like he's calling to me, trying to get my attention.

"Amy!"

I look up to see one of the girls from the exhibit reading my name from her tablet.

"Thank you for participating in this experiment. Here is the portrait of you taken as you entered the exhibit." She turns the screen to face me. "And here is how you could look if you chose to shake your cosmetic shackles."

She swipes to reveal a second image in which my face has been digitally altered to reveal a dewy, fresh-faced look.

"I'm not sure I'd look quite so radiant in real life," I note.

"You would if you hadn't spent the past twenty years worrying about your looks."

Wow. I blink back at her.

"Liberation?" A second girl offers me a facial wipe. Her T-shirt reads: "In a society that profits from your self-doubt, liking yourself is a rebellious act." I feel a stirring. I think of Alicia Keys hosting the Grammys au naturel in front of doll-faces like Gwen Stefani and how radiantly beautiful she looked because she was happy with herself.

"Okay! I'll do it!" I blurt.

I'm committed from the first swipe, rubbing the layers off

my brows, cheeks and jawline, exchanging looks with other girls who are choosing to be equally bold. As we remove the last traces of lipstick and liner I feel a kinship with them, a fun warmth. I can imagine us eyeing each other on the tube feeling a daring sense of sisterhood. I go to pull May into the fold but find her locked in some kind of sultry gaze-a-thon with a Ruby Rose lookalike, complete with raven Elvis quiff, electric blue eyes and hummingbird tattoos.

Even as an onlooker it feels like one of those freeze-frame moments where the world blurs to soft focus around the love-struck couple. Ruby makes her approach, stealthy as a panther, and I feel a flutter of nerves on May's behalf. I can't make out the details of their whispered exchange but I see Ruby passing a black and red matchbook around her fingers, then flipping it open to reveal what I assume is her phone number. It looks for a moment as if she is going to tuck it into May's cleavage but she diverts to her waistcoat pocket, lingering for just a second longer than necessary.

"Well, that was intense." May whistles as she returns to my side. "Did you see?"

"I did indeed," I coo admiringly. "You've still got it!"

"Apparently so!" she marvels, a-flush with attraction.

I couldn't be more delighted—seeing Teagan will now be purely incidental.

I'm babbling away about how my life has been changed forever by a facial wipe when May grips my arm with a stunned look on her face.

"Oh my god—I can't believe it!"

Here we go.

"Where is she?" I ask.

May shakes her head. "Not her, *him*!"

"Him?"

"Your waiter guy from the wedding—he's here, I just saw his shoes."

"What?" I turn around, instantly clocking his lanky form offering pale pink "rose water" cocktails to the guests. My heart gives a happy skip. "Oh, isn't he lovely?"

"Come on, let's go over!"

I come to a sudden halt as realization hits. "I've just taken off all my make-up!"

"You look fine!"

"Noooo!" I protest.

May is indignant. "Two minutes ago you were all *vive la révolution*!"

"I know, that's before I wanted a boy to like me."

May rolls her eyes. "You're such a terrible feminist. Isn't it possible he'll like you au naturel?"

"It seems unlikely."

"So you'd let him go, this genuine contender, for the sake of vanity?"

I pause. This definitely feels like a test from the universe.

"Just cut to the chase and ask him for a date," May insists. "Somewhere cheap because he probably doesn't have too much money."

"I doubt he'd even recognize me—my hair was up, I was in a glam dress and heels. Where's he gone?" My eyes dart every which way.

"Amy?"

Oh. My. God. My body tenses. He's standing behind me.

"Hiiiiii!" I say, turning around, amping up my smile. "I didn't think you'd recognize me!" I motion to my face.

"Of course I do!" He smiles, holding up his tray. "Cocktail?"

"Oh no, no. I'm still in Never Again mode after the wedding. I'm sorry if I was obnoxious."

"Think nothing of it."

Wait. Does that mean I was?

"Actually, I'm glad I ran into you." I charge in headfirst, aware that he's working a busy room. "I wanted to ask..."

"Yes?" He leans closer so he can hear over the hubbub.

I take a second to treasure the proximity of his dark hair and the faintly soapy scent from his neck. May nudges me, reminding me to speak. "I just wanted to know if you'd like to go for a walk sometime?"

"A walk?" He looks bemused.

"Like a walk in the park or..." I come to a rather premature halt. I haven't really thought this through. "Somewhere outdoors."

"You know, I'm actually going somewhere outdoors on Saturday," he grins. "It's not everyone's cup of tea but you're welcome to join me?"

"I'd love to!" I blurt, unconcerned with the details.

His hands being full with the drinks tray, he recites his number, I dial it and then realize just how close we're standing when his thigh buzzes against mine.

"Okay, we're all set. I'll text you the address later."

Simple as that.

I stand in a daze as he moves on. All these years, I've never had the nerve to ask anyone out but that went so smoothly. And swiftly. Is that really all it takes? And then I frown—am I going to arrive and find out he's part of some rambling group?

"What are you looking so worried about?" May asks. "He gave you his number!"

"Yes, yes," I rally, focusing on the facts. "His name is Ben and we're going for a walk on Saturday!"

"So the same day you're seeing Tristan," May observes.

"What? Oh no!" My face falls.

"That's okay—it's a daytime thing with Ben, isn't it?"

"Yes, I'm sure he'll be working in the evening."

"Well then, there's no problem."

"No," I say, biting my lip.

"And if you find out the identity of the third one, just remember to schedule him for breakfast."

I blanche. I've never been a proficient multitasker; suddenly I'm feeling quite stressed.

"It's all good," May soothes me. "A girl's gotta do what a girl's gotta do. And you pulled this one off with no make-up."

My hand goes to my face. "I can't believe it! So, what now?"

"Well, considering we've both scored, there's no sign of Teagan and it's fondue night at The Cheese Bar…"

"Let's go!" I cheer, linking arms with her as we barrel through the crowds toward the exit.

Which is where we find Teagan. Attempting to hit on the Ruby Rose lookalike.

"Unbelievable!" May curses, making a beeline for her.

"May!" Teagan seems a little taken aback by the intensity of her approach.

"All right? You remember Amy?"

"Of course." She nods to me.

"This is Lexi." Teagan motions to the Ruby Rose lookalike.

"I know," May says, reaching for the matchbook.

"Oh, I wondered if you'd heard."

"Heard what?"

"About our engagement."

Shut the front door! I know my mouth is gaping, so I don't know how May is holding it together. I see her flip the matchbook around her fingers, wondering which way she's going to go.

She could hold it up to Lexi and say, "I believe this is yours?"

She could laugh and say, "Good luck with that, twenty minutes ago she was hitting on me."

But instead, she serves up an enigmatic smile. "Matches made in heaven."

Teagan frowns. "You mean match?"

"Do I?" May gives a little smirk and moves on.

I scurry after her, waiting for her to start ranting and pacing, but instead she simply flips the matchbook in the first bin we come to.

"I was sure you were going to say something!" I gasp.

"What, like, 'Teagan babe, you're about to marry a cheater!'?"

"Something like that."

"I thought about it," May replies with a twinkle. "But why spoil the surprise!"

13

Today is double date day. Later I'll be fine-dining with Tristan but first I have a far less conventional date scenario with Ben.

"He's taking you to a cemetery?" May scoffs. "Are you about to discover his goth alter ego?"

"No," I tut. "He's just interested in architecture."

"Ohh!" May nods as she watches me try to find a top to go with my black skinny jeans. "If only we lived in a city that had architecturally interesting buildings which didn't come with rotting corpses."

"Well, I think it's cool," I say as I consider my loose-knit star jumper.

"It's a no to that shapeless item." May swipes it out of my hands. "I do, however, still have my skeleton bodysuit from Halloween if you want to borrow it? Or maybe we should drape you in Miss Havisham lace and have you carry a dried flower bouquet that crumbles a little every step you take..."

"I don't have time for your mockery, May," I sigh. "I have to leave in five minutes."

"All right, move over and let the professional handle this!" She flips through the hangers, pausing by a cream ribbed polo neck and then reaching for my teal cashmere jumper.

I've had it for years but it's still a favorite—the little puffs at the shoulders help create the illusion of a waist and it clings to my boobs but not my stomach.

I drop my dressing gown.

May rolls her eyes. "You really need to consider investing in some new underwear, especially now you're getting back in the game."

"It's not pretty but it does the job," I shrug as I adjust my straps which, admittedly, are quite wide.

"Does it?" May's nose wrinkles. "I know your boobs ask a lot of a bra but I think this wartime style could set you back a step or two in the bedroom."

"These are first dates," I remind her as I pull on my sweater. "I promise I'll have something presentable by date two."

"I'm going to hold you to that. Allow me." She pins a vintage brooch with milky aqua stones just below my right collarbone. "And switch to the suede pumps. You'll be able to get away quicker if you hear groans coming from one of the tombs."

I roll my eyes.

"Now, for your evening look…"

"Oh, I can figure that out when I get back," I dismiss her concern. I really need to get going.

"Last-minute outfit selection never ends well," May tuts. "This restaurant is in Mayfair?"

"Yes. I'm hoping it's not too fancy."

"It will be," she says, pulling out my rose-gold shimmery top. "And I know you hate to wear heels but..." Her face puckers. "Amy! These are still muddy from the wedding!"

"You say that like it was a year ago!" I protest. "Who has time to clean their shoes?"

"I'll sort it and leave them out for you."

I smile. "You're the best!" I give her an extra squeeze knowing that she will pick out a pair of earrings, and there may even be a small getting-ready snack on the side when I come home...

It's a curious thing, heading to a cemetery on a day when I feel so glad to be alive. Ben and I have exchanged a few cute texts since the photo exhibition but they have been more friendly than flirty so I don't feel any undue pressure to wow him, which makes a pleasant change. Plus, he's seen me sans make-up, which shouldn't be a big deal but is for someone like me who only really feels confident under a layer of honey-beige foundation.

As I step off the bus, the sun breaks out from behind the gray bulk of cloud to reinforce my optimism. Highgate may be the more obvious choice for a cemetery stroll—the last resting place for the likes of Karl Marx and George Eliot—but Ben has chosen lesser-known Abney Park in Stoke Newington.

The entrance has four grandly angular pillars linked by black wrought-iron gates. I give a little shiver as I observe a couple of less-than-savory characters disappearing into the greenery on the other side. If Ben doesn't turn up, would I venture in alone? I'm not sure that I would. I picture myself tripping on the uneven path as assorted tangled roots and vines lock around my limbs, dragging me from view and claiming me as their own...

"Amy!"

"Ben!" I jump, glad to have the reassurance of a hug to settle me down, albeit a rather awkward, lightweight affair.

"Good to see you!"

He's in jeans and a loose-knit star jumper—I knew I should've worn mine.

"Shall we?"

The second we step through the gates I can see the appeal—there's a forgotten-world feel to this place: overgrown and crumbling, the headstones sit off-kilter, almost like the ground has grumbled and groaned and tried to turn over to get more comfortable. And then I notice that each grave seems to be interspersed with a different plant or bush or tree.

"I feel like I'm seeing every possible leaf pattern, in every possible hue of green."

"Funny you should say that," Ben smiles. "The park was originally laid out as an arboretum with the trees planted in alphabetical order around the perimeter."

"Really? What a concept!"

"It fell into disrepair in the 1970s which is why it now has this unkempt look—but that's all the better for the bees."

Don't you just love a man who cares about the bees?

"I read that this is one of the 'Magnificent Seven' cemeteries from the Victorian era?" I try to sound casual as I throw out the one piece of knowledge I gleaned en route.

He nods. "For me, it's the coolest because this is where the dissenters and non-conformists were buried—those who refused to align themselves with a particular religion. Plus, Amy Winehouse filmed the video for 'Back to Black' here." He gives me a sideways glance and sings *"Amy, Amy, Amy"* giving me a teasing look.

My heart does a loop-the-loop.

"But mostly I just like how I feel when I'm here…"

I follow him in something of a trance. "And how do you feel?"

He lets his hand trail along the long grasses. "Suspended in time. Peaceful. Thankful. It helps me let go of the things that don't matter."

"I can see that," I say.

"When life gets overly complicated, this serves as a reminder that we can always step off the conveyor belt, live a simpler existence, and probably be more content."

I sigh. "I should definitely try to get out in nature more. If I go to the parks near me, there are just so many people having picnics, playing frisbee, chasing toddlers, I barely even notice the greenery. But here…" I take in the meandering paths, spiky branches and dangling vines. "There's a sense of intrigue—you can't help wonder what's around the next corner."

He nods his agreement. "I'm always discovering a new trail or secret nook—there's over thirty acres to explore…"

I make a mental note to return with Gareth so he can put a name to the myriad flora and fauna. Words like acacia and acanthus leaf are so soothing to my ear. One day I'll record him reading the index from a botany book and make it into a sleep meditation.

"Do you know the two most popular flowers for funerals are carnations and white stargazer lilies?" I venture.

"I did not know that," Ben replies, repeating "stargazer" with a wistful breath. "That seems apt."

No doubt Gareth would have brought a few stems to lay beside the graves. I wish I had thought about doing that. It feels a little voyeuristic to come empty-handed.

"So how long have you been taking walks in cemeteries?" I ask, hoping my question doesn't come off too "Do you come here often?"

He stops to think. "Well, I suppose it started when my grandmother died, so about six years now. That was my first time in a churchyard and I was surprised to find myself feeling something other than sad."

I tilt my head. "How do you mean?"

"Well, this is going to sound weird but I remember thinking, *She's not alone in this. Look at all these people who have gone before her, all these people who surround her.* There are way more people who have crossed over than there are still living on the planet. It helped me see this wasn't just a loss or an ending, it was a rite of passage. You have to respect the cycles of life."

"Hmmm."

"You don't agree?"

"No, it's just…" I trail off. "Sometimes you lose people too soon."

"Well, that's true. And that's very different." He eyes me and then asks gently, "Did you lose someone?"

I look away. "I'm more in the process of losing…" I begin, surprised to hear myself telling him about my mum's dementia. I haven't even told my work colleagues. "It's made me hyper aware of the little time I have left with her. You know, as herself."

"I'm so sorry," he whispers in sympathy. "My grandmother had dementia. I know how it feels to miss someone when they are stood right in front of you."

I stare back at him. It's rare for me to talk with someone who understands.

"I can't imagine what it would be like to have my mum be that way…That's got to be hard."

"It is," I say, fearing I may have brought the vibe too far down. "I'm sorry. I don't know why I mentioned it. I can't even bear to think about it. But then again, I'm always thinking about it…"

He tilts his head. "I know this is easier said than done but you don't want to be conjuring the loss over and over before it even happens."

"I know. But I honestly don't know how to break the cycle."

He looks around him, as if searching for answers in the moss-smudged inscriptions. "I'm not saying any of this will work or be easy but instead of saying you are losing her you could say you are celebrating her, or making the most of her or grateful for her—all of which are equally true."

I nod back at him.

"We have to find the beauty to balance out the despair. Like now, you can feel that pain but you can also look around and find some wonder too, right?"

At his invitation I scan the scene, choosing to point out the way the gold leaf lettering shines so brightly on a dull gray headstone, even though it dates back to 1890.

"There you go!" he encourages. "You know what my grand-father always says? 'Some days there won't be a song in your heart. Sing anyway.'"

My heart pangs. I feel so touched by his empathy. It's funny how a relative stranger can say a few words and bring about such a keen sense of comfort and relief.

"Thank you," I sigh, misty-eyed.

"So, do you want to see a fallen angel?" he asks.

"Of course," I cheer, glad to move on.

He takes me to the tomb where a sculpted, winged figure has toppled into the undergrowth, cheek to the earth. "Isn't she lovely?" he says, laying a gentle hand on her head.

"She is," I sigh, inhaling the woodsy scent as a breeze stirs the spirits around us.

It's easy to picture Ben in a billowing shirt, writing poetry with a quill pen. He seems a romantic soul, not quite of the modern world and thus not bound by its rules.

"All I ask when I go is that I leave behind one piece of work that is meaningful—I don't mind if I spend half my life schlepping drink trays trying to figure out what that is."

In a society filled with daily goal-setting and target-hitting, I find his long-game perspective refreshing. As he ambles on through a leafy archway, I find myself raising my phone camera, eager to memorialize this sentiment. And then I crouch beside the fallen angel, taking a close-up of her face nestled on a pillow of tiny white flowers. I smile as a little chiffchaff bird hops onto the headstone and poses perkily for me, giving me an assortment of angles and sweetly squeaky chirps.

When I stand upright again, Ben is nowhere to be seen.

"Hello?" I call. "Ben, are you there?"

How far would he have gone on without me? He could be chatting away presuming I'm right behind him and then not be able to retrace his steps because there are too many forks in the path. I experience a twang of nerves.

"Ben?" I hurry what I hope is after him, passing a couple who probably think I'm calling for my dog. "Ben?"

I round a corner, momentarily distracted by a set of sculptures on plinths, putting me in mind of a band rising up from the stage at an arena concert. And then I jump out of my skin as I feel a prickling-tickle on my neck.

I turn around to find Ben with a fern in his hand. "Did you see this headstone for the founder of the Salvation Army?"

I heave a sigh of relief.

"Are you okay?" he asks, suddenly concerned.

"I am now," I puff, waiting for the pounding in my chest to subside. "I thought I'd lost you."

"Oh, I'm sorry! Do you want to sit down for a moment?"

I nod gratefully and then blink in disbelief.

The setting he conjures couldn't be more enchanting—a double set of stone steps strewn with pink blossom petals.

"One staircase each?" I suggest and we scamper up in unison, sending the petals a-fluttering. If I twirled around, my outfit would become a chiffon dress and we'd break into a wafty-dreamy waltz before reclining on the balustrade, gazing breathlessly at each other.

"You wouldn't expect to find a terrace here," I muse as we rest upon the low wall. "Ooh, look!"

A hush descends as we track the air dance of a pale blue butterfly. When it finally moves on, Ben seems content to relax and let his thoughts drift, but I continue to take pictures, even though my battery is now on 5 percent. I discreetly switch to video as I zoom in on him—now reclining, gazing skyward, one hand on his chest, the other twisting his hair.

"What are you thinking about?" I ask.

He turns to the camera, giving it the sexiest look ever and murmurs, "Cake."

"Really?" I sigh.

"I know the perfect place to take you."

At which point he jumps up and grabs my hand.

I'm thrilled and can't wait to see what his idea of the perfect place for me would be...

"This way!" He ducks under a low canopy of leaves and as we emerge, an ominous swathe of gray blocks the sun and the air turns chilly.

"Oh no, rain!" I whimper as it starts to mist and then smatter.

He looks at me with curiosity, perhaps wondering how a light shower could ever be a surprise in England.

"It's just the hair situation," I explain, in case every woman he has ever met has been a festival freebird.

"I know, nightmare!" He scrumples his own mop until it stands askew in seven different directions but only serves to make him look more handsome.

"Can you do mine like that?" I ask.

"Seriously?" He falters.

"Why not?" I grin, feeling ridiculously daring.

I think my eyes close for a second as he pushes his hands through my hair, swirling and backcombing with his fingertips. This is the most intimate we've been since the wedding. I wish I knew how heated things got in the kitchen that night. I also wish he would kiss me right now. He is arranging a few straggles around my face and when our eyes meet it feels as if he's smiling right into my soul. My heart pounds in anticipation, but then an overhanging tree branch drops a big wet dollop on my nose and startles us apart.

"Come on," he laughs. "Let's make a run for it!"

14

I feel like a kid again—the smell of the damp earth, racing over twigs and stones, the promise of tea and cake...

I wasn't expecting Ben to have a car but when I see a dinky Fiat with a dent on the side panel it just seems to fit.

"Actually, this is me!" He points two cars back.

Suddenly the rain stops and the sun illuminates a shimmering gold sedan.

My head jerks back in surprise. "You drive a Mercedes?"

"It's an old one, I got it for three grand. Door's open."

"Oh, I love it!" I coo as I slide into the worn leather passenger seat. "Look at this dashboard!"

It has a glossy tortoiseshell finish with a chrome-trimmed cigarette lighter and narrow ivory steering wheel. As we pull away from the curb, Ben drapes his arm out of the window like he's on an American road trip, desert breeze wafting through his fingers. I can almost hear The Doobie Brothers playing, even though the stereo doesn't work.

In a little over ten minutes we're cruising down an unfamiliar high street with an enticingly quirky range of boutiques, cafes and knick-knack shops.

"A bookshop!" I cheer, twisting around—such a good reminder of all there is to know and wonder at in the world. "It always makes me happy to see one still going strong."

"There's actually three here."

"What?" I exclaim. "Where *are* we?"

"Crouch End."

"Is this where you live?"

He gives a little shrug. "Until Wednesday."

"You're moving?" I can barely conceal my dismay. Already I'd compiled fantasies of Sunday coffee in the open-fronted cafe, laughing in the local pub with his mates, resting my head on his shoulder in the cinema, picnics and piggy-backs in the park and sunbeam-streaked photos with the big shaggy dog we adopted the day we decided to share a postcode.

"I'll probably be back in the summer," he consoles me.

"Where will you be in between?"

"Let's see, next stop is Chiswick, then I've got a weekend in Chelsea, followed by nearly a month in Clapham."

"You only live in places beginning with C?"

"That's actually just a coincidence."

"Also a C." My eyes narrow.

He laughs as he slides neatly into a parking space. "I'm pet-sitting. This car is the closest thing I have to a fixed abode right now."

"So, are you in the process of looking for somewhere to live?"

"Well, I was. But then the sits kept coming so I put the flat-hunting on hold and now I just can't bring myself to pay a grand or so in rent when I can share a bed with three cats or an enormous Saint Bernard."

"Who on earth has a Saint Bernard in London?"

"I can't say, I had to sign a non-disclosure agreement."

"Seriously?" My eyes widen.

"Total C-lister, but all the same." He mimes zipping his lip.

"Is it a fancy place?"

"It's big, with a big garden. And that's really all I'm prepared to say."

"Wow."

"Come on." He gives my leg a little squeeze. "Cake time."

As we head down the street I ask, in my most casual tone, how this house-hopping has impacted his romantic life...

"In terms of bringing someone home? It hasn't really come up, I've only been doing it for six months."

I try not to look too pleased with his answer.

He tells me the bigger hassle is all the packing and unpacking—not so much his wardrobe but all the food items.

"There have been several leaky soy sauce and melted butter incidents," he grimaces. "Plus, I seem to lose something every time I switch places. And sometimes I finish work and just stand there in the street thinking, *Where am I staying?* I drove halfway to Camden last month before I remembered I'd moved on."

"To…?"

"Camberwell," he replies and then smiles. "You seem to have a point about the C thing…"

"How long do you think you can last doing this?" I ask. "I'm just curious, no judgment. I'm looking to buy a flat but now you're making me wonder about other options!" Like maybe housesitting for a year to add a bit more to my budget…

"Well," he muses. "I'm twenty-five now—"

"Wait! You're twenty-five!" I come to an abrupt halt. "I thought you were my age!"

"I've had a rough couple of weeks sleep-wise," he says, rubbing his eyes. "The dog snores and the cat gets her kicks scaling the wall to flip the light switch—usually around four a.m. I certainly feel like I've aged ten years lately."

Before I can fully process the decade age gap, he motions for me to step through the adjacent doorway.

"This is the place?"

He nods. "After you."

For a second, I think I've stepped into his grandmother's sitting room—there's chintz upholstery with lace antimacassars, standing lamps with peach tassels, framed photographs of kids with bowl cuts hung on floral wallpaper, a basket of yarn and knitting needles beside a chunky, wooden box TV, not to mention a pair of Noddy and Big Ears salt and pepper shakers.

"So, what do you think?"

"I truly couldn't love it any more," I sigh.

"I thought you'd like it." He looks chuffed.

It takes a very particular man to be able to enjoy homespun kitsch. Suddenly his age seems to be of very little consequence.

Rose and lemon loaf with glittery sprinkles. Banana bread with espresso butter. Chocolate Guinness cake with creamy frosting.

We order one of each to share, heeding the advice penned on a porcelain plate: THE MORE YOU WEIGH, THE HARDER YOU ARE TO KIDNAP. STAY SAFE – EAT CAKE!

My phone dies as I try to photograph it, though I may get it tattooed at a later date.

"And your choice of tea?" the waitress inquires.

We lean into the menu, sleeve to sleeve. I do like being in Ben's personal space. I linger over the description of the Oolong Iron Buddha just to prolong the proximity.

"How about this one?" He points to the Darjeeling Second Flush. "In case you don't know, a flush begins when the tea plant grows new leaves and ends when those leaves are harvested. I used to do the tea service at the Waldorf."

"I believe you, and yet you seem to have a particularly mischievous look on your face..."

"Did you see this plate?" He attempts – and succeeds – in distracting me with more quotes.

"My theory is that all Scottish cuisine is based on a dare," I read with a giggle.

"I saw one last week that has become my motto for life: *When nothing goes right, go left!*"

"Brilliant!" I enthuse. "If it's not working, make a different choice."

"Exactly! And speaking of going left…" He ushers me up a couple of steps and through a doorway.

If the initial area was styled after a front room, we are now entering the boudoir. There's a chaste single bed with floral sheets and a hot water bottle set alongside a vanity table with a three-fold mirror and a white plastic hairdryer, perfect for seventies flicks.

But the pièce de résistance—or should that be piss de résistance—is the powder pink bathroom suite: pink tiles, pink sink, pink loo with ultra-frilly nylon covering.

"Who would sit there?" I gasp. "I mean, someone would actually have to sit on the toilet!"

"And today that someone is you!"

"No way!" I shrink back.

"You have to—I called to reserve it!"

"You didn't!" I gasp, wondering if that was what he was up to when he seemed to disappear at the cemetery. "But where will you sit?"

"On the laundry basket." He points to the wicker unit, padded with a neatly folded pink towel.

I shake my head. "This is blowing my mind."

We slot into position to allow the waitress to place our order on a sheet of glass covering the sink.

"I can't believe I'm going to eat cake sat on a toilet!"

She holds up a teapot commemorating Charles and Diana's wedding. "Darjeeling?"

"Second flush, that's me!" I raise my hand.

As Ben hoots with mirth, the penny drops. I look down at the toilet then cover my face with my hands. "I knew you were up to something!"

"Would you mind taking a picture?" he asks the waitress, handing her his phone.

"What, now that my face is the same color as the fixtures?"

He tells me not to worry—I look great!—but the image tells a different story: between the rain spritzing and Ben's artistic tousling I now have the same frazzled locks as the doll covering the toilet roll.

"Isn't it funny how dolls' hair always ends up all matted and mad?" I muse. "I know I ruined mine with a mix of talc and my mum's tongs."

Ben takes a closer look at the doll's outfit—a voluminous pink crocheted number, a cross between a tea cozy and a Disney princess. "They need to do an updated version of this," he decides. "Something like Billy Porter's black velvet gown from the Oscars."

"Wasn't that sublime?" I sigh. "I actually know a brother and sister team that could make that happen."

As we tuck into our cakes, the conversation veers from friends to fashion to school uniforms, worst childhood hairstyles and then teenage crushes. I try to get him on the subject of more recent exes but all I glean is that his last girlfriend was a tattoo artist, which makes me question whether I'm remotely his type. Mind you, he's also very different to anyone I've dated. I'll say one thing about this "which cup is the ball under" style of dating—it's making me give men a chance that I wouldn't normally have thought I could have a future with.

"Fancy another cuppa?" he offers.

"I do indeed—and maybe we could try the scone with the fig jam?"

This time round I insist Ben gets the toilet seat and he pairs it with some toilet humor, showing me some graffiti he saw in a recent cubicle: "Dear Automatic Flush—I appreciate your enthusiasm but I wasn't done."

"I always seem to have the opposite experience," I confide. "I'm waving my hand trying to trigger the sensor, pressing everything that could pass for a button…"

"You know the C-lister's house? They have a toilet with an LED light in the lid for night-time peeing with six color options!"

"No! What did you choose?"

"Well, green felt too alien, red too Amsterdam but blue was quite soothing."

We've really run the conversational gamut today. Eventually we look up and realize we are the last people here. If the bed in the corner could accommodate two people, I'd happily snuggle up and keep chatting through till the vegan breakfast serving.

"You don't know if there are any estate agents around here?" I ask as I gather up my bag.

"You're thinking of moving here just to be near this place?"

"Well, it does feel like the next best thing to a guinea pig cafe with Phoebe Waller-Bridge behind the counter," I reply. "But honestly, I like the whole area, the cozy village feel..."

"Well then, let's go have a look."

Of course, the flat next door to Gareth would still be my first choice but given the slim chance of that coming to fruition, this would be an excellent consolation prize.

As it happens, the estate agents are all closed but several boutiques are calling to me with their multi-textured, muted-hue wares promising instant serenity if I just purchased a macramé plant holder, a set of sage smudging sticks and a bar of activated charcoal soap.

"You want to look inside, don't you?"

I feign indifference though internally I'm swooning at the idea of "desert ghost flower" scented candles. "Some other time."

"I really don't mind!"

My eyes narrow. "Is this some kind of trick?"

He leans in. "Haven't you heard—they've created this device for increasing the male shopping tolerance by up to five hundred percent?" He holds up his phone with a smirk.

Now I'm smiling. "I'll just be a few minutes."

As I step inside I almost feel like we're a boyfriend and girlfriend at that nice harmonious stage where you can tootle off and do your own thing and then happily reunite. At least I've heard of such things; I've never actually experienced it myself.

I'm rifling through a rail of cute sweaters with colored pom-pom bobbles when I come to a cluster of silk camis. I pull out the black one with the deep V of spidery lace at the décolletage and then look back through the window. Ben is leaning on the wall, contentedly tapping away on his phone. This could be just what I need to step up my game.

"May I try this?"

The petite assistant pushes back the curtain to the changing room and then swishes it semi-closed behind me. It's one of those cubicles that never quite seals you from view and makes you wonder how much of a peep show you are putting on, but I want to see what it looks like with nothing underneath so I quickly strip and slip it over my head at double-speed. It certainly feels pleasingly slinky on my skin. I give my hair a fluff, imagining inviting him over for dinner, putting on a little Nat King Cole, teaming the cami with a pair of jeans and a slinky gold chain like the Instagram babes do. I might even get some shimmery body lotion…Suddenly I'm so impatient for that moment I want to rush over and tap on the window and mouth, "What do you think?" but with my cleavage that's a move that needs to be reserved for a private viewing.

"I'll take it!" I say as I emerge.

My heart is racing at the till and I find myself adding a pair of pale blue drop earrings.

"You look happy!" Ben smiles as I exit, swinging my bag.

"I am!"

I want him to ask what I bought so I can say, "You'll have to wait and see…" but instead he tells me he was just texting his friends and they want to know if we'd like to join them at the cinema—he points across the street to the cool, glass-fronted movie theater. "And there's the option of an Italian after."

"*Italian!*" I jump, looking at my watch, then clamping my hand over my mouth. I'd completely forgotten about Tristan!

"That looks like a no…"

"Ben, I'm so sorry! I'm supposed to be having dinner with…" —I catch myself—"a potential client. For work. I completely lost track of time!" I spin around, unsure of the speediest route from here. I can't even use my phone for directions.

"Where do you need to get to?"

"Mayfair."

"Okay. Quickest option is the tube. I'll drop you at Finsbury Park so you can get the Piccadilly line straight down…"

"No, no I don't want to throw out your evening." I can't have Date Number One drive me to Date Number Two, it's just wrong. "I'll get a taxi."

"Come on, the car's right here." He's already striding toward it.

I scurry after him. "It's really so nice of you." I feel all jumbled up as we bundle in, then brace myself, hand on the dashboard, as we begin dipping and weaving through the traffic.

"You certainly know your way around!" I note.

He shrugs. "One of the benefits of house-hopping—all the different areas start to patchwork together…"

"I can't even imagine driving in London," I say, flinching at a near miss with a cyclist.

"It's one of those things where the only way to find it less scary is to do it more. Right. If the next lights are red, you're best jumping out. You see where to go?"

I nod vigorously, tucking my boutique bag into my tote and preparing to unclick the seat belt.

"Okay, go dazzle them!"

Oh god. "Thank you!" I squeal as I bundle out.

I feel decidedly off-key as I run toward the tube station. This is so absurd—cutting the flow on a date that is going well in order to start another one off on the wrong foot. I've even done myself out of a farewell embrace with Ben, leaving me with no sense of when—or even if—we're going to see each other again. Clattering down the escalator, I'm also aware of a guilty sensation—as if I've sold out Crouch End for Mayfair. It would serve me right if I get there and Tristan's already gone.

"Excuse me, sorry!" I squeeze into the carriage, find a rail to hold and take out my phone, clicking and depressing every button in the hope that it will magically come back to life. No such luck. I can't warn Tristan that I'm running late and I can't get May to meet me at the entrance with my change of outfit. What can I do? I go to rummage in my bag to see if I can at least find my lip gloss but another surge of people squish in at King's Cross and now all I can do is spend the next six stops hoping that a) he's later than me, b) the maître d' has us down for a low-lit booth tucked at the back of the restaurant and c) the strange sweaty-food smell coming from the man next to me isn't transferring onto my outfit...

15

The good news is that I am only twenty-six minutes late arriving. The bad news is that the restaurant is one of those vast, gleaming, nook-free spaces populated with Real Housewife clones, each one so botoxed and bedazzled I expect to be handed a selfie ring light and microblading kit at the host podium. It could happen—remember how men used to be given ties to wear if they didn't meet the dress code?

"*Buona sera, signorina.*" I am greeted by a sleek man with a shiny jaw. "How may I help you?"

He thinks I've strayed in to ask directions to Nando's.

"*Buono sera.*" I dip my head then whisper, "I'm afraid I'm a bit late for my dining companion, Tristan, um." Oh gosh, I don't know his last name. "Very handsome blond with a little dip in his chin here…"

"Ah, yes," he grimaces. "Allow me to escort you."

Even from this distance I can see my dinner date is peeved. I begin my fluster of apologies from two tables away. "I'm so sorry, I had a client meeting that overran and—"

"You look different."

My hand goes to my hair. "Well, yes, I am a little windswept…"

Was he expecting me to turn up with an updo and a silk dress like at the wedding?

"I wouldn't have recognized you."

By which he means, "I wouldn't have invited you…"

"I, er…" I falter. He doesn't seem overly keen on my joining him. I'm not convinced either—we're right next to the clattering and sizzling of the open kitchens, which just adds to the frazzled vibe.

"Are you going to sit down?" He seems fully exasperated now.

"Just give me five minutes to tidy myself up!" I rally, sidestepping a waiter bearing a tray of oysters.

I find myself hovering for a second beside the exit… Would it be awful if I just ran out into the night? We both seem to have had a loss of appetite—he'd rather be with the dolled-up girl from the wedding and I'd rather be with Ben. Or even just out in the cool air. Of course, there is a one-in-three chance that Tristan is my Big Love but I think the odds are higher. Or lower. Or whatever way round it is when the outcome is unlikely. Already I feel deflated and defensive.

"Could you at least try seeing it from his point of view?" I hear my mum playing devil's advocate as I step into the hall of mirrors they call the ladies'.

I have to concede that he's gone to a lot of trouble to groom and impress whereas I look like something that blew in from the moors. I mean, how would I have felt if I'd got a mani-pedi and a new frock, only to have him lurch in late in a crumpled football shirt? If my phone wasn't dead, I'd be tempted to ask May to swing by with my rose-gold top. The thought of doing three courses in cashmere right next to all the flambéing and grilling...

Unless.

I reach into my bag. The slippy silk of the camisole is pleasingly cool to the touch. I feel a bit guilty repurposing it for Tristan when I bought it with a Ben bedroom scenario in mind, but what other options do I have? I dart into the cubicle, wrangle it on but unfortunately May was right about my underwear situation. My comfort bra is not exactly showing off the spidery lace to its best advantage. I'm going to have to try and drape my jumper over that area. Or order lobster and hope they provide a bib.

The more pressing concern is my face. As much as I'd like to reconnect to the liberation I felt on the Disruptive Beauty night, this is not a conducive environment. I start rummaging in my bag for my make-up. Earlier this week I watched a YouTube video on how women prisoners do their make-up without cosmetics—using deodorant and vaseline to work the colored pigments from magazine pages into eyeshadows. I'd be willing to give it a try but for once I don't have a rolled-up copy of *Grazia* in my bag. I do, however, have concealer, so I sweep it under my eyes, around the corners of my nose and in a circle on my chin. Blend, blend. No eyeshadow but I can smudge my kohl into a smokey eye and my rosy lip sheen can double as blush. Oh, that's a bit sticky. I try to lift it off with a tissue but now have a layer of white paper stuck to my cheeks.

"*Goddammit!*"

I turn away as another woman enters the ladies', scrubbing at my cheeks as she enters the cubicle. On the upside, I now have an authentically pink flush.

I quickly wash my hands and then smooth a little of the scented hand cream behind my ears to double as perfume. All that remains is to loosely pile my hair up into a topknot, freeing a few waves around my face.

The other woman is stood beside me now. If I were her, I would be transfixed by my own reflection—the luminescence of her skin, the artistry of her brows—but she seems more interested in studying my outfit.

"You need to lose the bra."

My eyes widen. Is that a proposition?

"If it were black, you might have got away with it, but beige that's seen better days?"

I pull a face. "I'm worried about looking a bit *provocative* without it…"

She leans in. "You step out like this, your evening is only going to get worse. You lose the bra, he'll forgive you everything. Trust me, I know men."

"Really?" Suddenly I feel a little seedy.

She shrugs as she applies a layer of iridescent lip gloss. "It's your call."

And then she's gone.

I look back at the mirror, acknowledging just how much better it looked in the boutique and then sigh, "Well, here goes nothing!"

This time when I approach the table Tristan scrambles up to get my chair and, when the waiter approaches, he orders champagne. A magnum of Moët & Chandon no less.

I sneak a glance at my fairy godmother, who discreetly raises her glass to me and smiles.

This really is a different world—gleaming cutlery, attentive service, leather-framed menus as big as desk blotters...Rich people even sound different in their small talk.

"So, should we be toasting the success of your meeting?" Tristan asks as the waiter positions the ice bucket beside our table.

"My meeting?"

"The reason you were late..."

"Oh, I'd already forgotten about that." I swat away his comment, turning my attention to the pale gold bubbles filling my glass. "This place is so amazing. Any particular dishes you'd recommend?"

"Do you often work on a Saturday?"

He doesn't seem to want to let it go.

"Very rarely, it was just this one client was in town from Italy, and it was the only day he could do." I study the menu intently, hoping he'll do the same.

"What part of Italy?"

Oh, for the love of pizza.

"Bologna," I say, having dismissed the lesser-known towns of Carbonara and Amatriciana.

He nods. "I just got back from Milan the night before the wedding."

"Really?" I look up.

"Of course, it was business but I always try to take in some culture in my downtime. Opera in Italy is a much more visceral experience. And La Scala isn't to be missed, especially if you're a fan of Neo-classical design, which of course I am."

"Of course."

It feels like he's reciting a *Telegraph* city guide but he's certainly got it down pat, pausing only long enough for us to place our order. Happily we both go straight for the main course—apparently he ate his body weight in olives while he was waiting for me.

"And would you like wine with your meal?" the waiter asks.

"I'm fine with champagne," I say, as if I'm taking one for the team.

"I'll have a glass of the Bucci Villa Riserva Verdicchio," Tristan decides.

"An excellent choice, signor."

I wonder if a waiter has ever responded with a spitting motion and said, "What are you thinking? That one tastes like vinegar!"

"Anyway! Back to Milan," Tristan continues. "Did you know that Bellini premiered his first opera at La Scala?"

I want to say, "No, but give me some peach juice and I'll conjure a Bellini right now!" But I don't. Instead, I say, "Tell me more!"

Ordinarily I might find this lecturing style of talk tedious but I'm so glad to have the chance to catch my breath and for nothing to be asked of me, beyond the occasional "Really?" or "Oh, how wonderful!" It's amazing how much drinking you can get done that way. Especially when you have a waiter whose sole duty appears to be keeping you topped up.

"Of course, whenever I'm there I visit my tailor. He does the most superb bespoke suits."

"Is this one of them?" I ask, acknowledging his immaculate midnight navy ensemble.

He nods, visibly preening.

"Beautiful—very George Clooney."

His eyes light up. This is clearly a man who responds well to compliments. At least now I have a tactic for the meal: I'll simper and fawn and laugh like a bell and then go home and get in my pjs and strike his name from the list.

"More champagne?"

"Don't mind if I do."

I smile as I watch the waiter refill my glass. I'm finding the blurriness helpful, softening the edges of my brain. But then Tristan says, "So, Amy, tell me everything I need to know about you."

"That seems a little broad..."

"All right." He leans back on his chair. "What do you want from me and where do you want tonight to lead?"

"And that's incredibly specific."

He gives a cocky shrug. "Well, you were pretty detailed on the phone..."

I gulp.

"I liked it," he tells me. "I like a woman who knows her mind."

Oh jeez. I neither know my mind nor what I said. I take another sip of champagne. Is this why we're at such a fancy restaurant, because I made some highly explicit sexual promises? I should really watch my drinking tonight. Or drink more...

"You know, I knew as soon as you sat down at the wedding table that we were going to get together."

"Did you?"

He nods. "There's just something about you..." His eyes lower to the lace area of my camisole, making me so self-conscious that I fear even my breathing is causing an unnecessary rise and fall in that area.

I feel I might need to rein him in a little. I look for my fairy godmother, wondering if I could lure her back to the ladies' for some pointers, but she's gone—probably on a private helicopter by now.

"Your cappellacci di zucca."

Oh, praise be! The food has arrived, we can focus on that. Mine looks perfect—six pasta parcels in a brown butter sauce accented with crispy, deep-fried sage. I can't wait to tuck in!

"Spaghetti al nero di seppia con gamberi."

"Oh goodness!" I startle at Tristan's choice—I don't know if I've seen a less appetizing dish: squirms of shiny black spaghetti set with giant, pink, ridged prawns. It looks like a high-end Bush Tucker Trial—I think it might even be moving...

"You've never had squid ink pasta?"

I shake my head emphatically.

"You have to try it!"

"Oh no," I wince. I don't know which I find more distressing—eating it or the idea that he might try to feed me across the table.

"What does it taste of?"

"I think briny is the best description. Here..."

"Really, I'm fine!" I quickly fill my mouth with butternut squash and extend the necessary chewing period, adding a second one before I'm done.

For a moment I think I've got away with it. I've got him on to the subject of homemade tagliatelle. Gareth showed us how to do this on my last birthday dinner—flattening out the durum wheat dough to a paper-thin layer, rolling it up like a carpet, then cutting it into narrow slices that unravel into the delicate pasta strips. But then I see a heaped fork heading my way.

"Come on, one little bite..."

Oh god! I'd use my fingers to take the food but of course it's too slippery to handle so, reluctantly and resentfully, I lean forward.

The table is sufficiently wide that I have to rise up and bend forward, adding a peep show quality to the proceedings. I wonder just how far down my top he can see? Apparently he's wondering the same thing because when I lose my nerve and turn my face away at the last minute the spaghetti continues its motion, sliding neatly down my cleavage.

I gasp in grossed-out shock as the warm worms slither down to my belly button. I don't even know what to do—how to react, how to fix this.

Tristan's jaw is equally slack. "Oh my god!"

"I can't tell you how weird this feels right now."

Tristan bites his lip. "Can you just let it fall out onto the napkin?"

"Is anyone looking?" I hiss, pulling my seat closer to the table.

He glances around then tenses. "One sec!"

"And how are you enjoying your food tonight?" Naturally the waiter chooses this precise moment to check in.

"Delicious!" Tristan enthuses, reaching for his wine.

"Signorina?"

I bat my eyes. "I can feel it going straight to my hips!"

Tristan spurts his drink as he bursts out laughing.

"Oh my god!" I reel, shaking off the liquid. "I didn't need any wine with my food!"

"I'm so sorry!"

"You want to order the tiramisu now so you can just smear that all over me?"

He's really laughing now.

"You wish for me to bring the dessert menu?" The waiter looks confused.

"No, no!" I sigh. "But a couple of extra napkins would be nice."

"Certainly."

I raise an eyebrow at Tristan.

He tries to contain himself but bursts out laughing again. His eyes are streaming now, his nose pink, his teeth are on full display and not as flawless as they first appeared. And yet…he's never looked more attractive. It's as if a mannequin has come to life.

"What are you trying to say?" I ask as he points to my shoulders.

All he manages to get out is, "Spaghetti straps!" before he convulses again.

"You know, you wouldn't find it so funny if you were the one coated in squid ink."

"Well, at least it matches your outfit!"

I try to hide my smile. I would never have predicted this side to him. It's a world away from the terse individual who greeted me. And the conversational bore who made me wonder if the reason I kissed him at the wedding was to stop him talking.

Finally he catches his breath. "Any food, any body part—you choose."

"What do you mean?"

"I'm inviting you to return the favor—I have a whole fridge full of options."

Did he just ask me back to his?

I make a joke to stall for time. "A little orecchiette for your ears? Jelly beans for your belly button…"

"I've got a whole pork loin—"

"Now hold on a minute!" I raise my hand, which he takes in his.

And then my entire body chemistry alters. The mere act of him interlacing his fingers with mine sends a tingle through me and when his thumb begins tracing circles in my palm I become utterly entranced.

Finally I regain the ability to speak. "I would've thought you'd find all this mess and hysteria mortifying…"

"Why do you say that?" he asks, softly now, gazing directly into my eyes.

I give a little shrug. "Made-to-measure suits from Milan, Michelin-starred restaurants in Mayfair…"

"Well, you didn't seem like the kind of girl you could take to a taco truck."

"I'm exactly the kind of girl you can take to a taco truck!" I snuffle. "Mind you, if ever there was a cuisine that spills everywhere…"

"You know, my friend is hosting a Mexican street party next weekend…" He progresses his caresses up my arm. "There will be watermelon margaritas and a Mariachi band that does Lady Gaga covers."

"That sounds amazing!"

"So you'll come with me?"

I hesitate. I can't believe that an hour ago I was thinking of doing a runner and now I'm considering a second date. More than considering.

"I'd love to," I hear myself say.

He gives me a satisfied smile. And then peers over my side of the table. "I can't have you sitting there like that. My place is ten minutes from here. Let's get you cleaned up and start over."

My heart skips a beat—I'm going to see his place! But I'm definitely way too tipsy to navigate another posh restaurant. "Is there somewhere casual we can go?"

"There is an old-school pub near me that does the best pasties—"

"Bill, please!" I cut in.

Tristan takes out his wallet and then reaches over to the ice bucket to assess the remaining champagne. "Do you reckon we can finish this before he gets back?"

There's still the equivalent of a standard bottle left.

"Go for it!"

Suddenly everything seems a lot more fun. The champagne glugging only makes us giggle more and knowing that we're going to a scruffy pub where we don't have to worry about making a scene is such a relief. I don't even care about the state I'm in. All I want to do is to get this table out of the way so I can get closer to him. I'm longing for him to touch me again.

When he places his hand on the small of my back to escort me out, I have to bite back a squeal of excitement.

"Taxi!"

He hails one like a pro.

"Manhattan-trained," he acknowledges.

This time I am impressed, suddenly picturing myself on his arm on Fifth Avenue in a cocktail dress and satin heels.

He bows low as he opens the cab door for me. "My lady..."

"My man," I murmur as I step inside, wondering if he really could be The One.

16

The second the taxi is in motion, his lips are on mine. It's hard to coordinate with the bumping and the breaking and I'm feeling a little champagne-dizzy so it's a relief when he transfers his attention to my neck. He's wearing a different cologne to the wedding but it smells equally expensive. It makes me feel like I'm in the hands of a professional. And he is slick—I barely notice the transition from the cab to his place. From the key in the door to the steaming shower.

"It's all ready for you…"

I hover in the doorway, asking myself if I'm really going to shed my clothes right here, right now. I'm sure there must be a reason why I should hold back but I can't for the life of me think what it is. My eyes glance around the bathroom—it is exceptionally clean. Cleaning service clean. He has an after-shave collection to rival Selfridges and those towels look so plush…

"Never mind the towels!" I hear May huffing. "What are your instincts telling you about him?"

I don't know if I can even trust them anymore—I've been wrong so many times, utterly convinced I've met a quality guy only to flash-forward and see his dark side. Perhaps it's happening in reverse this time? The more layers I peel back, the more I like what I see.

Speaking of which...Tristan's jacket is off now and his unbuttoned shirt is giving me a preview of his tanned chest. He may have been at the opera by night in Milan but he was definitely on the hotel roof terrace by day.

"Everything okay?" he asks.

And that's when I hear a voice, which sounds a lot like Jay's, say, "Go on, treat yourself!"

And so I do.

It's dizzying to be desired with such intensity. I can't believe someone so attractive could be this into me! I'd forgotten the outrageous pleasure of exploring a man's body—how flawlessly silky his skin is, the firm lines, the boulder biceps...

It is clear now there will be no trip to the pub. Instead we kiss like we've been starved of contact for decades. Hearing his pleasure-drenched moans and knowing I am the cause is such an ego boost. My chin is going to be scorched tomorrow but I don't care. I just want to pull him closer, clamp him to me and feel that primal connection, bruised hip bones and all.

There's no gazing into each other's eyes, no still moments, no giggling—it's just full tilt sexual charge.

Eventually we fall apart, panting, shiny, trying to catch our breath. He reaches over and presses a button on his bedside remote and I feel a cool breeze whisk over my damp skin—it's as if I've been sunbathing in the tropics and now I'm being spritzed by an ice mister. Heaven!

I'm just thinking that no words can do justice to what just transpired when I realize he's fallen asleep. Oh, thank goodness. Finally a chance to steady my heart rate and give my body a chance to process what just happened. A few areas are clearly in shock from the excessive partying. I don't blame them—I'm kind of in shock myself. I didn't know I could be that amorous. I look over at his naked body. To think I wanted to do a runner from the restaurant!

I do, however, plan to do a runner from his bed—anything to avoid the morning-after anti-climax. I mean, that was so wild, I couldn't bear for hungover awkwardness to ruin the thrill of it all. Besides, if he was thrown by how I looked when I arrived at the restaurant, he'd be holding up a crucifix come the morning. I don't even need to look in the mirror to know that my hair has already gone full zombie apocalypse. The only problem is that my body is too spent to move. Perhaps if I just took the quickest nap, just enough to revive myself…

*

When I reopen my eyes, I see daylight taunting me from under the blind. Oh no. That is not tentative daybreak light, that's late morning on a gray day. I'd look at my watch but I don't want him to know I'm awake yet. First I need to come up with an exit plan.

I look around the room, which might as well be a hotel suite it's so immaculate and free from personal artifacts. There's even a bottle of designer water on the nightstand and—talk about service—two paracetamol. Did he do that last night or is that his version of a mint on the pillow for all his female guests?

I make a surreptitious, half-yawning movement to see if he responds.

Nothing.

I have got to take a slug of water.

I slowly move my hand toward the nightstand like I'm afraid of triggering a laser security system. Nice and easy does it. Oh no! Sparkling! I try to hush the hissing spurt of bubbles but still he doesn't stir. I raise the glass bottle to my lips, so grateful for the hydration. There's even a hint of refreshing mint so I feel like it's doubling as mouthwash. Now if I can just slip out unnoticed, I can send a cute text then get extra dolled up next time I see him. Far better that way.

I begin easing myself off the mattress. That's the first leg out, I'm working on the second but this bed frame is so high I think I'm going to have to employ a rolling motion.

"All right?"

I look up and see Tristan's form filling the doorway. I jerk my head back to the bed and find it empty—not quite sure what I was expecting to see there.

"You're up!" I say, grappling with the sheet.

"One moment…" He walks past me to the bathroom, returning with a velvety robe, pale ivory to his rich navy. "Now come with me…"

I go to protest—I just need to tidy myself up a bit, maybe take a thirty-second shower—but he is already leading me through to the kitchen, all black granite and brushed-chrome fixtures. But who's looking at the cabinetry when there is a breakfast spread to rival a boutique hotel: outsize chocolate croissants, Greek yogurt scattered with pink pomegranate seeds, heaps of diced tomato and grated cheese beside the omelet station (aka the frying pan), orange juice so fresh the citrus zest is tickling my nose…

"I thought you might need some fortification before we begin again." He pulls me toward him with the belt of the robe. "We can spend the whole day getting to know each other."

My shoulders slump. "I wish I could, truly, but I have to go." I catch sight of the oven clock. "In fact, I'm already late."

He releases me abruptly. "Another client?"

"No, no, my mum."

"Your mum?" he hoots then reaches for me again. "I'm sure you can miss one Sunday lunch." His lips begin at my neck, moving hungrily down to my collarbone as he teases open my robe. "Wouldn't she want her little girl to be happy?"

I jump back, startled by the sensations he's triggering. I have to nip this in the bud before I become another item on the buffet.

"Honestly, I can't let her down, if anything happened to her the one week I didn't visit…"

He frowns at me.

I hesitate. I don't want to reference her condition, it seems too personal. Which is odd since I didn't think twice about discussing it with Ben…"It's just a set-in-stone thing with us, but I really appreciate all the trouble you went to—it looks amazing."

"So, that's it?" he scowls. "You've had your fun and now you're walking out on me?"

Oh jeez.

"I'm not walking out on you, I'm just keeping a prior appointment." Is he really in a huff or just messing with me? I decide to give him a moment to cool off. "I'm just going to hop in the shower, if that's okay…"

"Mmm, sorry, you're going to have to skip that," he snips out. "I'll need to set the alarm so we have to leave together."

What? I frown back at him. "I'll be two minutes."

"I need to go now. I just remembered I'm meeting the guys." He clips my shoulder as he passes me on the way to the bedroom and starts pulling items from his wardrobe.

I can't believe how quickly he's switched from nuzzling my neck to throwing me out on my ear. This definitely feels like a punishment. And what a waste of this glorious breakfast. I look back longingly at the croissants. I get the feeling he'd smack my hand if I reached for one now.

As I collect my clothes to change in the toilet I wonder if I could have handled that better. Once again he's the one who's gone to an enormous amount of effort and I'm the one spoiling his romantic plans. And what's he going to say in response? "You hurt my feelings!" No. He's going to get surly. I decide I need to have a sincere moment with him—to let him know how amazing the whole evening was—but he looks away as he holds open the front door and I say nothing.

"Of course!" I mutter to myself as we step out from Tristan's building and into the rain.

I don't have a coat, let alone an umbrella. All I can do is run for the shelter of the tree while he bleeps his car, parked directly outside on the curb. I watch with incredulity as he steps into his low, sleek Jag. I don't even know what part of town I'm in and he's going to drive off and leave me? How was none of this in my premonition? Surely this is how it ends—me bedraggled and furious with myself for succumbing to his charms. Why isn't this scenario ringing any bells?

Speaking of ringing—my phone is still dead. Obviously. They really should have kept phone booths around for these sorts of situations. All I can do is walk until I find a busier road then ask directions or flag down yet another taxi. I seem to recall him mentioning there was a pub nearby…

I feel mildly teary but set myself in motion—arms folded

across my chest, head down to keep the rain from getting in my eyes. How can we have gone from crying with laughter at dinner to this? Never mind all the bedroom shenanigans...

"Amy, wait!"

Oh gosh, he's coming after me! I quicken my pace. *Too little too late, mate!*

Suddenly he's stepping in front of me, opening out a black executive-style umbrella and offering me shelter—the two of us now face to face in this dark, waterproof cocoon.

"I'm sorry," he says, his voice low and sincere, his eyes fully locked onto mine now. "I really like you, Amy. More than I should at this point. And I wanted you to stay—I'd gone to a lot of trouble with breakfast, I had all these fantasies..." He gives me a sly smile. "You can't blame me for wanting more of what we had last night..."

I don't know what to say. So much of my mind is taken up with the sensation of wet wool on my arms.

"The fact is, it's nice that you want to be with your mother. And that you keep your promises."

I look warily back at him, still not sure where this is leading.

"So can I take you there?"

Much as I'd like to spurn him, the rain is getting heavier. I heave a frustrated sigh. "I don't even know where we are—it might be a trek from here."

"I don't mind, wherever you need to go."

"What about your friends?"

He shrugs. "They can wait."

I push my hand through my wet hair. "Well, at least I got my shower!"

He looks sheepish. "You know, I've got a brand new Tolly McRae blanket in the boot, I can make you all cozy."

"I'm riding in the boot?"

"No," he splutters, laughing.

"Well, it's best to be sure about these things."

I'm grateful that he's keen to show off the capabilities of his car stereo so we don't have to talk, and even more delighted that I get to charge my phone from his lead.

When the screen comes back to life I surreptitiously tap on the map to check our route. We are in Chelsea. And not only are we on course for Battersea, we'll be there in a few minutes. I exhale in relief.

"Worried I was going to abduct you?" he smirks.

"Just checking our arrival time," I say, turning my phone face down and making a show of peering up at the pretty pastel paintwork of Albert Bridge. The strands of lightbulbs look like a cat's cradle of luminous pearls at night—my mum loves it when we sneak up onto the fire escape to see them. She says it makes her feel like we're Tinkerbell and Wendy, about to take flight…

"You know, I could wait for you…" Tristan suggests.

"No, no. I'll be here most of the afternoon," I say, sitting forward in anticipation of the turning. "Here we go. Anywhere here is fine!"

"Come on, let me drop you at the door."

"We're practically there."

"Well, let me take you *actually* there."

"Now we've gone past it."

He brakes, turning to me with a frown. "That was a nursing home."

"I know," I say, tensing, feeling as if I am somehow betraying my mum by revealing her whereabouts, and her circumstance.

"Your mother is in a nursing home?" He hangs his head. "Well, now I feel even more of an arse."

"Don't worry about it." I reach for the door handle.

"Wait! We're still on for next weekend, aren't we?" His hand is on my arm. "You have to let me make it up to you. I'll get you extra churros."

His eyes do a convincing job of conveying molten chocolate dipping sauce.

"Please," he insists. "I'm an arse. But I'm an arse that really likes you and wants to be less of an arse so you'll like me back." He leans closer. "The way you did last night."

My cheeks flush and I experience an acute sensory flashback to our sheet-tumbling.

"Amy..." he breathes my name, touching the side of my face and leaning in for a kiss.

One part of me feels I should keep him at a distance—that was a pretty weird moment back at the flat—the other part of me is already yielding.

When we come up for air he has a satisfied look on his face. He knows he's got me hooked.

"I guess we just had our first argument and make-up," he smiles. "I kind of liked it."

I'm still feeling conflicted so I focus on prising myself away from him and trying to sufficiently compose myself to make it to the nursing home entrance. As I reach the front door my phone bleeps a message.

Look at what you do to me…

And, yes, there's a visual.

I slam my phone to my chest, eyes darting around as if some passerby might have caught an X-rated glimpse. Now I feel even more jangled and riled up.

I'm also smiling way more than I should.

17

This is the second week running I've turned up at the nursing home hungover. At least last week I'd had a shower.

"Lidia, Lidia!" I beckon my mum's favorite carer over to the entrance.

"Oh!" She seems startled by my appearance—and this is someone who often sees ninety-year-olds naked. "Are you okay?"

"I stayed at a friend's house last night and had to leave in a bit of a hurry. I couldn't use the staff shower, could I?"

"Of course, my stuff is already in there, help yourself."

"Oh, you are a gem!"

She gives me a sideways glance as we head down the corridor. "Is this a new friend?"

I nod. "I've got mixed feelings about him. Oh, hello, Malcolm! Glad to see you're fully dressed this week."

He pulls a face. "You're the one who needs to check your reflection."

"Yes, yes, I know!" I pat my fuzzy hair. "I'm seeing to that now."

"Do you want me to throw your sweater in the dryer?" Lidia asks. "You seem a bit damp."

"I fear it would shrink, I'll borrow something of Mum's."

"The cream cable knit?"

"Perfect," I smile.

For a second I stand in the doorway thinking how marvelous it is that there are people in the world who you can trust whole-heartedly. Lidia feels like a safe haven after Storm Tristan.

Could it be that he's just too much for me? There is definitely something unsettling about him. If I'm honest, I think part of the problem is believing that someone that good-looking would be into me. I mean, a one-night-stand maybe, but an ongoing thing seems like a stretch. Don't men like him need women with longer legs and higher heels and beauticians on speed dial?

"Enough with the self-sabotage!" I hear my body complain. "Can we please just enjoy the attention he is paying us?"

I sigh. I'll process the pros and cons of this union later. For now, I simply attempt to sluice away any misgivings with the shower.

When I emerge all shiny of locks and freckly of face I feel mar-ginally better, or at the very least clean. It's also dawning on me just how hungry I am—small wonder since very little food was consumed last night and I had nothing more than a visual feast for breakfast. Imagine my joy when I find warm-from-the-oven ginger cake and a pot of tea beside my mum.

"Oh, that's a sight for sore eyes!" I cheer as I enter her room. "Shall I pour?"

"That's for my daughter." She raises a protective hand. "She's coming to see me."

My heart sinks. I should be used to this by now but I always experience it as if it were a physical blow. There's something so disconcerting about your own flesh and blood not recognizing you. In these moments I feel so disconnected, like I've lost part of my identity.

"I'm here, Mum. It's Amy." I gently take her hand, hoping that her muscle memory will trigger her mind memory and gaze imploringly into her eyes. "You remember me!"

She peers closer, studying my face. "Oh yes, I recognize those freckles. How was school today?"

"Good," I reply with a sigh. Always easiest to go with the flow. "What did you do?"

"Um, physical education mostly."

"You smell nice," she says as I lean over with her cup of tea. "Is that coconut?"

I nod. "It's like being at the beach, isn't it? Remember our holiday to Spain? We played the *Guardians of the Galaxy* soundtrack every night when we were getting ready for dinner."

I ask Alexa to play "The Piña Colada Song" and her face lights up. She's singing along by the chorus, happy as a lark, while I feel overwhelmed with nostalgia, wishing I could rewind to those days, when she was herself all day every day.

For all the times I've skipped forward, would it be too much to ask to skip back, just once? Imagine if I could rewind to the night before the wedding and not drink so much so I actually knew which was my guy. Then again, would I have kissed any of them sober?

I reach to top up our tea, frowning at a sudden overlapping in tunes. I'm just wondering if Alexa has a new DJ mix option when I realize the second tune is coming from my phone. I'm about to turn it off, concerned it might be Tristan, but then I see Charlotte's name on the screen.

"Aren't you still in South Africa?" I gasp as I answer, hurrying over toward the window.

"Yes! But I had to tell you—the photographer sent me the link to the wedding pics. There's hundreds of them. We're just leaving for our afternoon tea at the Mount Nelson but I thought you could start going through them?"

"I'm at my mum's!"

"Well, she's got a tablet, hasn't she? She can be an extra pair of eyes for you."

Ever calm and wise. "Thank you, Charlotte," I sigh. "I'll let you know what I find."

"Okay, gotta go! Good luck!"

I turn back to my mother. "I've got a game for us."

"What kind of game?"

"We're going to be detectives looking for clues in a set of photographs."

"You're so dramatic."

"I know. But it'll be fun." I prop the tablet in front of us. "Not to sound like an egomaniac but we're looking for any shots of me interacting with a man."

"There's one, there's one!" She points excitedly at the screen.

"That's Jay."

"So?"

"Okay, any man except Jay."

"I've found another!" she cheers.

"That's Ernie, Marcus's grandfather."

"I suppose he doesn't count, either?"

"Not for this particular game but you've got a good eye so let's keep going."

There's a lot of exclaiming and cooing as we scan through the highlights of the wedding. Charlotte is going to be thrilled, especially with the first dance sequence—she looks exquisite and Marcus is clearly smitten. It really is all so romantic.

"Ooh! My waiter!"

"Well, he's lovely."

"Isn't he? His name is Ben. I had a date with him yesterday, though it feels like a lifetime ago."

"Are you going to see him again? Your face is telling me that you want to."

"I do. I just left in a bit of a hurry and haven't had a chance to contact him since." I casually bring my phone to life and startle as I see there is a text from him. "Oh my gosh, he's messaged me!" I bite my lip as I read it.

"Not good?"

"No, he's just being really sweet."

"Is that a problem?"

"Only because I feel guilty at leaving him rather abruptly to go on a date with another man. You'll see him in a minute. Here. This one." I point to Tristan.

"Oh."

"What do you think?"

"Well, of course, he's very handsome..."

"But?"

"I don't know. There's something about his eyes." She zooms in on his face.

I get a little shudder myself. "Moving on!"

There is a noticeable change in the poses as the booze kicks in—way more lunging and hugging, faces smooshed up together with exaggerated pouts. As ever, the dance floor freeze-frames are good for comedy value.

"You danced with a lot of different men," my mum observes.

"That I did," I confirm. "But none of these ones are ringing a bell."

"Wait, go back!" My mum grabs my arm. "That picture in the hall—go in closer on the background."

I squint at the figures and then jerk back in shock—it's me and Elliot.

"Who's he? It looks like you're having cross words."

"That's Charlotte's cousin," I murmur. "You met him once years ago. I'm not a fan but I don't remember an argument." Although I am now getting the sensation of being riled up and indignant.

"See if there's any more of him."

I continue to scroll.

"There!" she exclaims. "What's that down his shirt?"

My stomach drops. "Red wine."

"Is that significant?" She looks at me.

I nod. "I think I threw it at him."

"Why?"

"I don't know. I can't remember anything we said."

"Maybe things went beyond conversation."

Now I'm feeling seriously queasy. She's right. He must have been one of the kisses. And if the red wine was the end of the relationship, that means it really is between Tristan and Ben. But did Elliot and I really kiss? I shudder.

I sit back and tap my lip. I know where he works, I could just show up and ask him what happened. But would he tell me the truth? I have to at least try to get the facts.

"Are you okay?"

I nod dumbly.

"Okay, let's keep going."

By the end of the photo viewing I am all the more amazed that Ben agreed to meet up with me after bearing witness to my drunken debauchery. I pick up my phone and look back at his text.

Hope you landed the client. The movie was a yawn so you didn't miss much. Have a super chill Sunday.

I type my reply:

> *Just having tea and ginger cake with my mum—definitely no chance of anyone kidnapping me now!*

I smile, thinking of the sign at the Crouch End cafe. I can't wait to go back there. But for now I turn off my phone and turn all my attention to my mum.

"Fancy a little mani?"

I walk away from the nursing home in something of a daze. The manicure somewhat soothed me—the warm water, the attention to detail, the prettiness of the pearlized ivory we opted for this week. For half an hour I didn't have to make any decisions greater than how many coats to apply.

As I head down the street, I take out my phone and tentatively bring it back to life. I send a quick update to Charlotte and then ponder who I should follow up with first—Tristan or Ben? The sex text or the sweetie who, now I reread his text, isn't exactly hounding me for a second date. Hmm. I was the one who asked him out on the walk, so it really should be his turn now. Though I guess he did ask me to the cinema. Maybe he thinks because I'm the older woman I should lead the way?

I jump as my phone buzzes in my hand. Who's this?

> *Welllllllll?????*

It's May, via text, wanting to know how the dates went. This is not something I can summarize in a line or two. Or even do justice to on the phone.

Meet me for lunch tomorrow? I type.

I can't wait that long! she complains.

8 a.m. coffee at The Pour House?

Isn't that where Elliot works?

It is indeed.

There's a pause and then my phone starts to ring.

"Please tell me he's not a candidate!" May gasps down the line.

"He had red wine on his shirt in the wedding pictures."

"Noooooo! The scoundrel!"

"I just need to hear what happened from the horse's mouth."

"The ass's mouth!" she scoffs. "I've got to get back to the shoot but I need every detail tomorrow. I'll see you on the corner so we can walk in together."

"Deal," I confirm.

I feel so much better about the prospect of confronting Elliot with May by my side.

In fact, I think it's best if I wait until that is dealt with before I engage any more with Tristan or Ben. I've had quite enough action for one weekend. Just one more deed to be done—returning Gareth's phone—and then it's home to bed.

As I arrive at his door my gaze inadvertently slides to the left, wondering whether Julianne has sealed the deal yet. A week ago the thought of calling this place home seemed so thrilling but now, without Gareth around to get into the nitty-gritty, it's been relegated to a passing fancy. I'd still like to run the idea by him out of curiosity but the house is in darkness so I'm guessing he's still not back. I sigh to myself. So, what now?

I reach for his phone, which I've been carrying around all week, thinking he might get in touch. If I had a Jiffy bag, I could just put it through the letter box and have done with it. Perhaps I could wrap it in something? I rummage through my bag, pulling out my multi-purpose cami. Now that would start a whole different conversation.

Suddenly the door opens. "Oh!" Gareth startles.

"You're back!" I exclaim.

"Did you ring the bell?"

"I was just about to—are you leaving?"

"No, I was just going to get my things from the car."

"You're just getting home now?"

He nods.

"Well, that's good timing—I brought your phone!" I hold it up.

He looks between that and the black silk cami.

"I…" I try to speak but I'm lost for words.

"Did you want to come in?"

"Not if you're busy…" Why does this feel so awkward?

"It can wait," he says, leading me inside. "Tea or rosemary ale?"

"A very small ale, please." I perch on the edge of the sofa with the cats, awaiting my hair of the dog. "Your lip looks better."

"It is," he nods, running his thumb over it. "Are you coming from your mum's?"

"I am."

"How is she?"

"Good. In fact, they're having a fancy dress party the weekend after next, if you'd be game? I'm hoping the whole gang will be there…"

"Of course," he nods, handing me my drink and then turning back to the counter. "Oh, I got your favorites."

He throws two packets of crisps at me, causing me to exclaim, "Mackie's Haggis! I can't believe you found these in Sweden!"

"Sweden?"

"Oh! I presumed…" I bite my lip. "Dharmesh said you hopped on a flight…"

"I went to see my dad." He puts me out of my misery. "In Scotland. Hence the Haggis crisps."

"Well, of course, that makes a lot more sense."

He sits down in his old recliner. "I hadn't seen him in a while and I was right there at the airport with my overnight bag…"

I nod, understanding. There's nothing like the comfort of home when you're feeling down. Plus, Freya and Gareth lived with his dad for a while so he could chime in more than the rest of us, despite being a man of few words.

"How's he doing, your dad?"

"Good. He's got a new lady friend. Maggie. She's nice." There's a hint of sadness behind his smile, I note. I wonder if he's thinking of his mother.

I wait a moment and then ask, "Do you want to talk about Freya?"

"I don't but it feels like you do," he half smiles.

"It's just, it was such a surprise to us all…"

"I know." His voice softens. "But it wasn't for me. We might have similar interests but we have a very different approach to life. She's more global messaging, I'm just planting seeds in my small corner of Battersea hoping the word will spread. It got to the point where she needed to be with someone louder, more vocal."

"Like Lucas?"

"Yes, how did you…?"

"Just a hunch."

"Okay, so that part was a little galling. He was always coming up with new promotional partnerships for the pair of them." He shakes his head. "Then again, they are probably the better match."

"So you really are okay with this?"

"I really am. Honestly, it was a bit of a relief. All the back and forth to Stockholm, feeling like we were pulling in different directions."

"Can I be nosy?"

He gives me a look as if to say, "Aren't you always!" But not in a totally exasperated way.

"Do you know why she was calling you the day after the wedding?"

"She wanted me at her ceremony."

"*What?*"

"She wanted to show that there were no hard feelings. A lot of local press had pictures of us from a recent event so she said for 'optics' it was important to show a harmonious transition."

I raise my eyebrows. "And what did you say to that?"

"Well, I didn't get the chance to reply—she was on speaker-phone and my dad chimed in with a few choice Glaswegian phrases from his youth."

I laugh. "I love your dad."

"He loves you too."

"Not as much as May."

"He loves drinking and arguing with May."

"But aren't those two of his favorite things?" I tease.

"You have a point." He takes a sip of ale. "So, what's the theme of this fancy dress party?"

"Sitcom characters!" I brighten, equally ready to move on. "You have to go as Tom from *The Good Life!* And wouldn't Char-lotte and Marcus make a great Margo and Jerry? She loves a seventies dress with billowing sleeves and apparently he's got a whole drawer of cravats he's saving for retirement!"

"You know, with the right wigs they would be excellent."

I lean over to the other side of the sofa and grab Gareth's heavy green knit jumper. "Team this with a pair of Wellies and you're golden."

"Not much of a stretch, is it?"

"Well, no, but…"

"What are you going as?"

"I haven't decided, it depends on who I bring as my date."

"And how's all that going?"

I decide to spare him the whole Ben/Tristan saga but I do reveal that it looks like Elliot has been identified as the missing third kiss.

"Elliot?" He's not convinced. "You've always said he gave you the creeps."

"He still does, but one of the premonitions involved throwing red wine on a white shirt and he fits the bill there."

"Is it possible you kissed more than three men?"

I shake my head. "Three bottle tops, three premonitions. Was that your doorbell?"

He looks down at his watch. "She's early."

"Who?" I'm not making any more assumptions.

"Peony," he replies, not looking exactly thrilled at the prospect. "Maggie talked me into it."

"Do you want me to leave by the back door?"

"Of course not!" he tuts.

"Okay, well, I'm out of here." I swig back my drink.

We both head for the front door but I step to the side as we get there. "You should answer it."

"Right."

I will now be hidden behind the door as he opens it. I really hope she hasn't gone for a flasher mac and suspenders entrance.

"Oh! Mr. Atkins!"

"I hope you don't mind, I saw you'd got back. Oh, hello, Amy!" he addresses me as I peek out from behind Gareth. "I was thinking about what you said about the joint purchase or shares in the cafe—"

"Sorry?" Gareth interjects.

"Um," I grimace, squeezing to the fore and giving Mr. Atkins a significant look. "I've yet to have that conversation with Gareth."

"Oh." His shoulders slump. "I see. Well, goodnight to you both."

"Goodnight. Thanks for coming by!" I chime.

As I close the door I hear Gareth's voice behind me. "You offered him shares in a cafe that doesn't exist?"

"No, well, I was just trying to think of a way to persuade him to sell to you rather than this Julianne character and Charlotte had suggested making a joint purchase—"

"With Julianne?"

"No, um, with me."

"What?"

"Well, you know I'm looking to buy and you want this place but it's too expensive so if we split it and I took upstairs and you had downstairs…"

He looks completely thrown.

"Or not. It was just a random thought."

He leans back on the wall.

"It's obviously a terrible idea," I fluster. All these years of being friends and I still have no idea what is going on behind those eyes.

"It's not the idea, it's the timing," he tells me. "I mean, aren't you about to fall in love?"

"I don't know about that…"

"But that's not true, is it?" he counters. "You do know. You know that one of those men is your happy ever after. Don't you want to be making plans with him?"

I purse my lips.

"And that's not to say you can't make your own choices and live anywhere you please, it's just–"

"No, no, you're quite right. I just got carried away thinking it was so close to Mum's and there was the added bonus of the cats…"

"The cats?"

"And you," I say.

And for a moment it seems as if the world stops. The way those two words came out of my mouth wasn't jokey or cavalier. I flush, suddenly very conscious of how close we are in the corridor.

"Amy–"

The doorbell rings again, causing us both to jump out of our skins.

"Okay, now it's Peony."

I shake off my daze and pull myself together. "Should I?" I am now closest to the latch.

"Go ahead."

It's no surprise to see her face fall at the sight of me. If I'm not answering his phone, I'm answering his door.

"I'm just leaving," I say, not waiting for her to reply. As soon as I'm out of the door I jog a few paces in an attempt to put some distance between myself and the awkward triangle.

"Amy!"

I turn to see Gareth coming after me. For a moment I think he's running to tell me that the idea of us co-buying the house is brilliant and The Botanist dream can finally be made a reality. But of course, it's not that.

"You forgot your crisps."

"Oh," I say, taking them from him. "Thank you."

"See you here next Thursday?"

I give him a blank look.

"The dinner to hear about Charlotte's honeymoon?"

"Of course! And then the fancy dress party is that Sunday. Feel free to invite Peony, by the way. She could be Grace Adler with that beautiful red hair."

"Good call. Okay, I should get back." He reaches to give me one of our customary hugs.

I hold on a little longer, trying to convey how sorry I am about Freya, closing my eyes and imagining him surrounded in a glow of healing love. It takes him a moment to respond but then he leans his head against mine and, for a fleeting moment, I feel a direct connection to his heart.

"Thank you for thinking about buying the flat, I know you meant well."

I sigh. I want to say my offer still stands but that doesn't seem to be what he wants to hear. At least he's no longer mad that I went behind his back with Mr. Atkins.

"Have a good night with Peony!" I give him a cheery wave.

"Have a good week with your beaus."

Oh jeez, I'd almost forgotten about them.

I head for the bus stop in a daze. All the times I wished for more romance in my life, I never expected it to feel this confusing. Still, hopefully by next Sunday things will be a lot clearer.

18

It's a wonderful thing to wake up without a hangover. It's also quite fun to be having a pre-work rendezvous. I typically avoid The Pour House because of Elliot and that has meant I've been cruelly deprived of their Nutella bombolone. Now the prospect of that deep-fried crispiness and oozy filling has me singing in the shower. Of course, if I was having to confront Elliot by myself, I would be riddled with dread but I always feel pretty much invincible when May is by my side. Which is why it's something of a blow to emerge from the tube station and find out she got a last-minute job shooting her first cover for a new magazine client.

I'm just weighing whether I could stop a total stranger heading into the cafe and ask them to get me a doughnut when Jay appears in his superhero cape. Literally.

"Even on a Monday morning?" I marvel at his get-up.

"Especially on a Monday morning," he replies, standing

proud in knee-high lace-up boots, hair styled to Dr. Strange perfection.

I lean in for a hug. "Thank you for coming to my aid."

"You know I love a bit of drama."

My face falls. "You don't think this is a mistake, approaching him at work?"

Jay shrugs. "It's not ideal but then you don't want to make a date to see him *after* work, do you?"

"I do not."

"And a phone call isn't going to cut it because you really need to see his facial reaction."

"Agreed. Come on then, let's do this."

I see only female baristas when we enter. It never occurred to me that Monday could be his day off.

"What now?" I ask Jay.

"We're here, we might as well have a little treat."

"Okay, you grab that table in the far corner. I'll get the goodies. What do you want?"

"Surprise me with something pretty."

I look up at the menu, considering the options. "Is the beetroot latte the pale pink one?"

"Yes," the young server replies.

"And does it come in a glass with foam art?"

She nods. And then she looks down at her buzzing phone. "Can you excuse me just a moment?"

"No problem." I let my eyes rove the pastry and dessert bar. Isn't it just like life that all the cutest items are the most calorific? I mean, look at that mini cheesecake with the orchid on top.

"Have you decided?" The young server returns to me.

"Yes, I'll have one beetroot latte, one matcha latte, one Nutella bombolone and three macarons—one lilac, one pale blue, one peach." Jay's going to love arranging those around his pink drink.

"Is that everything?"

"Yes, thank you."

"Okay, that's £52.70, please."

I burst out laughing. "Oh my god, I thought you said it was fifty quid."

"That's right."

"What? How is that possible?"

"Two lattes, one doughnut, three macarons and one replacement shirt."

"Shirt?" It is at that moment I catch sight of Elliot, lurking in the back room.

And so it begins.

I heave a sigh. "Could you ask him to come out, please?"

"Who?" She blinks innocently.

I roll my eyes. "Elliot."

She looks conflicted.

"And cancel my order."

"Even the doughnut?" she gasps.

I jut my chin in the air. "Even the doughnut."

I walk over to the far end of the counter and drum my nails on the black laminate surface.

"Really?" I say when he finally appears.

"That was my best shirt."

"That was a really good glass of wine."

"Then why did you throw it at me?"

"Why do you think?" I bluff.

He huffs. "I don't see the big deal, everyone else was taking a pop at you, why is it suddenly a big no-no when it's me?"

My jaw drops. I don't quite know where to begin.

I take a breath. "So, what you're saying is—"

"I don't think it's fair!" he pouts. "You know I like you, I've always liked you. And suddenly I'm seeing you getting off with this guy and that one, why wouldn't I take a chance?"

I almost feel like he has a point.

"When you say this guy and that one..."

"You want me to name names?"

"If you could..."

He makes a scoffing sound and turns away from me, reaching for a surface cleaner. "Unbelievable."

"Why do you like me anyway?" I follow him along the counter. "It's not like we've ever really got on. In all the years we've known each other we've barely exchanged two words."

"Only because you've never given me the time of day."

I scratch the side of my face. "I've never felt comfortable around you. It's just a feeling I had."

"I had a feeling too—that you were The One."

My jaw drops again. I look him in the eyes, probably for the first time. They are small but with a shock of amber around the

216

pupil and ringed with dark denim at the edge. I still get a resounding full-body no when I look at him, but now it comes with an element of sympathy.

He looks sheepish now. "I just wanted to know what it would be like to kiss you. I've thought about it for so long. I didn't know when I'd get another chance."

"So, what happened exactly?"

"You really don't remember?"

"Just flashes..." I say.

He glances around the cafe. It's still quiet. Jay has got his headphones on and is grooving away, oblivious. He lowers his voice. "I followed you into the main hall. I asked if you wanted to come to the bar for a drink with me, you said no. I tried to get you to change your mind." He looks uneasy.

"Go on."

"You were going to walk away—to go back to that Tristan guy. How could I compete with him? So I grabbed you and I... well, I kissed you." He hangs his head. "In my mind I thought it would change everything—you see it in the movies, the girl resists and then goes all weak and compliant in the guy's arms. But that didn't happen."

"No."

He sighs, fiddling with the cardboard cup holders. "It seemed like you were in shock for a minute. You had this weird look on your face and then the next thing I know you're chucking wine on me."

I bite my lip.

"I left after that. How could I stay?"

For a moment I'm silent, and then I hear myself saying the last words I would ever have expected to spill from my lips. "I'm sorry. And not in a woman taking the blame kind of way. I'm just sorry. I know what it's like to like someone who doesn't like you back."

"It sucks."

"Yes, it does," I say.

"At least you didn't punch me—I heard what you did to Gareth."

I wince. "It was quite a night."

The bell rings as a bevy of girls come in, cooing over the decor and ordering beetroot lattes to match their all-pink outfits.

"I should let you go."

He shrugs, letting the young girl serve them.

"It wouldn't have worked out between us," I tell him.

"Apparently not," he huffs. "But I'll always have the stain on my shirt to remember you by."

"You know, you can just soak it in—"

He holds up his hand. "I'm kidding, I don't care about the shirt."

I don't know what to say. This hasn't gone quite how I expected. I turn and motion to Jay that it's time for us to leave.

It's hard to find the right parting words when none of the usual pleasantries apply. Instead, I try to offer some dating wisdom.

"My only recommendation for future encounters would be to try and ease into making a move."

"Really?" he snorts. "How's that working for you?"

He has a point. I certainly didn't take a gradual or subtle approach to Tristan and Ben. "Touché," I concede.

"Sorry," the young server interrupts. "Elliot, how much do we charge for a beetroot latte with no beetroot?"

"I'll leave you to it." I step away.

Jay is already out the door and I'm just pushing it open to join him when Elliot reaches his arm across, blocking my path.

"Here," he says, handing me a little box containing a Nutella bombolone. "On me."

I'm more than a little taken aback. Now this is my kind of love token. "Thank you," I gush, adding with sincerity, "I hope you find your person."

He gives a grudging shrug. "I hope you find yours too."

19

"Well, well, well." Jay arches a brow as I take his arm. "And then there were two…"

"What?" I say, still thrown by the whole experience.

"Elliot was one of the kisses?"

"Yes."

"But not a romantic possibility?"

"No." I feel a little sad as I say it.

"So that means we're down to either Tristan or Ben as the absolute love of your life."

My facial expression doesn't change.

He sighs. "I think you need to eat that bombolone."

"It's literally all I can think about," I confirm.

Jay directs me around the corner to a cafe by the name of Slim Pickings. It's table service and we're lucky enough to get the back booth so I can stealth-eat my bounty in this squeaky-clean land of Pilates ponytails and jutting hip bones.

"So, where were we?" I say, licking my sugary fingers and checking the box for any last smears of Nutella.

"Tristan versus Ben—who will win our fair maiden's heart?"

"Who indeed?" I sigh, reaching for my ginseng brew.

"Is the hesitation in your voice because you are now reconsidering Elliot on the basis of free bombolone?"

"Definitely not," I assert. "The flash-forward with his kiss went no further than the throwing of the wine—there is no romantic future for us. Nada."

"So why the lackluster response? We're a step closer to the big reveal—I thought you'd be on tenterhooks."

"I know," I say, looking uneasy.

"You can tell me anything." Jay's voice softens. "You know I won't judge."

"I know, it's just…"

"Yes?"

"Out of all the men in all the world, I wouldn't have narrowed it down to these two. Which immediately sounds ungrateful, I'm lucky to have anyone be interested…"

Jay sits forward, adopting his counselor pose. "I understand your reservation with Tristan because, aside from being visual manna from heaven, he's kinda moody and a potential psychopath. But Ben seems decent."

"Oh, and I like him so much, I really do. But he's twenty-five."

"Ten years is nothing when you're in love. Look at Tom Daley and Dustin Lance Black."

"Okay, so they are completely awesome, obviously. It's just

where Ben is at in his life—the whole nomad thing, moving from place to place. And he's such a dreamer. Which is really appealing but…"

"But?"

"I was sort of hoping for someone I could build a life with, not just be enchanted by. Though I definitely feel I could learn a thing or two from him."

"Perhaps that relationship is meant to be a slow bloomer. I mean, if this is the person you're going to grow old with, you've got all the time in the world to get together. Besides, tea on a toilet? In Crouch End? I mean, he's the clear winner for me."

I smile. "I did love being with him. And I think I'd be completely swooning over him now if I hadn't barrelled straight into bed with Tristan." I give a little shudder. "So now when I think of him I just feel guilty and a bit sleazy."

"Well then, the sooner you can see him again, the better."

"That's easier said than done. He's got a new dog sit on top of the lunch and dinner shift at a local restaurant which basically means he's either walking the dog or being a waiter during the only hours I could see him."

"So walk the dog with him or go eat at his restaurant."

"Doesn't that smack of stalker—imagine my face appearing from behind the menu: *Surprise!*"

Jay smiles. "Maybe the dog walk is the better bet, work on that."

"Will do."

"What about Tristan?"

"He's invited me to this Mexican street party thing. I'm conflicted because he'll likely expect us to sleep together again and I don't want to do that before I've given Ben a proper shot. But then again, it's only happening this one weekend and I do love a churro."

"Don't we all. You said he sent pictures of his?"

I roll my eyes. "I'm not showing you."

He gives a shrug. "Worth a try."

And then I sigh, running my nail along the groove of the wooden table. "I just thought I'd be more certain. You know, in that 'I just knew!' way. Wouldn't you think I'd be able to tell which one is my guy? I mean, if he really was my life partner?"

"I think you're expecting too many guarantees and love doesn't work like that. Not even for you."

I look down at Jay's taro root crisps. "Are you going to eat those?"

He pushes the bowl toward me. "Turns out I'm more tarot card than taro root."

I perk up. "I suppose I could go to a fortune teller."

"Oh Amy, you're already your own fortune teller! Besides, I don't think you should be so fatalistic about this. Don't you want to feel you've made up your own mind about who you're going to be with?"

"Yes, but I've just got this niggling feeling that my supposed superpower has got it wrong."

"You want to go back to square one?"

"I don't know! I mean, look what happened when my mum pursued the man her premonition warned her against."

"Okay, why don't you take a breath and give it another week, then see how you feel?"

We're momentarily distracted as a yoga fan performs "dancer pose" while waiting for her table and then I turn back to Jay.

"What's your secret?"

"Which one?"

"The one that means you never get riled up about love stuff. I mean, no one is more dramatic than you in everyday life but when it comes to the thing that unravels the most even-keel folks, you're so zen."

He shrugs his caped shoulders. "It never made sense to me to bet the farm on one person. I mean, the idea that in a world of seven and a half billion people there's only one way to live your life—paired up like the animals filing into the ark? No. That can't be right."

"So why do so many of us want that?"

"Century upon century of conditioning? Sex on tap? I'm not saying I'm a total solo artist, you know I like my flings."

"That I do."

"But I haven't got time to have a broken heart, there's too much life to live. Besides, I don't watch enough TV."

"What's that got to do with it?"

"Well, that's the main point of being in a relationship, isn't it? Having someone to binge-watch shows with? I'm not home enough to do that."

He has a point. It's certainly one of my life's great pleasures.

"Speaking of TV…" I decide to move the topic on. "Have you settled on your fancy dress costume for the party?"

His face takes on a grave expression. "This has been very challenging for me, researching all these sitcoms and having to look at so much shapeless loungewear, not to mention those nineties suits that just hovered over the body—I can't believe how much excess fabric the men were dragging around."

I give a chuckle.

"Anyway. I've decided to go as Tahani from *The Good Place*."

My eyes light up. I can already picture the bold-print gown and décolletage bling.

"I'm trying to persuade May to go as Jason, you know she looks great in a tracksuit."

"Now that would be perfect." I rub my hands together in glee. "You?"

"I still don't know who I want to be," I admit.

"And therein lies your problem."

Jay gets to his feet, adjusting his outfit in preparation for sweeping out the door.

"That's how we're going to end our chat?" I splutter.

"I've got an appointment at the wigmaker's. You've got your character and ideals to assess." He pauses beside the table and then gives me a sympathetic look. "You're looking at these men for all the answers but all you really have to do is check in with yourself. When you're with them, ask yourself, *How does being with this person make me feel about myself?* If you feel like the bee's knees, that's great; if you feel in any way 'less than,' move on. It really doesn't need to be any more complicated than that."

I sit motionless for a good five minutes after he's gone. Could it really be that simple?

I text Ben on my afternoon break as part of our daily back and forth. It definitely falls short of flirtatious (not for lack of trying on my part) but I do get a thrill every time I see his name pop up on my phone. It started with me requesting pictures of his Saint Bernard charge Nessa and led to him sending me a snap every time she offered a new facial expression or sleeping position. In return, I sent him pictures of me with my childhood cat, which led to pics of him as a skinny little boy out fishing with his dad. He had the shiniest mop of dark hair and looked like a dreamer even at that age. It sounds strange, but I miss him. He seems so elusive. I want him to be the one to suggest we meet up again so I can be sure he likes me but he seems happy to just be text pals.

"There's a lot of it about," May notes when I complain that I'm not making any progress. "People would rather present the cute sound bite version of themselves than bring the 360-degree reality. I mean, you can text and watch TV at the same time, text and eat, text and ride the bus, no one wants to have to stop what they are doing and give their full attention anymore."

"First of all, that's really depressing. Second of all, he was great company when we were together."

"So, suggest a meet-up!"

"It just makes me feel slightly sick, the thought of me initiating it again. I don't want to come off needy."

"So Tristan is too forward and Ben is too laid-back. Don't you think you're being a bit Goldilocks about this?"

"Maybe you're right."

And so I try this tack: *If you and Nessa ever want company on your walk, I'd love to join you!*

He comes back with an invitation to join the pair of them on Saturday morning. It's just a sixty-minute slot but I decide to tell Tristan that I won't be able to come to the Mexican street party that afternoon because I don't want a repeat of last week's farrago. I mean, imagine if Ben's shift suddenly got cancelled and I'd have to say I couldn't hang out because I had another "work meeting." No. I'm going to be grown-up and show a little restraint. I don't have to fill my every waking minute with potential suitors. Besides, it will be nice to turn up at the nursing home on Sunday sans hangover and looking presentable for once. There we are, I feel calmer already.

Within the hour I have a piñata donkey on my desk.

You know those outsize papier-mâché creations filled with sweets? All colorful and kitschy and cute—everything Tristan is not.

I send May a text saying I'm having trouble reconciling this playful gesture with the wine snob I met at the wedding.

"You said he was fun at dinner."

"Well, yes, eventually," I concede.

"We human beings are complex creatures," she replies. "Besides, this might be less reflective of his tastes and more about what he knows would appeal to you. In which case, he's right on the money."

I can't deny that I love it. You see these featured in movies but I've never seen one in real life. I trace my fingers along the fringed layers of tissue paper and then pick it up and rattle it. I wonder what kind of sweets it has inside. More to the point, I wonder what kind of metaphorical sweets are inside of Tristan. I suspect he's like that BeanBoozled game where you spin a wheel and you don't know whether you're going to be eating a jelly bean flavored as a toasted marshmallow or a stinky sock. Chocolate pudding or canned dog food. I'm not making up these flavors. And they really do taste like their labels! Jay brought the game back from his trip to New York Fashion Week.

I try jabbing a hole in the side of the donkey with my pen, to no avail. I can't start thrashing at it because my boss recently introduced an afternoon nap hour that is supposed to increase productivity and so everything is on mute.

"Here!" Becky from the Art Department beckons me over. "Are you trying to find a way in?"

I nod back.

She walks the rainbow donkey over to the guillotine and, in one ruthless move, slices off a leg. She hands it back to me to shake the goodies out.

"Oh." Our shoulders slump in unison.

"They look like those little hard-boiled sweets that cut your tongue when you suck on them."

"I think you're right…" I say, holding up a tiny purple sphere in a clear plastic wrapper. I can almost taste the grape, with a dash of metallic blood.

"The person who gave this to you is a real ass, am I right?"

"How did you know?" I gasp.

"What? No! I was just joking—ass as in donkey?"

"Oh yes, of course!"

And then I walk back over to my desk and shake the sweets directly into the bin.

I really need to concentrate on doing some actual work. I've managed to get away with fiddle-faddling for a week but now I have to get a move on with the pitch for our new client. The trouble is, it's such a blank slate and I have nothing to riff off. Give me a concept, a theme, even a color palette and the ideas spontaneously ping around my brain but this time all we have is the product—a new skincare range for men. Mid-range. Decent quality. No distinctive smell or trending ingredient. The company wants to target younger men starting to care for their skin for the first time and has a willingness to give a percentage of the proceeds to support a cause because, in their words, "that business model seems to be working right now."

This is actually the most exciting part for me—I've been wheedling at my boss to take on at least a couple of non-paying clients a year, to feel like we are giving back. I think it would genuinely help with our team's morale and motivation. Last year I watched an interview with a former newsman and his theory was that the first surge of your career tends to be self-centered, all about what's in it for me? But then the older you get, the more satisfaction you derive from there being a service element to your work, as in how are you benefitting others? Typically this doesn't hit till your forties or fifties but I say the sooner the better.

So this is a good project which could have a positive impact in the world, provided we position it just right. They've even given us carte blanche with the name. Something simple and memorable that prompts an emotional response, like Zeus or Adonis but less male stripper. They also want something with a great origin story—like San Diego's Hydraman, created by a former Navy SEAL. But without actually having a great origin story of their own.

I sit toying with the products, working the moisturizer into the back of my hand as I scroll through the competitors, amused to see how organic ingredients are typically described as gentle when relating to female skin but become "powerful" for the male market. Women get less wrinkles, men get more manly. Women get smaller pores, men get to feel heroic for simply applying SPF.

Within twenty minutes I find myself reaching into the bin. I knew this would happen. I should've opened each wrapper and rolled each sweetie on the carpet until they were covered in fluff and street grime. Only then would I be safe from temptation. I opt for a green one. Is that kiwi? I move it around my mouth, rather enjoying the tang on my tastebuds as I return to my screen, sensing too late the crack in the surface. Within seconds it has made a blade-like slash at my tongue. I put my finger in my mouth. Yup. Bleeding.

I shake my head. I knew better and I did it anyway.

20

Saturday morning in Primrose Hill.

Well, this is a reassuringly pleasant start to the weekend. The sun is shining, coffee beans are roasting and there may even be a whiff of romance in the air...

I smile to myself as the odd couple approach—long, slimline Ben and the hulking bulk of droopy-faced fur that is Nessa.

"Wow! She's massive!" My face lights up as she lunges in my direction. "May I smoosh her?"

"You may!"

I lean in and bury my face in her fur, feeling the great rucks of skin around her neck and then gazing into her steady brown eyes as I rumple her velvety ears. She takes it all in her stride, panting warm breath over me.

"Is she too hot?" I ask, squinting up at Ben. "Hello, by the way! I didn't mean to ignore you."

He smiles back at me. "That's okay, I accept my role as her

humble footman. I was going to get her some ice when we stop for coffee."

"Sounds like a plan," I say, getting to my feet but still unable to take my eyes off her. "The size of those paws! They're like Yeti boots!"

"You want to know what else is giant?"

I look back at him. "Oh no."

"Oh yes," he grimaces. "You virtually have to use a shopping bag to pick it up."

"Oh gosh, is she going to do that now?"

"Lucky for you that's already taken place, she's like clockwork."

"That's Swiss precision for you."

"Funny you should mention that…" he says, directing me down a side street. "I always cut through here, it's a little shadier. It turns out that the reason the owners are away is that they are scoping out a second home in Switzerland."

"Really?"

He nods. "The wife read this book about doggie DNA and now she feels Nessa will never reach her full potential unless she gets to romp a snowy mountain range at five thousand feet."

"Primrose Hill's elevation just not cutting it?"

"Exactly."

"I feel a Facebook video coming on—Nessa experiencing snow for the first time…"

"Of course, it's going to be sunshine and green meadows in the summer but she'll love that fresh air."

"How glorious."

"Yeah, I can't wait."

I do a double take. "Are you going with her?"

"Well, it's just wishful thinking at this point. They're talking about spending the summer in Europe using their new Swiss home as a base. Some places they can drive to—Lake Como is just four hours away, for example—but when they are in Capri or Monaco they'd need someone to stay with Nessa."

"And you're volunteering?"

He nods. "If it was just me and Nessa and a mountain-view desk, I could make some progress with my script."

"Of course."

I resist the urge to say I could come out and visit, because that's the opposite of his plan for peace and solitude. I feel a little stung by the realization that I'm not remotely a factor in his future planning. Which isn't surprising since we just met, but also makes me question how we could progress romantically. I suppose all I can do is try and make the most of him while he's here. We chat a little about how his writing is going and then I casually throw out an invite to my mum's fancy dress party.

"Though I completely understand if that is the opposite of appealing."

"No, of course not, why would it be?"

"Well, a dementia nursing home isn't everyone's idea of a good time."

"When is it?"

234

"Next Sunday afternoon—so you're probably working?" I give him an easy out.

"I'll see if I can switch shifts. You don't suppose there's any chance I could bring Nessa?"

I give an excited gasp. "We could say she's a therapy dog!" I look down at her. "How would you feel about that?"

"I think she'd be a natural," Ben asserts. "A spirit-lifter by trade."

"And speaking of spirits...She could double as a waitress if we got her a barrel filled with party punch."

"You know, if you're looking for any entertainment, I have a small repertoire of magic tricks!"

"That would be great!" I enthuse. "I know some of the old folks won't be able to join in the dancing so perhaps you could do some armchair magic with them?"

"You're on."

I feel a swell of anticipation. I've never had a boyfriend who was so game. Not that he's my boyfriend but all the same, I love the fact that he'd actually think this would be fun. I thought Gareth was the only man who would humor me in this way. Of course, Jay will be coming too but that's really because of the fancy dress element.

"Woah!" Nessa suddenly starts pulling ahead.

"I take it we're near the cafe?"

"Yes, they give her treats so we don't really have a choice where we go."

"It's all fine with me," I say, though I do express mild

disappointment that the chairs are metal-framed with wooden slats, as opposed to a cluster of ceramic toilets.

Ben gives a little wave through the window to let the waitress know we're taking a table.

"Everyone is so dressed up around here," I say, noting that even the staff seem catwalk ready.

"Apparently Michael B. Jordan came here last week so everyone has been upping their game ever since."

"Really?" I give my sloppy Joe sweater a self-conscious tug.

He shrugs. "The coffee tastes the same whatever you wear."

I smile back at him. "Actually, I feel we should have hot chocolate in honor of Nessa and your potential Swiss trip."

"Nice!" he beams.

"Are you going to sit for me, Nessa?" the slender blonde waitress asks as she approaches our table. Nessa's bottom slams down onto the pavement, pink tongue lolling in anticipation. The waitress witholds her foie gras dog biscuit a little too long and a globule of drool splats onto her shoe. "Oh, gross!" She jumps back.

I bite back a smile.

Ben simply offers one napkin to the waitress and uses the other to mop Nessa's chops. "My apologies!"

"Oh, it's totally fine, we love our dog customers!" She forces a smile. "What can I get you?"

"Two hot chocolates, please."

"Whipped cream?"

"The works," I confirm. "And a bowl of iced Evian for Nessa."

"Ooh, she's getting spoiled today."

I smooth her head and then run my hands down the wavy fur of her back. "Do you know what part of Switzerland they're looking at?" I ask, as if I am intimately familiar with the country's geography, as opposed to planning to google the location and fantasize about being invited out for a fireside fondue.

"Verbier," he replies. "They stayed at Richard Branson's chalet one ski season and fell in love with it. It does look pretty idyllic. Plus, it's less than an hour from the Saint Bernard Pass monastery where these dogs were first bred, so Nessa can be with her own tribe."

"That's so cool."

I want to go more than ever now.

We chat about skiing—neither of us have ever felt the inclination to go hurtling down a mountain but both of us like the idea of winching up in a ski lift.

"Do you know there's a restaurant at one of the Italian ski resorts where you have dinner at the top of this mountain and then go hurtling back down to town on a toboggan in pitch-black darkness with only a headlamp to light the way?" I marvel. "Who would do that?"

"I would!"

"Nooooo!" I gasp.

It's pleasant conversation but I'm feeling an underlying frustration knowing how little time we have and that, once again, this doesn't feel like it is leading to anything amorous. I definitely need to wangle an after-dark date or we're going to end up squarely in the friend zone.

"Can I get you anything else?" The waitress returns to clear our table, carefully sidestepping Nessa.

"Just the bill, please," I say.

Ben reaches for his wallet.

"Allow me." I hold up my hand. "You brought the dog, the least I can do is get the drinks."

"Well, if you're sure?"

"I am."

And so we amble back to where we met.

"Well, that was a lovely way to start the day," I sigh.

"It was indeed. Thank you for treating us."

"You're welcome," I smile, loitering expectantly. Now would be the perfect time for him to make a move.

Instead, he leans in and gives me a casual half-body hug. "Come on then, Ness, let's get you home."

"Um, Ben?"

"Yes?" He turns back.

"Do you mind if I ask you a weird question?"

"I love weird," he grins. "Go ahead!"

I move over to the side of the pavement, as if that affords any degree of privacy to our conversation. "When we were in the kitchen at the wedding…"—I give him what I hope is a beguiling smile—"what is the last thing you remember?"

He tilts his head. "Well, we were in the middle of seeing how many petit fours we could fit in our mouths in one go—"

"What? No—we did that?"

He nods. "You came into the kitchen and said you were hungry and was there anything left over…"

I think for a moment, attempting to picture the little squares of frosted sponge. I do have a vague recollection of the red velvet ones, now he comes to mention it…

"Just out of interest, how many did I…?"

"Five."

"Really?" I gulp. "That must have been attractive."

He smiles. "You told me that petit four means 'little oven' in French."

"With my mouth full?"

He bursts out laughing. "Maybe."

"What I'm trying to say is…" I shuffle closer to him. "When we kissed, did I seem to have a particular reaction or say anything unusual, or even mention a premonition?"

"Well," he begins. "First of all, we didn't kiss—"

"What?" I startle. "What do you mean?"

"We've never kissed."

"But—"

"I feel like if a woman is swaying as though she's on the deck of a ship, it's best to wait for calmer seas. Plus, you know, I was working. We were in the middle of polishing off the petit fours when my boss came in and said it was time to start clearing the tables."

I hang my head.

"Nothing wrong with being drunk at a wedding," he assures me. "I'm not being judgmental."

"No, no, I know you're not—I just…I thought…"

He waits patiently for me to process the bombshell. It wasn't him. And if it wasn't him, it means it was someone else and now I'm back to square one. Unless…If we haven't kissed, then he's not ruled out. There could still be a dreamy premonition waiting on those lips. All I have to do is make contact…

"So, if we didn't kiss, then…" I hook a playful finger in his belt loop but instantly feel him tense up. Oh, the utter mortification. I quickly withdraw my hand.

His shoulders lower and he smiles kindly. "Amy…"

"Oh god," I say, backing away, flustered. This is the worst! I could just die. "Sorry, I don't know what I was thinking!"

"It's okay. It's just…There's a good chance I'm going to be leaving and I don't think it's wise to form any ties."

I hate to be thought of as any kind of tie or obligation and find myself reaching for Nessa's fur like it's a security blanket. "Quite right, I understand."

"I'm sorry, Amy, I hope I haven't misled you?" he continues.

"No, no, it's fine. You're right. There's no point, really."

He nods.

"Anyway!" I rally. "I really need to get going—I have to get ready for a Mexican street party. Frida Kahlo eyebrows don't connect themselves."

He gives a little chuckle and then says, "Okay, I'll see you for your mum's party next week!"

"What?" My jaw gapes. I wasn't expecting that.

"If I'm still invited?"

"Yes, yes, of course!" I brazen. "See you then. Gotta run!"

I turn and stride off, trying to walk normally while my face contorts and scrunches up as if I've just taken a sip from a super-sour margarita. They say the course of true love never did run smooth but *really*?

21

I can't face the confinements of the tube yet so I decide to walk on to the next stop. Oh, this is just excruciating! The look on his face when I tried to make a move. Of course, it's not a crime that he didn't want to reciprocate but it just feels so utterly humiliating. I can't believe I've been caught out like this! Ever since the wedding I've been on this absurd wild goose chase leading me nowhere and only bringing me more disappointment.

I look at my watch. It's only eleven a.m. I've got the entire day ahead of me. I have to think of something I can do to short-circuit this feeling. Shopping won't cut it; I don't want to be around mirrors, it'll only make me think he turned me down because of my assorted flaws. I suppose I could go to a movie. Sitting in a cool, darkened room and immersing myself in someone else's life sounds hugely appealing right now.

I take out my phone to google what's on in the West End.

Why don't I go all out and go to Leicester Square? Maybe I'll see two back-to-back, I've always wanted to do that. I'll load up with Poppets and popcorn and just power through. I'm busily scrolling through showtimes when a text appears.

From Tristan. An image. But not of a body part this time. It's the menu from his friend's food truck.

He's playing to two weaknesses now—hunger and the need to feel desired. I flashback to his hands on me, the depth of his kisses. And then I read about fried avocado tacos with poblano ranch slaw and ahi tuna burritos with citrus ponzu...

I mean, a girl has to eat.

And I still have plenty of time to go home and change—no fashion faux pas will hinder me this time. I find myself coming to a standstill. I need to get a grip on this situation—there are only two candidates left in the running now: Tristan and a man of unknown identity. Mystery man has disappeared without a trace and has made no attempt to contact me. (And as one of the bridesmaids, it really wouldn't be at all hard to track me down.) Which brings us back to Tristan—indisputably hot, into me and offering a fun activity for a Saturday afternoon. And maybe even Saturday night...

I still feel a bit uneasy about his weird tantrum last week but if it was a one-off blip, this could be a golden opportunity for a re-do...He has been trying to make it up to me ever since so at least he regrets his behavior.

Still, I can't bring myself to text him back. Apparently, I need outside permission, so I dial May. She sounds genuinely disappointed about Ben but quickly bounces back with a dismissive, "Nice shoes but too young—on to the next."

"I feel I might need to give Tristan another go," I venture.

"I bet you do!" she hoots.

"Is that wrong, though? He isn't really my type and I already told him I wasn't going to see him today."

"So don't."

Oh.

"I feel I should probably give him another chance, just to be sure. I have very limited options at this point."

"So do."

"You're saying it's up to me? What happened to my wedding pimp who dictated my every move?"

"I'm returning to my role as stylist."

"Well, in that case—what should I wear to a Mexican street party?"

"Ha!" she laughs. "Where are you now?"

"Just about to head into Belsize Park tube."

"I'll meet you at yours."

"Really? Do you want to come with me?" Now that would be fun.

"Nope. I've got a date of my own."

"Whaaat?"

"I don't want to talk about it."

"Unbelievable! You get to be all stealth and yet my love life is by committee!"

"Well, you are a blabbermouth and obviously need more assistance."

"Fair point!" I faux pout.

May chuckles. "See you at home."

I can't deny, May offers a great service. She has a set of my house keys so by the time I arrive (thanks to sitting in a tunnel for ten minutes), she has my whole outfit picked out, beginning with my *Mask of Zorro* dress from last year's Halloween. I couldn't be happier with that choice—the flounces of lace-trimmed red cotton hide a multitude of sins and make me feel like dancing.

"How did you even remember I had this?"

"It's all logged in here." May taps her head as she begins plaiting my hair into two long braids. "So, how do you feel about seeing Tristan now that you know the odds are further stacked in his favor?"

I think for a moment. "I suppose it makes me more curious, like there may be more to him than meets the eye. You don't expect people that good-looking to have any insecurities but he does always seem to be trying to prove himself."

"Maybe he's always been in competition with his even hotter brother or had a girlfriend leave him for a Hemsworth." May shrugs. "There's really no point in speculating when you can find out for yourself in an hour or two. What did he say when you told him you were coming?"

I reach for my phone and show her the gif he sent of a blindfolded woman hitting a heart-shaped piñata, unleashing a shower of red and pink confetti.

"Quite the romantic."

"Well, it did come with a comment about how he'll be blind-folding me later but I can't say the sexual overture was unwelcome after the Ben rejection."

"I guess there's no reason to hold back in that department anymore."

"No."

"You don't sound entirely convinced…"

"Enough about me!" I look back at May in the mirror. "Are you going to tell me *anything* about your date?"

"Nope."

"Where did you meet her?" I persist. "Online?"

"Pass me the hairbands."

"It's not the Ruby Rose lookalike, is it?" I gasp.

"No!" She looks affronted.

"Sorry."

"Clips…" I watch her fix my two braids on the top of my head and then pull open my knick-knack drawer so she can add a row of pink silk flowers.

"I knew these would come in useful one day," I cheer, delighted with the result. I feel like I'm gearing up to be photographed for a "Mexican Summer" fashion spread.

"Okay, I've got to go but this is what I want you to do to your face." May pings over an image of a woman with strong brows, heavy liner and a bold red lip. "And here's the jewelry." She points to a pile of my jangliest, most colorful pieces.

"Got it," I say, then give her a pleading look. "Can't you tell me anything about your date? Just one little nugget?"

She holds my gaze and for a minute I think she's going to cave but then she says, "No," one last, definitive time. "And remember, you can say no to Tristan at any time if he gets weird again."

"Right," I nod, hugging her goodbye. "Have fun tonight!"

Back in my room I decide I need a little music to keep the good vibes going. I grew up with my mum playing the soundtrack to *Don Juan DeMarco* and as soon as I summon the guitar-strumming, flamenco-clapping sounds on YouTube I feel utterly in the mood for all that lies ahead. Within half an hour the transformation is complete and, I have to say, I love the feminine but foxy look—the abundant layers of fabric definitely give me an extra sass and swish to my gait. I turn the music up and do a few dramatic flourishes around my flat, shaking off my earlier humiliation with Ben and wishing I had a ruched satin garter to wear under my skirts. I'm feeling almost daring now.

It's a teensy bit of a dampener to ride the tube but I sit there feeling like I have a secret and can't stop a smile playing on my lips. Mischief is on the horizon and I'm ready for it. When I get within five minutes of the address I breathe in, tighten my belt a notch, push my shoulders back and prepare to make my big, sassy entrance.

My eyes widen as I round the corner. Joyfully clashing fiesta bunting is strung from one side of the street to the other— fluttery paper panels in orange, aqua, purple and red with cut-outs in the shape of hearts, roses, cacti, even jalapeños! I love how the sun is casting stencil-style patterns on the road. I pass a vibrant stall selling Mexican blankets incorporating stripes of Day-Glo pink, another with heavily embroidered smock tops and a wall hanging that says, "It's okay to fall apart sometimes. Tacos fall apart and we still love them." I want it all. As the trumpets toot with almost comical joy from the speakers, it makes me wish my mum was here with me—it would feel like a trip abroad for her.

"Oh, thank you," I say as I'm handed a flyer, delighted to see it's on tomorrow too. I'm going to try to spring her from the home and bring her. Maybe a little earlier when it's not so crowded. She needs a change of scene.

And then I stop in my tracks. There he is, as promised—by the Mexican folk art stand opposite the bar truck.

Suddenly I can't wait to feel his eyes upon me.

"Tristan!" I wave, striding confidently up to him, hand on hip, giving it the full signorina sway.

"That's a lot of dress." He looks me over.

I ruffle my flounces. "I thought it was in keeping."

"I guess." He glances over at a woman spilling out of a tight red top and hot pants and instantly I deflate.

He doesn't get it.

Suddenly the same fabric that seemed so flirty and floaty feels overly bulky and costumey.

"Love your hair," says a passing girl with eye make-up in the green, white and red of the Mexican flag.

"Thank you," I smile after her. She gets me.

"You coming?" My date is already heading over to the bar truck.

I request the longed-for watermelon margarita but Tristan decides the sugar content is too high so opts for a shot of tequila and a Modelo beer. He takes a swig and then looks back at me, hooking a finger onto the elastic of my neckline. "Isn't this supposed to be off the shoulder?"

"It's easier to wear like this," I say, pulling it back into place. I really must update my underwear.

"Spoilsport."

I shrug and turn away, pretending to take in the scene.

"It's such a great culture, isn't it? So colorful, so much energy."

"Weird how so many of them are so short."

I frown back at him. "I don't know that it's weird—"

"That's my mate's taco truck." He talks over me, pointing ahead. "You ready to get messy?"

"At least this time my dress comes with built-in napkins!" I joke, flipping up the top layer.

He doesn't reply, just forges ahead through the crowd. I get that urge to run again, like I did at the Italian restaurant. I could let the crowd obscure me then turn and run, skirts hitched up at the front, fluttering in red waves behind me. But then the breeze carries a waft of sizzling flavor to me and I move forward in a trance.

He opts for the carnitas. I go for fish with extra lime. It's so zesty-fresh with a tingling kick, I actually feel my mood improving.

"Two more?"

I nod, taking an extra-long slurp of margarita as Tristan drops a piece of braised pork into his mouth. "Mmm, so tender."

"What are your feelings about mole sauce?" I ask, as a plate layered in rich brown passes by.

"Hmm…Initially I felt chocolate had no place in any sauce you might have with chicken," he begins.

"Right?"

"But I'm coming around to it, especially if it's heavy on the chili and garlic. You want to share some enchiladas?"

I nod.

As we bandy around words like *tomatillo* and *chilaquiles*, I feel my uneasiness subsiding. He does love his food. That's something we have in common so at least three times a day we could be compatible. We'd be at work most of Monday to Friday. If we found a series we both liked on Netflix, that would take care of our evenings. We're definitely good to go in the bedroom and I'm sure he'd want to see his friends some weekends. And I could see mine, still go off on jaunts with them. If we went on holiday to his grandparents' vineyard, we'd have them to talk to as well. I guess it's doable. If he was The One.

For a while we pause our eating and turn our attention to the stage where a three-piece mock mariachi band has launched into Lady Gaga's "Poker Face." Their costumes are fantastic— neat black bolero jackets with silver buttons and embroidery, bold red neckties and matching satin cummerbunds, felt sombreros with metallic threads and sequins glinting in the sun.

I look down at Tristan's trousers — black with silver trim running along the outer seam. "You could fit right in with them in your outfit."

"Maybe I will…"

"Can you sing?" I ask.

"Of course."

"Why of course?" I laugh.

"You know who my dad is?"

"No," I frown.

"Seriously?" he scoffs.

"Is he a musician?"

"I can't believe no one told you."

I squint at his features. He looks too polished to be rocker offspring. "Who is it?"

"You'll figure it out."

I go to speak but he turns away and starts singing along to "All About That Bass." I try to tune into his voice alone but it's not ringing any bells. It's also not as amazing as one might expect with that build-up. It crosses my mind that he might be delusional. Like, maybe his mother got pregnant on a one-night stand and she told him his father was Gavin Rossdale or Simon Le Bon or someone.

"Churros?" I suggest as the band announce a short break.

He nods and we join the line, watching the crispy, grooved coils of doughnut-like yumminess enter the deep fryer and then get sliced into sticks.

We take our cardboard tray of calories over to the spare

corner of a picnic bench and dip them in the silky, chocolate custard.

"Now this is a chocolate sauce I can get behind," I note, relishing every bite. "Not too sweet, clings to every contour."

"Maybe we should get a little pot for later?" He leans in and nuzzles my bare neck. It strikes me that this is the first affection he's shown me today—he didn't kiss me hello but apparently booze has once again overridden his initial disdain for my appearance and now he's eager to move on to the next stage. Not so fast, young man. I try to get him back onto a non-sexual conversational tack.

"Did you ever see that Netflix series where people spent a month living with a group that they had a deep-seated prejudice about?"

He frowns a no.

"There was this one guy who volunteered to patrol the American border just to keep the Mexicans out and they put him with this amazing immigrant family…"

"Do you want another drink?"

"Okay," I say, waiting patiently until he returns to continue. "Anyway, this guy found himself having so much respect for the super intelligent teenage daughter, you could see his mind changing and him gaining an understanding of the other side of the story for the very first time."

"Mmm-hmm."

"He even went with the father of the family to their former home in Mexico and saw just how desperate their situation had been and why they wanted a better life. And it was all so heart-warming and hopeful but you know what? Just a few weeks after, he was back patrolling the border."

Tristan gives a disinterested shrug and takes another swig of beer. "Are you going to drink that?" He nods to my margarita.

"In a minute," I reply, feeling a little peeved. "Are you looking for someone?" His attention is all over the place.

"Andy! Over here!" He waves over his friend, the trumpeter of the mariachi trio, and then stands talking to him.

I prepare my face to be introduced, making sure I have no chocolate smirches around my mouth, but Andy moves on before I get to give him my most winning smile.

Oh.

"Come on, I'm up in ten. You'll want to get a good spot."

"Up as in up on stage?" I say as he hurries me, moving me along with a hand on my elbow.

"I help them pull in a bigger crowd."

There's no denying that the second he steps on stage all the single females start moving in for a closer look, flipping their hair, whispering and giggling. I wish I felt the same. It's hard to see him as 100 percent handsome when you've had first-hand experience of his personality. He really is a bit of a twat. I'm definitely having second thoughts about going home with him tonight. I know my body is normally of the "make hay while the sun shines" persuasion but right now I feel like it's saying, "Nah, I'm good."

Of course, that could change if he gets all rock god on stage.

I watch with interest as he confers with the guys, confirming the song choice.

An expectant hush falls across the crowd as he takes center stage. A lone voice cries out, "Shake Your Bon Bon!" but he goes a different way.

"Oh no!" I hear myself murmur as the band launch into a mariachi version of Right Said Fred's "I'm Too Sexy."

On the upside, it's not like Tristan's comparing vocals with Tom Jones.

I watch with mortification as he struts and parades, doing his catwalk turns and whooping up the audience while unbuttoning his white shirt.

"You're vibrating."

"What?" I turn to the girl next to me. It's the same girl who was kind enough to compliment me on my hair earlier. I notice now that aside from her Mexican flag eye make-up she's wearing really cool earrings—gold filigree that look like they came from a street market in Oaxaca.

"I think your phone is ringing in your bag," she tries again. "Or something has switched itself on…" She gives me a wink.

"Oh! I'm sorry!" I say, trying to rummage with one hand, holding my margarita in the other.

"Here!" She offers to hold my drink for me.

"Thank you," I say, managing to locate it now. But my stomach plummets when I see the number. It's the nursing home. This can't be good.

"Are you okay?" the girl asks.

"I've got to go." I turn to push through the crowd.

"Your drink!" she calls after me.

"You have it, I haven't touched it."

"Sweet!" she says, raising the plastic glass to me.

I weave through the people, continuing to walk even as I press the button to return the call, trying to get away from the noise.

"Hello, can you hear me? This is Sophie's daughter, Amy."

"She's had a fall."

The words halt me.

"The medics are on their way."

"Is she okay?" I ask, though of course she is far from okay, I just need to know the severity.

They tell me there was a little blood as she hit her head but she's quite calm.

Blood. Blood from her head. I feel faint with concern. I look back to the stage, trying to motion to Tristan that I need to leave but he's playing to the girls in the front row and I can't get his attention.

With hands shaking, I call an Uber, relieved to see it will be here in three minutes. I think ahead to my arrival. Saturday is Lidia's day off. I need someone I trust to watch over Mum until I get there.

"Gareth?" I blurt.

"This is Dharmesh."

"Dharmesh, I need to speak to Gareth."

"He's just with a customer, can I—"

"Tell him it's Amy, my mum's had a fall," I cut in.

The phone is muffled for a moment and then Gareth's voice comes on the line. "I'm on my way."

"I'm not even there yet," I bleat. "Can you—"

"Of course! I'll keep you updated."

"Thank you." My hand goes to my heart. "I should be there in twenty."

"Okay. Be safe."

I allow my first exhale. It's so reassuring to reach out and find something steady to hold on to. I begin pacing as I wait for the car to arrive. Oh Mum, how did you fall? It makes you sound so frail, so unstable. I can't bear the thought of her being in any pain. What if they have to take her to hospital? I wonder if I should divert the ride there? No, Gareth will let me know if there's a change.

Here's the car now.

I slide into the back seat and then look at my phone again. I suppose I should let Tristan know where I've gone.

Had to leave, I text. *My mum has had a fall. Speak later.*

I stare out of the car window, feeling such a jumble of emotions. I wonder if it's the new medication they are trying her on. I wish I'd taken more time off work, just to sit with her, and make the most of the times she is present. And I wonder, as I always do, how I will be able to take a breath when the time comes that she leaves me for good. *Just don't let it be now. Please don't let it be now.*

I jump as my phone buzzes. Tristan calling. I turn it face down. I'm not answering. I need to keep the line clear.

In fact, I want to clear that line for good. Even if he is my destiny, that's not a destiny I want a part of. I can't keep ignoring the uneasiness I feel around him. I shudder as I recall the scornful look he gave me when I arrived...I want someone who looks pleased to see me, not as if they are grading me in a contest.

But right now, all I *really* want is for my mum to be okay and for life to feel safe again. Romance can wait.

22

I've had many cab drivers in my time – counselors, comedians, cultural ambassadors, some who complain about every other driver on the road, others who ask inappropriate questions with amorous undertones – but today, mercifully, I get one who is blissfully quiet and not trying to get extra points for dazzling conversation.

A full five minutes before we arrive I am positioning myself ready to leap out of the vehicle the second we come to a standstill outside the nursing home.

"Amy!" Gareth is there to greet me as I step through the door. I see a flicker of confusion as he takes in my outfit but he knows this isn't the time to quiz me over it. "The medics are just checking her over."

"In her room? Can I go in?" I ask in earnest.

"Claire wanted you to stop by her office first."

"Really?" Claire is the manager. I rarely see her, which makes me feel this is even more serious.

"I'll wait here," Gareth notes. "Keep an eye."

"Thank you," I say as I hurry down the corridor, still feeling light-headed as I tap on her door.

Claire's face is grave as she invites me to take a seat.

"Do you think it was the new medication, unbalancing her?" I cut to the chase as I pull the chair closer to her desk.

"I'm concerned there's a little more to it than that." She folds her hands neatly in front of her.

"Oh?" My stomach drops.

"Your mother was up on the fire escape. I don't want to alarm you but there is a concern that she wanted to end her life."

"Oh no, no," I sigh in relief. "It's not that."

"I know it's hard to face—"

"No, really. That's not why she was up there."

Claire tilts her head.

"She just wanted to look at the view," I insist.

Claire doesn't look convinced. "She's never attempted anything like this before…"

"Well…" I squirm.

Claire raises an eyebrow.

"I may have taken her up there."

"You may have?"

I feel like a naughty pupil in the headmistress's office. "I did take her up there," I blurt. "She loved looking out over London at night, the lights reflecting on the river. She said it made her feel like Wendy in *Peter Pan*."

"Which brings me back to my concern for her taking flight."

"I can see that." I bite my lip. "I'm so sorry. I didn't think she'd try and go up there without me."

"Well, now you mention it, she did say she was looking for you."

"Oh gosh," I say. My heart squeezes with pain. It's my fault. I brought on this fall.

"I'm not saying that to make you feel responsible. I just want you to know what happened."

"Right," I gulp. "How bad is it?"

"They want to take her into hospital for a scan, just as a precaution."

"What part of her do they want to scan?"

"Shall we go through and see her?" She avoids responding.

"Yes, of course," I say, leaping to my feet. "And I promise I won't take her near the roof ever again."

"Well, you wouldn't be able to even if you wanted to. We'll be locking the door now."

"Right. Good idea."

I follow sheepishly behind her, beckoning Gareth to join me.

"This is Sophie's daughter, Amy." Claire introduces me to the two medics—both women, both warm and welcoming—and then dips out, saying, "I'll leave you to the experts."

Apparently if you've seen one resident fall, you've seen them all.

And then the medics step aside.

"Oh Mum!" I exclaim, taking in the pile of bloodied tissues next to her. "Look at your poor head!" My hand hovers over the gash at her temple.

"We're just cleaning it up."

"Right…"

I crouch down to take my mum's hand, asking, "Does it hurt?"

"I'm all right, just embarrassed. I shouldn't have tried to climb in my flip-flops."

"She lost her footing and hit her head on one of the metal steps."

"Oh god!" I grimace.

"We're going to take her to hospital once she's had a chance to catch her breath."

"Thank you," I say. I hate feeling so helpless. I hate it when I can't make things right for her.

Suddenly I feel Gareth's hand on my shoulder and it has the same effect as a heated lavender-scented neck pillow, morphing my anxiety to gratitude—I'm so glad he's here, glad my mum is fully present, glad the medics are so kind.

"We're just going to get the wheelchair so we can take her to the ambulance."

"Wheelchair?" Mum recoils. "Not today, Satan!"

I roll my eyes. She's been watching *Queer Eye* again.

"It's just a formality," I assure her.

"You won't get your joyride to the hospital if you look like nothing is wrong," Gareth whispers.

"Good point," she acknowledges. "Are you coming too?"

"We'll be following right behind you."

She smiles contentedly but I get a little teary as I see them securing her and then closing the doors to the ambulance.

"Come here," Gareth says, opening his arms to me.

I can't resist a moment's surrender, leaning into his chest and exhaling. Mum seems okay. She'll get checked out and who knows, they might even tell me the bump to her head has set her right again. I slide my arms up Gareth's back, hugging him tight, drawing from his strength.

"You little bitch!"

I leap back as these words blast from right beside me on the pavement.

"Tristan!" I gasp, startled to see him standing so close—his face contorted with disgust. Where did he come from?

"So you walk out on me and run straight into this luddite's arms."

"Luddite?"

"You've been screwing him the whole time, haven't you?"

"What? Gareth and I have been friends since school! He's just here to help me."

"Is that what they're calling it?"

"Yes, when someone helps you out that's exactly what they call it."

"You dirty little slut!"

Gareth goes to step in but I assure him I can handle this.

"Are you suggesting we're on a hot date at a nursing home?" I gesture at the building only to notice assorted faces clustered at the window. Oh great, now we're causing a scene. "My mother has just gone to hospital in an ambulance," I hiss. "We're following her there now."

I motion for Gareth to get in the car but Tristan steps in front of me as I try to reach for the passenger door.

"You're lying to me!"

"Please move out of the way!"

"I know you're sleeping with him."

"I am not!" I hoot, exasperated. "I'm also not sleeping with you. Ever again. Whatever we had was clearly a mistake."

I try to move past him but he blocks me, every which way.

"Ohhh! Look, it's like a scene from a show!" Malcolm is now at the door with Mum's next-door neighbor Beverly.

"I think they're doing the paso doble," she opines. "Look at their costumes, all Spanishy."

"Amy?" Gareth hesitates—seemingly unsure whether to get in the car or come to my aid.

"I have to go. I have to get to my mother. We'll talk about this later." Which we absolutely won't but I'll say anything to get away.

"Show me your phone!" he demands.

"*What?*"

"Prove you're not sleeping with him and I'll let you go."

"I don't have to prove anything to you!" I'm incredulous. Even more so when he tries to make a grab for it.

As we tussle for it, my phone flies out of my hand, hitting the tarmac hard. Tristan lurches into the road to retrieve it, just as a taxi rounds the corner—it's the premonition! I grab him by the arm and pull him clear, just as the cab crunches over my phone.

"Ha! Karma!" he taunts, looking back at the pulverized glass.

"No, mate, this is karma!" In one swoop Gareth levels him.

Tristan rocks back on his heels, landing squarely on his rear. He peers up at Gareth in a daze. "You just hit me!"

"And she just saved your life." He scoops up what is left of my phone and then opens the car door for me. "Come on," he urges. "We need to get to the hospital."

23

For the first few minutes I sit in silent shock.

"I can't believe that just happened," I say finally, turning to Gareth. "I can't believe you hit him! That's so not you!"

"It seemed appropriate."

"It was appropriate. Wow." I shake my head and then grimace. "I think we put on quite a show for the nursing home."

Gareth raises his brows. "I'm not sure how we're going to top that for the fancy dress party."

"Fire-eating? Or some kind of trapeze act?" I look down at my lap. "My poor phone."

"Your screen was cracked anyway."

"It was," I concede. "I didn't see any point getting it fixed because I knew this was coming."

"From the premonition?"

I nod. "I didn't know when it was coming exactly. I certainly didn't think it was going to be today. But I'm glad it's over with Tristan. It wasn't right."

"Really?"

"I just wanted to be sure I wasn't missing anything," I say. "And now I'm *really, really, really* sure."

Gareth nods and then looks a little distant.

"I think it was that turn!"

"Oh yes." His attention returns as he makes a swift U-turn.

"Don't forget your phone," I say, handing it to him as we park.

I noticed it buzzing repeatedly on our journey but didn't say anything in case it was another burst of Freya calls.

"Oh crap!" he exclaims as the screen illuminates.

"What is it?"

"I completely forgot—I'm supposed to be picking up Peony, she got us tickets to a play. Let me just call her."

I put my hand over his phone. "You have to go."

"I couldn't possibly—"

"You can possibly and, in fact, you will definitely. You've already done your bit. More than your bit," I emphasize. "Now will just be a lot of waiting around."

"But—"

"The scan is just a precaution. You've seen my mum, she's fine."

"But what about you?"

My heart pangs with appreciation. "I'll call you if there's a problem."

"You haven't got a phone!"

"I'll use one at the hospital."

"Do you even know my number?"

"I've got it on your card." I reach into my bag and pull out my purse to show him. "See!"

"You still have that?"

"Of course, I love that little smiling cactus."

He chews his lip. "It doesn't feel right leaving you alone."

"I won't be on my own, I'll be with my mum," I assert. "I need to get in and check on her, you go enjoy the play!"

I quickly slide out of the car before he can protest further and march through the automatic glass doors, cruising on false bravado.

I'm surprised to find the atmosphere at the hospital quite tranquil—there's a flood of natural daylight in the lobby and a distinct absence of patients, though I suppose we're ahead of Saturday night's rush of drunken incidents. It's jarring to think that Tristan could have been one of them. That taxi wouldn't have seen him in time to brake. I shudder at the thought. But then I feel a sense of relief. That was the darkest element to my merged premonitions and it's over. I am now free to use all of my worry tokens on my mum.

I get directions to her ward from the kind woman on reception, and then regret not having Gareth's help to keep me on the right path. I'm sure I've already been down this corridor— she said second on the left, but they all look the same. Lino flooring stretching to infinity, shiny surfaces, signs taking you through the A to Z of ailments, clusters of old-fashioned chairs, swing doors with glass panels offering glimpses of people who'd rather not be seen.

It's such a relief to finally find my mum's ward. The nurse tells me she went straight in for her scan so she is already in situ in a bed—they want to keep her in overnight, just to be sure.

I nod and ask to see her, bracing myself before I do. It's not a sight you ever want to see—a loved one in a hospital bed.

She looks so fragile in this brightly lit, sterile environment. I try not to stare at the strangers on either side of her, separated only by a curtain. Everyone looks a bit worn and dazed but the nurses are chirpy as can be.

"Did you see my doctor?" Mum asks as soon as she sees me.

"Not yet," I tell her.

"So handsome. He's got hair like Tan France. There he is!"

She's quite right—it's a whisked-up, salt and pepper quiff, looking all the more monochromatic and stylish against his white coat. He smiles warmly as he approaches, assuring me that my mother is doing fine but they have given her something to help her sleep as they want her to get a good night's rest. It's possible it's already kicking in, or is it that she's looking dreamy and heavy-lidded because she's gazing at him?

"I see no reason why you can't go back to your party."

"My party?" I frown at him.

"Sorry, I just thought from your outfit?" He waves a hand over my scarlet flounces.

"Oh," I shrug, "that party is over."

"Well, in that case, you're welcome to visit again at nine a.m."

He clearly wants me to leave her in peace.

I nod but I have no intention of going home, I want to stay close by in case something happens. I'll find the nearest waiting room then let the nurses know that's where I'll be if they need me. For now, I gently take her hand, resting my cheek on it, wishing she would reach out and stroke my hair like she used to do when I was a little girl. But instead, I stroke hers. And then remove the flowers from my headdress and cluster them like a mini bouquet into the plastic cup by her bedside.

"Have a lovely sleep, Mum. Sweet dreams."

The nearest collection of seats is nothing more than that. It's going to be weird sitting there without the distraction of a phone. I think I'd better source some vending machine snacks to keep me amused. I suppose it would be too much to ask for it to dispense some jogging bottoms and a sweatshirt? Although if I had some bamboo poles, I could probably make this dress into a personal teepee.

"Excuse me, is there a snack machine nearby?" I ask a passing nurse.

"I'm one step ahead of you!"

I turn toward the voice. "Gareth!" I gasp, amazed to see him laden down with crisps, Crunchies and three bottles of orange Lucozade.

"I thought you'd probably be peckish."

"What about the play?" I gawp at him.

"I couldn't leave you. I'll go some other time."

I look around me. "I want to hug you but I'm afraid Tristan will jump off some passing trolley."

"Just let him try!" Gareth raises his free hand in a Bruce Lee slice.

"Oh, I love this new side of you!"

"So how is she doing?" he asks, nodding down the corridor.

"Good. She's taken a shine to her doctor. He's given her something to sleep so she's resting now."

He nods then looks down at the snacks. "You know, I could cook us some real food instead. We'd just be five minutes away. And you're welcome to stay over, in case they called."

I look at the uncomfortable chairs and then back at Gareth.

"We can leave my number as the contact," he continues, not realizing I'm already sold. "And I could do your favorite baked feta or a quick tamarind coconut stir-fry…"

"Do you know what I really fancy?" I say, after we've left his details with the front desk.

"Tell me."

"Cheese on toast with Marmite."

"Really?"

"If you had that squishy, grainy bread."

"I do have that squishy, grainy bread," he confirms. "I can also do a mix of three different cheeses."

"Now you're just showing off."

As we head out, we pass a worried-looking woman trying to

settle three young kids. Even the iPad has lost its appeal. The eldest is trying to do a headstand on the chair, the middle one is pulling on her sleeve, the smallest is anxiously nibbling at her tiny nails.

"Would you like some snacks?" Gareth offers his armful. "We just got them but we don't need them now."

The kids' eyes suddenly brighten, looking imploringly at their mum.

She looks at Gareth with cautious gratitude. "If you're sure?"

"Of course. Though I apologize in advance for any sugar rush antics."

"Oh, I'm having the chocolate," she assures him.

I chuckle and then smile at Gareth as he holds open the door for me. "You're such a kind person."

He looks back at me, almost baffled. As in, why would anyone be anything but kind?

"I don't think you realize how special you are."

24

It's funny how friends take on different roles in your life – the friend who makes you snort with laughter, the friend who tells you the truth no matter what, the friend who styles you, the friend who brings out the minx in you...With Gareth, I always feel I can relax and take a breath. I think it could be because I know that anything could happen and it wouldn't phase him. Today is a prime example. And right now, I know he understands my concerns but he doesn't let me dwell on them. If the hospital calls, we'll respond swiftly. But for now, we are entering the sanctuary that is his home...

"Hello to you too!" I respond to the meowing as the cats wind impatiently around our legs, slightly impeding our path along the corridor.

As we reach the lounge Gareth raises Zazel high up above his head, her purring volume increasing as his arms lock and she reaches maximum elevation.

I give a little chuckle. "Do you remember when you did that move with Jay?"

Gareth buckles and clasps Zazel to his chest. "Not quite the under-the-radar debut I was hoping to make as the school newbie!"

I remember it like yesterday: our PE teacher had us working on iconic lifts from the movies and, of course, nothing is more iconic than Baby being lifted by Swayze in *Dirty Dancing*. The only snag was that Jay wanted to be Baby, and none of the boys would place their hands on his hips and raise his groin over their heads, no matter how balletic he promised to be.

"So all those muscles are just for show?" May had taunted the wannabe class studs but they refused to be baited and the others simply turned away.

We were about to move on to the twirl and catch from the barn dance scene in *Seven Brides for Seven Brothers* when we heard a voice coming from the back of the room: "I'll do it." We all turned and looked at Gareth—pretty much his worst nightmare. He didn't make a big show, just set his feet apart and gave Jay the nod. I saw May hesitate—you had to have full trust in the person doing the lifting and Gareth had only been there a week or so. But Jay has always been a good judge of character and so he just took off running toward him and in one move Gareth lifted him sky-high, arms dead straight, not a tremble or strain or waver.

"I'm still kind of in awe that you did that!" I say as I watch him feed the cats.

"You know, Jay asked me to re-create that moment at the wedding?"

"Oh my god!" I hoot. "Our old classmates would have lost their minds!"

"I didn't think Charlotte would thank me."

I give a little shrug. "I think she would have been cheering along with the rest of us. The mother-in-law maybe not so much…"

Gareth points down to where Frankie has managed to get his claw stuck in my flamenco-esque ruffles.

"I am so over this dress!" I tut as I free him. And then I squint up at Gareth. "You know how I always borrow your jumper?"

"I do indeed. It hasn't gone unnoticed that I sometimes smell of jasmine with notes of vanilla."

I smile. "I was just wondering if you had something I could borrow for the bottom half this time?"

He thinks for a moment. "Is it too early for pajamas?"

"It's never too early for pajamas!" I cheer.

"Follow me!"

I look on as he jiggles open his heavy wooden dresser and pulls out a pair in a sage green check. "You'll actually be christening the top half."

"Quite the honor," I beam, hugging the set to me on the way to the bathroom, eager to revel in their coziness. Unsurprisingly they are huge on me, even with a roll-up on the trouser cuffs and sleeves. Not that I mind; I may even start shopping at men's stores now, I've never felt so petite. However, with the braids pinned on top of my head I'm feeling a bit too like a kid playing dress-up. I think it's time to take them down. In fact, it would be a relief to unplait them as May did pull the strands a little tight. I shake out the zigzag waves. And then fluff them to full Diana Ross volume.

"How do I look?"

As I strike a pose in the door frame, the breeze from an open window lifts my hair and makes it dance.

"Woah!" Gareth looks delighted, insisting I hold the pose. "I've got the perfect song for you."

He sets down the crusty loaf and rushes to the stereo, carefully sliding one of his vinyl records from its sleeve and then lowering the needle into position.

Kate Bush's "Wuthering Heights."

I duly flail around looking for Heathcliff. "Do I look like a woman possessed?"

"You look perfect," he smiles.

For a second I just hear my own heartbeat. And then I rub my hands together. "How's the cheese on toast coming?"

I could watch Gareth in the kitchen like other people watch a cooking show. Especially because his version comes with zero chatter or commentary. He likes to put on an old LP and get into the groove as he preps his dishes. Even something as simple as cheese on toast. He never rushes, every step is done with care—the slicing of the homemade bread, the grating of three different types of cheese for added flavor and texture, the golden bronzing under the grill.

"Everything always tastes better here," I sigh as he hands me one of his enamel plates.

"I did a little diced salad to have on the side." He sets down a bowl of cubed tomato and cucumber in a homemade vinaigrette.

"Always with the extra flair."

Gareth takes a seat opposite me and raises his glass. "To your mum's good health."

"To Mum," I concur.

I take a bite and study the man opposite me. Something feels different tonight. Maybe it's because we're usually chowing down in front of the TV, maybe it's because I don't have to keep an eye on the clock to get the last bus home. Either way, we have time to talk.

"Soooo, how's it going with Peony?" I ask.

"It's going," he replies, nodding at his plate, cryptic as ever.

"I'm really sorry about you missing the play."

"Don't be, you got me out of having a haircut."

"Was that part of the show?" I frown.

"No." He hesitates. "She was going to cut it prior."

"Really? Your wild, beautiful mane?" I say, eyeing his tawny curls.

"She says I'd look good with a buzz cut."

"Nooo!" I gasp.

"I'm kidding. I don't know what she had in mind. She said she'd seen some picture," he shrugs.

"You're not concerned?"

"It's just hair."

Hmm. I'm not keen on her remodeling him to suit some alternative vision she has but instead of interfering I go for a sing-song platitude. "Well, she's very lucky to have you."

"I don't know that she does have me…" He falters as he reaches over to top up my ale.

Is that a small sense of relief I feel? I take a sip and then say, "I saw your new pet-friendly plant range on Instagram…"

"Dharmesh did that, of course. He understood how important it is to let people know how toxic lilies are to cats."

And back he goes, into his comfort zone.

After we've eaten, we move over to the lounge area. Typically, I lie out on the sofa and Gareth sits in his retro recliner but tonight Frankie has fallen sound asleep there, on his back, furry belly exposed, head lolling to the side. To touch him would risk giving him such a fright you might as well put your hand directly into a metal-pronged trap.

"Do you mind if I join you?" Gareth motions to the sofa.

"I love how you're asking my permission to sit on your own furniture!"

"Well." He gives a little shrug.

"Help yourself," I say, tucking my feet under me.

For the next hour our conversation weaves from least favorite desserts to childhood duvet covers, and how we'd both like to contribute to Habitat for Humanity. At one point I consider asking him whether Julianne has closed the deal on the house next door but it's been a weird day with the knock-back from Ben, my mum's fall and Tristan's freak-out, so I decide I'd rather not add that to the mix.

"Fancy a cuppa?" Gareth yawns.

He looks ready for bed but I can't help but want to prolong the coziness so I hop up, telling him I'll make it. "What'll it be?" I call from the kitchen, scrutinizing the options from immunity-boosting to stress-relieving.

"Surprise me."

I reach for both the turmeric and the apple flavors, deciding to create a blend. It could work.

I smile to myself as I pick out a toning pair of misshapen mugs—one with an aqua glaze, the other looking like it's been dipped in glossy caramel. As I lean back to wait for the kettle to boil, I muse upon what a mismatched kitchen we'd have if we co-habited—all his rustic, hand-hewn wares alongside my cheeky kitsch. Every item in his home has a history and a memory—a pottery class, an antique find abroad, a family hand-me-down. With me it would be more a case of, "Ah yes, I remember that trip to TK Maxx in 2017. The checkout queues were particularly bad that day."

"Here we go," I say as I walk back in with the steaming mugs, and then stop in my tracks as I realize he's fallen asleep.

Oh-so-gently I set the mugs on the side table. And then I crouch down beside him, wondering if I should nudge him or let him be. My hand hovers over his. I look at the knuckles that punched Tristan, then up at the face I know so well—those soft lashes, that thick, tousled hair, the sculpted slant of his jaw. And then I notice the tiny dark line on his lip where I clunked him and experience a strange swirling sensation that makes me want to reach out and touch it. More than that. *I want to kiss him.* Which is ridiculous.

Or is it?

I mean, I've kissed practically everyone else, even May. What harm could there be in sneaking a peek at our premonition? It could be a fun anecdote to share—something we laugh about.

Of course, there is the issue that I'd be stealing a kiss without his consent, which technically would make me no better than Elliot. Not to mention the fact that he is seeing Peony.

Then again…It's not like I'd be going for a big, invasive smooch, it would just be the lightest touch, a chaste goodnight. I feel myself drawn toward him, almost like my actions aren't my own. I'm about to make contact when the wind from the open window suddenly whisks up my hair, sweeping it directly into his face.

"Pwah!" Gareth bats it away as if he's walked into a spider's web.

"Sorry, sorry!" I jump back. "That was just my hair! I was…I was going to put a cushion under your head!"

He looks over at the mugs. "How long was I out?"

"Just a few minutes."

He rubs his face then looks concerned. "Did I say anything? In my sleep?"

"No," I reply, standing awkwardly by his side. "Why?"

"I was just dreaming…"

"Well, why don't you get back to it?" I suggest. "Definitely time to call it a night."

He still seems a little disorientated but rallies and gets to his feet. "Okay, let me get my bed set up for you. I'll sleep here."

"No chance," I assert. "You know how much I love this sofa. Just give me a blanket and I'll be happy."

"It doesn't seem right," he falters.

"Oh, but it is." I scoot into place, the fabric still warm from his body. "See—perfect fit."

He lingers beside me. "Are you sure? My bed is so comfortable..."

For a heart-stopping millisecond I think he's asking me to share it with him.

But of course, he isn't.

It's like our teenage mistletoe misunderstanding all over again.

"Honestly, I'll be snug as a bug." I scrunch down, squeezing my eyes closed as if feigning sleep, but really just trying to bury my mortification.

"Well, if you insist," he sighs. "Let me get you a duvet."

When he returns, he's also carrying a pillow and a towel.

"Are you trying for a five-star Tripadvisor rating?" I tease.

"At the very least." He winks, floating the duvet over me. As I pull the pillow under my head, he crouches by my side, as I had done with him. "Can I get you anything else?"

I don't want him to go. I don't want to be alone. But I tell him I'm fine.

"Okay," he says, scooping up Frankie. "I'll leave Zazel with you."

I smile gratefully. "Thank you for being such a wonderful friend."

He gives a modest shrug and then pads over to his room. "Night."

For a few minutes I am comforted by the amber glow at the base of his door but then, in one abrupt click, it's gone.

There's just moonlight now, seeping in through the lounge window. Everything feels so still. Even the breeze has settled.

I sigh to myself and place my hand over my heart. "Soon," I whisper to it. "Soon I will find someone who loves you."

25

I didn't think I'd sleep, but after such a draining day I was out the minute I closed my eyes, only to wake up with Zazel's furry body in my face.

I pick the fluff from my mouth and slide her down under my chin.

"Is your lord and master awake?" I whisper in her dainty ear.

She stretches out her paws, extending her limbs, and then looks back at me as if to say, "Funny that you think he's in charge."

I listen for movement from his direction. All is quiet.

It gives me a chance to gather my thoughts...I wonder if we could take my mum out for the day? If Gareth was with me, with his strength and wheels and reassuring presence, so many possibilities could open up. Though perhaps she should be resting after her fall. Either way, I want to treat Gareth to a bumper Sunday lunch to say thank you for everything. Maybe afterward he could give me a tour of the neighborhood. I'm certain

I want to reside closer to the nursing home now and it would be nice to explore and really get a feel for what it would be like to live in this part of town. I'll propose it over coffee.

Not for Gareth a sleek Nespresso machine or cafetiere. He favors a Greek briki—a hammered copper vessel with a wooden handle—heated directly over the flame.

"You're up!" I cheer as he stumbles out from his room. "How many times do I have to let it bubble to the boil? I've done two already…"

"One sec!" he calls as he heads for the bathroom.

I take a deep breath. He's shirtless, still just in his pajama bottoms, and when he joins me I have to turn away so he can't read my desire to trace every curve of every muscle and each faint scar left by a rogue garden thorn.

What is up with my hormones since the wedding?

"Just let it simmer down and then put it back on the heat one more time," he instructs.

"Simmer down," I repeat as he leans across me to get the petite cups and saucers from the cupboard. "You know, I was going to wait on you."

"It's more fun if we do it together," he says. "So, you know, I wouldn't normally serve Turkish Delight until the afternoon coffee but I want you to try the new lemon one. They just got them in at the international market. I think I prefer it, it's not as chewy."

As my hands are full bringing the cups to the table he pops one in my mouth.

"Mmmm, I love that!" I say as we take a seat opposite each other.

He sips the dark brown liquid, making the required inhaling-slurping sound.

I do the same and then burst out laughing. "This is my favorite thing about this coffee—making weird noises."

"Feels like we're back in Kefalonia," he smiles.

"Remember you didn't want to go initially, because of the taramasalata."

"Well, it seems silly when you put it like that."

"Wasn't that the reason?"

"You know I only have to look at it to feel nauseous."

"I think that's true for a lot of people. Especially if they once mistook it for strawberry mousse."

"Noooo!" In a bid to distract himself from thoughts of pink goop he starts manically spinning a teaspoon on the table.

"Okay, now it's my turn to feel nauseous," I say, reaching out to stop the spinning.

"That makes you dizzy?"

"No, it's reminding me of Elliot's spin-the bottle party!"

"Oh god." He cringes, rubbing his face with his hands. "Not my finest hour."

I raise an eyebrow. "Does anyone have their finest hour at a spin-the-bottle party?"

He gives me a grateful smile.

"You know, when the bottle stopped halfway between you and Elliot, I thought it was curtains for me—the idea of spending three minutes in the coatroom with him…" I instinctively cross my hands across my boobs, at which point I realize one of the pajama buttons is undone. How long has that been gaping?

Gareth seems oblivious, too busy reliving that teenage night. He gallantly stepped up to the task of what was slated to have been my first premonition kiss but things took a different turn. The space was way smaller than we expected, and jammed with the family's parkas, waterproofs, fleeces and a lifetime of shoes. It was also pitch black. I put my hands out trying to judge how close Gareth was to me and found his chest rising and falling apace. His breathing was unusually heavy. For a moment I thought things were going to take an unexpectedly lusty turn but then I realized this wasn't amorous breathing, it was anxiety.

"Are you okay?" I whispered.

"I—I just…" He panted out his words. "So close. The walls."

As he shifted and twisted, he accidentally dislodged some of the boxes on the shelf, one narrowly missing my head.

I tried banging on the door but the party jailers insisted we still had two minutes to go. I felt for his hands, praying I wouldn't further exacerbate his claustrophobia. "It's going to be okay, deep breath in…Oh my god! What's that smell?" I recoiled.

"I think it's Elliot's trainers," he muttered.

And then we burst out laughing.

"You were so gracious, never revealing what happened in there," Gareth tells me.

"Oh, come on, the combination of Elliot's trainers and the hideous pressure of being my first premonition kiss? Even The Rock would crack."

"Actually, I kind of wanted it to be me."

I look up at him.

"I was worried about you having a bad experience with some stranger. Instead, you had a bad experience with me!"

I smile, toying with my cup. "You know, when I first heard you breathing so hard, I thought, *Oh hello, things are about to get steamy!*"

"Did you?" He holds my gaze and suddenly I have that feeling again.

I want to kiss him.

And I want him to kiss me.

As my mouth opens to say his name, the table buzzes. He tilts his phone toward him. Peony.

My hand moves to stop him answering—but then the doorbell rings.

He looks confused then presses the green button on his phone. "Hello?" There's a pause. He looks directly at me. "You're outside? Now?"

Oh, you've got to be kidding.

"Coffee and pastries?" He winces, getting to his feet and sluicing the last of his coffee down the sink. "I'll be right there."

"Is she going to freak out that I'm here?" I call as he heads to his room.

"No, I told her you were staying, it's not a problem."

Hmm. No wonder she's here so early.

I watch him pull on a T-shirt and then remember I'm still in his pajamas, so grab my bundle of clothes and run into the bathroom. As soon as the door closes, I lean on the wall, feeling light-headed, then catch sight of my stunned face in the mirror. What just happened? Did we have a moment?

Hearing voices, I jolt myself into action. I don't want Peony thinking I'm hiding. I slip out of the pajamas but hesitate as I go to put them in his laundry basket, diverting them instead to my bag. I want to return them clean, I think to myself, but what I actually want to do is climb back into them as soon as I get home.

But for now, it's bravado time.

"This *is* a lot of dress," I mutter to myself as I pull it on and try to revive the flounces. And just *so* red. Not the most discreet look. Scarlet lipstick seems inappropriate and I know I won't be able to do the plaits like May so I opt for a quick topknot. Now I look like a flamenco dancer. Oh well, in for a pound, in for a peseta.

I approach the kitchen and call "*Ole!*" from the doorway, arms raised clicking imaginary castanets. It's a good call—I couldn't look any less of a match for Gareth if I tried.

Peony, meanwhile, looks like a tumble of bluebells to his woodland dell, perched on his knee in a skimpy floral dress, slender limbs entwining with his.

"How's your mother?" she asks.

"I'm just heading out to get an update," I reply.

"I brought you a latte," she says, sliding the cup toward me. "And help yourself to the apricot galette."

"Wow! That looks delicious, where did you get it?"

"I made it."

Of course she did.

"I had to do something with my Saturday night."

I wince and then apologize for throwing off her plans.

"No worries. We'll make up for it today." She nuzzles Gareth.

"Well, I'd better be off." I hold up my drink. "I'll take this with me, if that's okay?"

"Of course. And please take a couple of slices of the pastry."

I'd love to say no but I suspect it is as delicious as it looks.

I thank her as I fold them into a paper napkin and then look at Gareth, or rather *near* Gareth because I don't want my eyes to give me away. "I really appreciate you helping me with Mum and letting me stay."

"Do you want me to run you there?"

"No, no. I could do with the walk. I'll see myself out."

I try to make a swift exit but struggle at the door, trying to not spill my coffee or crumple my pastries. Naturally my bag slips off my shoulder as I attempt to grapple with the lock.

"Here, allow me."

Gareth appears behind me, reaching over my shoulder to undo the bolt. I can feel the heat from him all down my back. I'd do anything to lean into him, to feel his breath on my cheek, then slowly turn my face toward his. But now is not the time.

"Thanks again," I mutter as I make my ungainly exit through the now open door.

I keep my head down until I round the corner and then I expel a long breath. I need to sit down…

I catch sight of a small, deserted square and make a beeline for it, squeaking open the gate and finding a little bench amid the brambles. As I sit there, I try to replay the scene. But there's nothing concrete for me to cling to—two friends reminiscing. A boy and a girl talking about an almost kiss from twenty years ago.

But that look he gave me!

My body tingles as I re-experience the thrill. What am I supposed to do with that?

I go to reach for my phone, as if it might have the answer, but remember it's been smashed to smithereens. Who would I call anyway? Charlotte's still away and it's too early to be calling May or Jay on a Sunday. Besides, it would be weird to discuss any romantic feelings for Gareth with them.

I reach for the coffee cup and take a sip, lukewarm now. And then I look at the pastries but I don't take a bite. Perhaps my mum would like them?

When I'm told that I can't see her for another two hours I decide to make the pilgrimage to the Regent Street Apple store and get the new phone I've been putting off buying for months, stopping off at H&M en route to buy some cheap jogging bottoms and a slouchy top. Finally I can relax.

"All set," Tony the Apple guy nods to my phone.

"This really is magic," I smile appreciatively as all my personal info appears on screen. "Ooh! A text from May!"

"Say hi from me," he jokes as he heads to his next customer.

It's from last night, sent at one a.m.

It just occurred to me what we overlooked on the night of the wedding...

26

What? *What?* I stare at May's one message. She just leaves me hanging?

Or I suppose technically I left her hanging, seeing as I didn't respond due to my smashed phone.

I reread her words.

> *It just occurred to me what we overlooked on the night of the wedding...*

Does she mean there's a new contender? A new clue. Could it be the vicar? I don't even remember what he looks like. He wasn't at the dinner but perhaps he came back for the party?

Call me when you surface! I tap to May, wondering if she's still with her date. *I'm just headed to see Mum.*

I won't mention that I'm seeing her in hospital in a text.

When I do get there, Mum is sitting up in bed, looking

physically fine but having one of her "away days" mentally. Which is okay because I'm hardly with it myself. She keeps talking about Jimmy, looking around the ward, wondering where the love of her life has got to. I can certainly relate to that.

I have a pleasant, positive chat with the doctor who says she's ready to go back to the nursing home and I'm delighted to see Lidia arriving to help facilitate that.

"So, on a lighter note, your mum has decided on her outfit for the party," Lidia tells me as we wait for the parting paperwork. "But I don't know how you're going to feel about it."

I brace myself for Karen from *Will & Grace* but instead she tells me it's Roz from *Frasier.*

"Oh well, that's easy. She's already got a cashmere sweater and a pencil skirt."

"Well, it's a little more elaborate than that, we might need a fitting…"

"With Jay? Sure thing, I can arrange that," I say, tapping him a text as we speak, including her number so they can speak directly. "Did you want any help with your outfit?"

"I'm actually all set."

"As…?"

"You'll have to wait and see!" She winks. "What about you?"

"I still can't decide."

Lidia gives me a sympathetic look, all too familiar with the emotionally vulnerable. "It's Sunday, why don't you go home, get into your pjs and binge-watch sitcoms until you find one that resonates?"

I take her suggestion like it's a prescription and, as it happens, hit a home run with my first sitcom selection. Even Jay would approve of the retro vibe of Zooey Deschanel's outfits in *New Girl* and I could easily get some black-framed glasses and a clip-on fringe...

The more I watch, the more hooked I get. It's so great when you've missed out on a series when it first aired and then discover you now have 146 episodes to power through. I can even justify my compulsive viewing as a form of research into the masculine psyche for the skincare account thanks to Jess's three male roommates, who range from metrosexual to someone who cuts their own hair. The bathroom scenes are especially helpful in terms of filling the gaps left by my personal reference points, i.e., Jay, who could take over a beauty counter at the bat of an eye, and Gareth who probably wouldn't notice if you removed his bathroom mirror.

I'm just wondering why none of the characters are acknowledging the ringing phone when I realize it is my own shiny new phone set to an unfamiliar ringtone. Better yet, it's May calling.

"Finally!" I crow, excited to chat.

"I can't talk now, meet me at Zannoni's at six p.m. tomorrow."

I give a startled laugh. "Sounds like a line from a thriller! Please don't get murdered en route."

"What?"

"You know how the person who has discovered the identity

of the killer always gets bumped off en route to the meeting place."

"What am I missing?"

"Your text? From last night." I roll my eyes. "The thing we overlooked at the wedding?"

"Oh god, what was that? It came to me in a flash but I was drunk at the time…"

"May!" I despair.

"It'll come back to me. I've got to go, the show is about to start."

I don't get to ask her what show or whether this is an extension of her date because the line cuts out. For a minute I sit in a daze. So much for a breakthrough.

I decide to finish off the last of my blackberry gelato then press play and watch another episode and another until my eyelids droop. I then fall asleep for nine hours straight and have a sex dream about, of all people, *Elliot*.

The next morning at work we dive directly into mocking up packaging ideas, in all the neutral tones you would expect men's skincare to come in—charcoals, tans, leather browns. We look at fonts that imply everything from cowboy swagger to camera-ready sophistication. And then we have a team meeting to look at the possible charities we could pair up with.

"You know, one simple option would be to join that global network of businesses giving one percent of profits to environmental non-profit organizations. Collectively they've given back more than two hundred million dollars to save the planet. You can be any size business—from a household name to someone like my friend Gareth with his flower shop." I pause. "You don't look convinced?"

"I think they might think that's a bit airy-fairy," Boss Lindsey says, wincing.

"How do you mean?"

"Saving the planet. I mean, it's not going to happen, is it? I think they'd probably prefer something a bit more tangible with actual faces and stories of people impacted. You know— we raised fifty thousand pounds and we bought this life-changing item for this disadvantaged group."

I open my mouth to offer a counter argument but Becky chimes in, "Can't it be for animals? Everyone likes animals."

"Not everyone," Lindsey sneers.

"What about mental illness? That's trending now."

Oh my goodness. It's a good thing our business meetings aren't recorded.

I come away more confused than ever. As usual, there are way too many cooks. I mean, you put six different personalities in a room, everyone is going to be pulling in different directions. And don't even get me started on focus groups.

By the end of the day I'm feeling keen to let off a bit of steam and all but run to Zannoni's.

"Hey, girl!" May gives me a faux *Valley Girl* wave.

"Hey, May!" I say, falling heavily into her arms.

"Right back atcha," she sighs, gripping me tight.

"How was the date?" I say as we slide into our regular booth.

She gives a "whatever" shrug. "I've got to stop messing with these fashion girls."

"You're a fashion girl."

"Exactly—how can I be surprised and amazed when I'm looking in the mirror?"

"Ladies. Your pizza."

We've got this down to a fine art—May orders en route to the restaurant and the pizza arrives at our pre-reserved table minutes after we do. I mean, it's the start of the week, you have to cut to the chase.

We normally get a couple of Peroni to go with the oozy slices but today the waitress is recommending cider to offset the six-cheese topping. Yes, six.

"Ooh, now that's a good call," I say as I take a swig of the chilled apple bubbles.

"Almost sherbetty," May notes as she reads the label. "Devon Mist—doesn't that sound alluring?"

I make a grab for her hand. "Why don't we just run away to Devon for the weekend? Forget our city girl woes, just for a night!"

"I'm listening." She leans in.

"We can take the train to Torquay on Friday, be there in time for a fish and chip dinner, do the Agatha Christie escape room at Torre Abbey on Saturday and be back in time for the fancy dress party on Sunday. No dates, no drama, just cream teas, cider and crime-solving."

"I can't say I'm entirely opposed to this."

I beam back at her. "If the others want to come, great. If not, we'll have a fun trip and a blast of sea air." I take another bite of pizza and get a dob of bright red sauce on my top. "Every flipping time."

"You need to get cold running water on that now. And then some soap."

I huff irritatedly. May will have gone off the idea by the time I come back—found at least three reasons why it's bad timing or the train fares are too jacked up this close to travel, which is probably true. I just want to believe there's a place I could go where I wouldn't feel so frustrated. It's tiring chasing down a man who doesn't want to be found.

"Do you know there are a ton of female farmers in Devon?" May looks up from her phone when I return to the table, now with a wet splotch across my tummy.

"Are we going there looking for love now?"

"Not necessarily but I thought I'd give it a quick google on the off-chance that my dream gal has a farmhouse and a herd of cattle."

I give a little snuffle but May looks sincere. "I just feel like something has to change. I think I may have reached my limit of flawless faces with vacant stares. I go to put my pictures up on Instagram and every one could be captioned, 'Unclouded by thought…' It might be nice to see some ruddy cheeks and muddy boots."

I flashback to my snug bar under the stairs at the wedding,

thinking fondly of that tweed dog bed and how the Wellies were calling to me to kick off my stilettos and slide into their solid rubbery form. And then my heart dips and I feel as if magical fairy dust is being sprinkled over my inner organs.

"Mmmm..." I give an involuntary gurgle of pleasure.

"What was that?" May looks vaguely grossed out.

I sit upright, trying to get a firm grip on the sensation. "Something happened by the staircase at the wedding. I remember hiding under there early on and talking to Ben but this is different." I swoon again. "Whoever this mystery guy is, he's gorgeous!" I say. "My whole body is in love with him."

May suddenly grips my hand. "That's it—mystery guy!"

"What?"

"This is what I was thinking last night—what if there were other guests staying the same night as us? I mean, I know it was supposed to be exclusive use for the wedding party but what if the owner had a friend or relative in town?"

"I guess it's worth getting Charlotte to look into it when she gets back."

"Of course it is," May insists. "For all we know there's a younger, hotter, less gratingly posh brother of the owner, also blighted by a lifetime of first kiss premonitions and disappointments!"

My eyes widen. "Well, that would be something."

"He could have snuck out from their quarters to take a peek at the wedding and spied a vision in lilac..."

"He wonders how she's still standing having consumed so much booze," I chime in.

"Perhaps he reaches out a hand to steady her just as 'Someone to Watch Over Me' comes on."

"Was there a slow dance section?"

"Of course! They sway to the music, lost in their own world."

"Go on." I'm warming to this now.

"He wants to hold her in his arms forever but her friends are calling her, like midnight calling to Cinderella."

"That's very poetic," I note.

"Thank you. She turns back, raises up on her tiptoes and kisses him."

"So he's tall?"

"You've taken off your shoes by this point so it's hard to say. Anyway, there's a kiss and you have a shared premonition of a long and happy life together."

I sit back and take a large gulp of cider. "That's awesome. So where is he now?"

"Well, I imagine in his excitement at having found you he took the stairs two at a time, tripped on some family heirloom and has been out with a concussion and amnesia ever since."

"Oh," I say.

"Ladies, would you like to see the dessert menu?" The waitress makes her peppy inquiry.

"Share a lemon mascarpone cake?" I suggest.

"Always," May confirms.

As soon as the waitress has gone I ask, "Is he going to get his memory back, my mystery man?"

"It's touch and go."

"May!"

"Of course," she laughs. "The minute he sees you."

I smile back at her. "Okay, so that's me all sorted, what about you?"

She scoots closer so I can join in her farm girl scrolling. "Could you see me living in Truro with eighty-five thousand free-range hens?"

"Um…"

"This chick at St. Ewe looks hot. She's even made Poultry Farmer of the Year shortlist. *Twice*."

I raise a brow.

"What? I don't think it's as far-fetched as it sounds. We could get Charlotte to host some events on the farm—give a whole new meaning to hen party…"

We burst out laughing.

"I feel like this cider is filling our heads with crazy notions," I note, wiping a tear from my eye.

"It is. Shall we have another one?"

"Let's have another two!"

27

Tuesday (hungover) and Wednesday (still feeling rough) are spent finalizing the pitches for Friday's meeting, not that any of them particularly sound like winners to me. Mind you, if someone had proposed Bull Dog as a brand name, I wouldn't have predicted that to be the huge success it is. Or that "intelligently designed" would be the phrase you lead with when describing skincare.

But, honestly, I feel like I don't know anything about anything anymore.

"What do you think of Face Off as a concept?" I keep pitching to Becky, hoping something will give me that "Jackpot!" feeling. "Touch of testosterone in the inferred conflict, as well as removing the grime of the day. Hold on!" I reach for my ringing phone. It's reception.

"Hi, this is Amy."

"Amy, there's someone here to see you."

"Who—" The line goes dead. "Every time." I shake my head.

"She likes to keep us guessing."

I huff as I get to my feet. "I bet it's not even for me. Remember last time I signed for that package and then got accused of stealing five hundred latex gloves from the botox doctor down the hall?"

Becky has already stopped listening. "See you tomorrow!"

"What?"

She points to the clock, never one to work a minute longer than our official close of business. It's a good thing she reminded me—I promised Charlotte I'd come straight over to hers. In fact, it could well be her coming to meet me. I grab my bags and take the stairs at a clip.

"Face Off, off your face...BEN!" I exclaim coming to a sudden halt as I enter reception.

"Hi!" He smiles broadly as I approach.

"Is everything all right?" I look around, though I don't know what I'm looking for.

"Yes, everything's fine—I hope it's okay I came to your work? Nessa is at the groomer's around the corner so I thought I'd chance it and see if you wanted to grab a drink."

I was not expecting this. After the awkwardness of our last encounter I thought he'd just discreetly back out of my life.

"Oh gosh, any other time I would," I respond. "But I'm just heading to Charlotte's, we're all getting together to hear about her honeymoon."

"Oh, no worries."

"But you could walk with me if you like, she's just down the road from here…"

"Perfect!" He brightens. "Let me carry one of your bags, you look a bit laden down."

I give him a grateful smile and hand him my farmer's market tote. "It's dragon fruit, if you're wondering—my contribution to the dinner party, selected in accordance with my culinary skills."

"I'm sure you'll do a beautiful job slicing them."

"I do have a particular flair for arranging fruit," I acknowledge as we sidestep a straggle of teenagers. "So, what's the latest on Switzerland? Is there yodeling in your future?"

"Actually, that's why I wanted to see you—I leave first thing tomorrow."

"*Tomorrow?*"

He nods. "Still haven't packed but I wanted to apologize in person, for not being able to come to your mum's party."

"Oh, don't worry about that!" I assure him, actually quite relieved that he won't be there. We continue on. "Gosh, so you're really going up the Alps?"

"I am. Of course, I'm suddenly thinking of a million reasons not to go now that it's real."

"I think I can re-convince you in three words."

"Go on…"

"Lindt Lindor Truffles."

"They are the smoothest," he acknowledges.

"Like silk," I confirm. "Besides, this is what you want—the chance to focus on your screenplay."

"Maybe that's why I'm nervous. I'd be all out of excuses there."

"Then all the more reason to go," I insist. "I see it all the time—young people today behaving like they've got all the time in the world to achieve their dreams. They haven't. The older you get, the harder it is to run on adrenaline and optimism. You start to lose your nerve, second-guess yourself, worry about mortgage payments. It's so much better to go all in when you haven't got so much to lose, you know, when you are naturally more daring."

"Did you just call me a young person?"

"You are a young person," I grin. "So go to the mountaintop. Fill your lungs with that zingingly fresh air and the page with your best work."

He blinks back at me, a sheen to his eyes. "Thank you. I needed to hear that. All of my friends have been saying I'll get cabin fever in a week."

"Do any of them visit fallen angel statues in cemeteries?"

"No," he admits.

"Well then. I'm sure you'll miss them but they'll all be here when you come back. Opportunities like this don't come along every day and you're the right man for the job—you've got the kind of heart that needs to be filled up with wonder."

He heaves an extended sigh. "I really hope we can stay in touch."

I give a little shrug. "Of course." Though I'm fairly certain he'll forget me at the first glimpse of a snow bunny hottie.

"And if you ever want to talk about your mum..."

I look up at him.

"You know I understand what you're going through."

Now it's my turn to get an eye sheen going.

"Sometimes I want to reminisce about my grandmother but when I speak to my family they just say they miss her too and change the subject." He pushes back his floppy hair. "If you wanted to tell me everything about your mum from the beginning, just to practice remembering all the good bits, I'd be happy to listen."

"That's really lovely of you," I sigh. "And I'd like to hear everything about your grandmother."

He smiles. "Do I deduce from the fact that we've stopped that we've reached your friend's house?"

I nod, suddenly feeling like I am going to miss this person I hardly know.

"Okay, well, I won't hold you up. I'm glad I got the chance to say goodbye." He moves toward me, arms outstretched. In my bid to make it very clear I'm not in any way angling for a kiss, I somehow misjudge the direction of his head and our lips meet, just fleetingly but it's enough...

I wait for the rush, for the barrage of images and emotions.

None come.

"Well, what do you know?" I blink back at him. "We were always meant to just be friends."

"That bad?" His fingertips go to his mouth.

"No!" I burst out laughing and then look at him fondly. "Say goodbye to Nessa for me."

"I will," he beams back.

As I wave him off I feel a strange sense of calm wash over me.

I turn to give an extra jaunty rap to Charlotte's heavy brass knocker but the door opens before I even get the chance.

"Oh my god! Is Ben back in the game?"

"Were you watching us?"

"Obviously!" she hoots. "But I couldn't hear anything!"

"You look gorgeous, by the way," I say, taking in her khaki silk maxi and golden tan.

"You too! No one wears a shirtdress like you."

"All white and I didn't spill anything on it all day!" I say proudly. Today really is turning out to be a good day.

"Come on, we haven't got long before Marcus gets home." She hustles me through to the lounge, still very much an interior design showroom as opposed to a home—I half expect to be handed a swatch of fabric samples as we sink into the sofa.

"So how were the penguins?"

"We can talk about the honeymoon when we're all together," Charlotte says briskly. "Right now we need to focus on your romantic situation—I have two items to discuss but you go first as the new Ben dynamic could change everything."

"There's nothing new to tell—except that he's moving to Switzerland tomorrow…"

Charlotte looks deflated. "But the way he was looking at you…"

I smile. "It was nice. But I kissed him and nothing."

"Really?"

"Zero romance," I confirm.

"And you're okay with this because…?"

"Because I actually think we're going to be friends." I clap my hands together. "So, what are your two items?"

"They are not great items."

"Oh. Do we have to address them now?" Just as I was starting to feel good.

"The sooner we face reality, the sooner we can move on."

Reality? This is never fun.

"Firstly, May's hunch was right—the venue owner did have a guest that night."

My hand goes to my heart. Here we go again.

"But it was a woman. His mother, who is in her eighties."

"Ah."

"I also checked if there were any extra staff that we hadn't accounted for but that was another dead end."

"And the second thing?" I ask, keen to move on.

"Marcus got the film developed. The sepia one from May's camera."

I give a little shudder.

"He's bringing the pictures home with him from work. We took a few snaps on the honeymoon so we didn't want to ask May to develop it."

"Say no more."

"I mean, she said sepia was really flattering and there was just so much good wine…"

"Really...Say. No. More!" I hold up my hand for emphasis. And then I get a wary look. "I feel like you are trying to prepare me for some bad news."

"Not at all. We haven't seen them yet, it's just..."

"You don't think they are going to provide any revelations," I finish her sentence for her.

She sighs. "I've been over the guest list so many times. I may have even made a few discreet enquiries while I was away..."

"What do you mean?"

"I just wanted to do my due diligence. You know I'm a very thorough person."

"That I do." My eyes narrow. "What did you find?"

"That's just it—I drew blank after blank." And then her expression changes. "Please don't take this the wrong way but I have to ask..."

"What?" I gulp, not liking where this is going. I pull one of the overstuffed cushions onto my lap for comfort but then find myself prickled by tiny white feathers trying to poke their way to freedom.

"Look, you were pretty drunk—we all were. Is it possible that the premonitions got muddled up with a dream. A really vivid one?"

My mouth opens but nothing comes out.

"I'm not doubting you, Amy. But the wedding setting..."

"You think the happy ending premonition was just wishful thinking?"

"I don't know. I don't know how else to explain it now that

Ben and Tristan are out of the picture and we know you're not going to have a sudden change of heart about Elliot."

I sigh. What if she's right? What if this has all been a wild goose chase of my own invention.

"Hi, honey, I'm home!" a voice calls from the hall.

"Marcus," Charlotte mouths, though I think even I could have deduced that.

"Heyyy, how are you?" I say, getting to my feet so I can shake his hand like a politician while he opts for a hug.

"Is that appropriate?" He darts a look at his wife. "I never know these days."

"It's fine, you're family now." I pat his pinstripe shoulder. "You're looking very well."

"I am well. The only bore is having to go back to work after all that bliss."

"I bet," I say, clinging to the small talk.

"The photos, darling..." Charlotte reaches out her hand.

He gives her a cautionary look. "Perhaps we should quickly vet them first?"

"Yes, why don't you do that?" I falter, not sure where to position myself. "Shall I put the kettle on?"

A sugary tea sounds appealing right now.

"No need, it won't take a second."

As the newlyweds begin sorting through the pictures, giggling and nudging, gazing and reminiscing, my mind wanders. Could Charlotte be right? Is it possible that my happy ending vision was nothing more than a dream? Certainly all the memories were tangled in my boozy brain. But why would only the bad ones be verified? And why would the good one feel the most real of all?

"Oh my god! I told you that was a bad angle!" Charlotte suddenly exclaims, shredding one picture on the spot.

"Wedding, wedding…" Marcus begins to drop the vetted images on the sofa cushion beside me.

I hold them up one by one trying to bring my blurry eyes into focus. It's surreal to be taken back to that night once more, remembering the giddiness as I careened between assorted men. Would I do things differently if I could guide myself with the knowledge I have now? Of course I would. I'd avoid Tristan for one thing. When I look at his face now I just feel repulsed. I can't wait for that whole scenario to become a distant memory. Oddly the sight of Elliot makes me feel almost fond now, but that could be because he will be forever associated with free Nutella bombolone.

"You look so beautiful in this one," I say to Charlotte, pointing to an image of her looking lovingly at Marcus.

"Am I the luckiest guy in the world or what?" he smiles.

"Don't get distracted," Charlotte chides. "This is our last chance to find a clue." She flips through a series of similar images. "What are all these ones of the entrance?"

"You told me to get a picture of the main staircase," Marcus defends himself. "It kept coming out wonky."

"I think it was a bit wonky," I concede.

"Oh my god!" Charlotte clasps a photo to her chest.

"What?"

"Marcus—get your grandmother's magnifying glass."

"What did you see?" I clamor.

She reaches for my hand and grips it tight. "I just need to be sure."

She takes the jeweled handle and walks over to the window, holds up the picture and squints at it like Miss Marple.

"It's him," she whispers in a stunned voice.

"Him who?"

"Your third kiss."

"What?" I lunge toward her.

"It doesn't make any sense…" She trails off, limply handing me the magnifying glass. "Look to the left of the staircase…"

"To the left…" My heart stops. I can't believe it—there I am, lost in the dreamiest embrace.

With Gareth.

All the feelings come flooding back—the warmth, the heart-swirling joy, the certainty, the comfort, the desire.

"How can this be?" I croak.

Charlotte shakes her head, stunned. "I don't know. Why would he deny this?"

I can't take my eyes off the picture.

Marcus shifts awkwardly, lightly clearing his throat.

We both turn to him.

"Do you have some kind of man insight?" I ask. "Why would he be so insistent he's not The One? Why wouldn't he speak up?"

"Um." Marcus looks trapped.

"You can say," I urge him. "Is it obvious to you that he doesn't want anyone to know? Or that he just wants to forget it because he thinks of it as a mistake?"

"I was going to say he might be peeved because it meant the world to him and then he saw you kissing another man. Or that he's hurt because you didn't even remember kissing him."

"Oh god, he's got a point—how could I not remember?" I turn to Charlotte. "I mean, of all the people…"

She looks as lost as me.

My shoulders slump. "He's my happy ever after and he wants no part of it."

"You need to ask him outright. He's the only one that knows what actually happened. Remember, he wasn't really drinking."

"No way," I reply.

"No way?"

"He's had multiple opportunities to tell me and besides, he's seeing Peony now."

"I'm not so sure about that," Marcus grimaces. "I saw her at work today and when I asked how things were going, she looked like she wanted to kill me."

"Really?"

Marcus leans forward. "You know I'm a man and thus would never recommend talking as a solution to a problem…"

"Exactly!" I turn to Charlotte.

"But in this case, I really think you should clear the air."

"What?" I turn on him.

"For the sake of your friendship and the group dynamic."

"It worked out with Ben," Charlotte encourages.

"Well, that's a little bit different—I haven't been in love with *him* for the last twenty years!"

The pair of them raise their brows at me.

I blink in shock. "Did I just say what I think I just said?"

They nod back at me.

"Oh my god—I think it's true," I mutter in a daze. "I think I've loved him since that first day he walked into the classroom."

I flump down on the sofa, releasing the photograph to the table so I can let my head fall into my hands.

"Are you okay?" Charlotte sits beside me.

I shake my head. "I'm sorry to spill out all these crazy emotions, this is supposed to be a fun night."

"Not at all," Marcus soothes, taking a seat on the other side of me, putting his hand on top of Charlotte's.

Is this how children feel when parents join forces to rally around them? It's really quite nice.

"There's no time like the present," Charlotte insists. "If we leave now, we might get to Gareth's before the others and then Marcus and I can make ourselves scarce."

"Oh no. Not tonight. I don't want to spoil the evening."

"I know you, Amy," Charlotte tuts. "You're just going to spiral if you don't nip this in the bud."

I turn back to face her, eyes welling up again. "I kissed him! I kissed Gareth."

"You know the weirdest thing? It suddenly makes perfect

sense, the two of you, together." She hands the photograph back to me. "Look at the pair of you!"

I gaze at it and then gaze some more. This kiss looks so ardent, so real. "At least we know now I didn't dream it."

Charlotte nods. "We just need to find out what happened next."

"I spoiled it," I sigh. "Whatever the reason, it has to come down to that."

"Well," she shrugs, slotting the photograph into my shirtdress pocket above my heart. "There's only one way to find out for sure."

28

"If I start wailing, '*Why don't you love me?*,' you'll gag me and send me home, won't you?"

"No."

"What?" I twist to face Charlotte, sat beside me in the back of the cab.

"That's actually the main question you need to ask."

"Oh yes, because it always nets such great results," I huff. "I'm actually thinking of opening with, 'Why didn't you tell me you were the mystery kiss?' I'm kind of mad about that. It's not like him to be so deceitful."

"If I may?" Marcus chimes in as we pull up outside Gareth's door. "I think we should halt the speculation train at this station. Wait until you've heard his side of the story."

"Must you always be so reasonable?"

"I'm sorry," he apologizes.

"Don't forget the booze," Charlotte nudges him, reminding the driver to pop the boot.

"That's my party plans out the window," the driver chuckles before leaning toward me. "Good luck, love. And if you need a rebound fling…"

I smile back at him. "I always wondered what the Above & Beyond ranking was for, now I know."

"I'm serious."

"I'm tempted."

"Amy!" Charlotte prises me out of the cab. "Now is not the time to experiment with dating men twice your age. You have to face this."

I lean heavily on the bell.

"Happy?" I say. And then jump behind Charlotte and Marcus as I hear the latch click.

"Welcome home!" Gareth cheers as he opens the door.

He hugs Charlotte, then me but Marcus has his hands full.

"I bought some wine," he says as he hoicks up the case of bottles.

"Is there a coach party joining us?" Gareth looks past him to the street.

"Well, now that I'm married to an event planner I don't want to get caught short," Marcus explains. "Mind if I pop a few bottles in the fridge?"

"Help yourself."

"Corkscrew?" Charlotte prompts.

"Already on the table. Come on through."

I'm so relieved we're eating in the garden, I would've felt totally claustrophobic indoors. My intention is to latch on to Frankie and/or Zazel to avoid any possible eye contact, but instead I find myself gazing in wonder as we dip under the draped canvas canopy of a makeshift safari camp. The long table is set with raffia mats and candle lanterns while the winking tea lights and surrounding potted palms give the impression that we're being watched from the bushes by amber eyes.

"Was that an elephant trumpet?"

"The soundtrack is all Jay," Gareth explains as the man himself appears, looking like a cross between a tribal leader in a 1970s Bond movie and Cher at an animal conservation fundraiser.

"I think you've just broken the record for the most animal prints incorporated into one outfit," I marvel. "Ginger giraffe, monochrome zebra, cheetah spot, tiger stripe…"

"Well, they say animal print is like a neutral."

"I feel like you are single-handedly disproving that theory."

And then May steps out from behind him, looking like she's guarding the area from poachers. I'm about to check Marcus's pathway for traps when she sees Charlotte.

"You came back!" May gasps.

"Of course I did," she says, embracing her. "And I come bearing gifts!"

Charlotte opens her leather tote and begins handing out an array of brightly beaded Zulu accessories. For May an eye-catching camera strap, for Jay a bold bib necklace with strands extending all the way to his waist, for me a diamond-patterned cuff and for Gareth a pair of cat collars — cobalt blue and white for Frankie, lilac and bronze for Zazel.

The joy is only amplified when Marcus uncorks and pours the South African wine, a Pinotage for the red-lovers, Chenin Blanc for the white. I stick to kombucha so I can keep a clear head. And boost my digestion. Which could come in handy with this South African themed dinner featuring *bobotie* — which appears to be a kind of curry moussaka — and *pap* which is sold as similar to American grits but is a little too much like porridge for my liking.

"So, tell us everything!" I say, loading on the salad.

We hear about trips to Table Mountain, the beach penguins, afternoon tea at the baby pink Mount Nelson Hotel…Charlotte is just explaining how she had to take off her dangly earrings when approaching a strokable cheetah at a conservation project when Marcus interjects, "Sorry, quick question, do we have enough takers for me to open another bottle of wine?"

"Soon you will know us well enough to never have to ask that question," May says, sliding over her glass toward him.

Once topped up, we hear about the inspiring trip to see Nelson Mandela's cell on Robben Island and how it made them grateful for all their freedoms but also consider their potential legacy.

"And then Marcus had an *Aha!* moment while we were on safari."

"Well, technically it was more of an *Aaaaarghh!* moment,"

Marcus confesses. "I went out with one of the guides while Charlotte was in the spa and we came across this herd of buffalo. They are so massive—six hundred kilograms—with these huge horns and we were watching them pass and then I don't know if the wind changed or what happened exactly but this one beast stopped, hung back and locked eyes with me."

"What?" I squeak.

"And the guide is telling me not to panic but he says he's gearing up to charge. And I'm thinking, I knew it was too good to be true—marrying a woman like Charlotte and now I'm going to get skewered and, that's it, my life is over."

"Please tell me the guide didn't shoot him!" May growls.

Marcus shakes his head. "The buffalo looked deep into my soul and it was as if he decided to give me a second chance."

May rolls her eyes.

"I'm not even kidding. I have never been so grateful in my entire life, so all the way back to the hotel I'm thinking about how I can show that buffalo that he made the right choice."

"Did you exchange email addresses?" May asks. "How's he going to keep updated?"

Charlotte shushes her and explains that he's already made a donation to a local conservation group.

"But that's not all—that night at dinner we're seated with this French couple and we get onto the topic of aristocracy and they used that phrase 'noblesse oblige'—you've heard of it, right?"

The general consensus is that we've heard of it and we can

definitely see it has a French origin but we don't really know what it means.

Charlotte holds up her phone and reads the dictionary definition.

"'Noblesse oblige is the inferred responsibility of privileged people to act with generosity and nobility toward those less privileged.' Or, as wikipedia says, 'Nobility extends beyond mere entitlements and requires the person who holds such a status to fulfill social responsibilities.'"

"So that's what I'm going to do," Marcus cheers. "I am going to dedicate the rest of my life to using my privilege to help others."

"Oh my god!" I gasp. "Noble!"

"Are you just getting this?" May frowns.

"Noooo! I've been trying to come up with a name and a concept for this new skincare range we're branding and this would be perfect! Noble! Be a Noble Man!" I enthuse.

"It's definitely catchy," May concedes.

"We wanted a socially conscious aspect to it so maybe we could even let people choose where their donation portion of the profits will go. Like, you register online and scroll through the options until you find a cause that really fires you up, and then you get to feel like a Noble Man when you donate."

"Wouldn't it be great if whenever you are feeling bad about yourself, instead of looking up exes on Facebook, you made a donation—just whatever you could afford—and then you'd feel all benevolent and gracious and good!" Charlotte joins in.

"Of course, not everyone is interested in doing good," Jay notes.

"Well, we wouldn't be marketing to those people. When you speak to everyone you speak to no one."

"But does the skincare company itself even care about doing good?"

"I don't think that matters," I reply. "If you were a charity, who would you appreciate more—the person with good intentions or the person who actually made a contribution?"

"This is interesting ethical territory," Gareth notes.

"You know, I met this twenty-something editorial assistant at a shoot the other day and though her salary is tiny she supports her favorite YouTube filmmaker via Patreon—six quid a month and it makes her feel like a patron of the arts!" May notes.

I listen as the ideas ping around, tapping notes into my phone, feeling like we're really on to something.

Eventually my head is spinning so much I dip out to prepare the dragon fruit. I find a strange satisfaction slicing into the magenta pink, artichoke-like outer layer to reveal the bright white flesh, speckled with tiny black seeds.

"Look how pretty you are!"

"Are you talking to the fruit?"

I turn to find Jay behind me.

"I just ask because that's the chattiest you've been all night."

"What? I just came up with a whole new campaign for work!"

"Aside from that you were totally zoning out. Don't think I didn't notice."

"Well," I sigh. "I've just got a lot on my mind."

"No joy with the flat-hunting?"

"I'm taking a break from that at the moment. It turns out you can't look for love and flats simultaneously or your head will explode."

"Don't forget you need a new bra too," May chimes in as she comes in search of glasses for the liqueur.

"Are you trying to push me over the edge?"

"Oh, let me make you a custom one!" Jay enthuses. "The structuring on the bridesmaid dress worked a treat, didn't it?"

"Yes," I confess.

"I think lifting your boobs could really help lift your mood."

"That sounds like an idea for a Netflix series," May sniggers as she sets the glasses on a wooden tray. "The life-changing magic of underwear."

"We could go out into the street and rip people's shirts open like Superman."

"*Really?*" I query.

As we head back to the safari camp the pair of them banter excitedly about the possibilities of episodes for the trans community and post-surgery options. And clothing alternatives for people who find Spanx too hot.

"Now that one I would watch," I concede.

You wouldn't think a fruit as striking as the dragon fruit could be easily upstaged but when Marcus pours the Amarula liqueur and explains that it is made from the native marula fruit, which contains four times as much vitamin C as an orange, it quickly becomes the darling of the hour. Even my abstaining self asks for a top-up—it's like a fruity Baileys. Charlotte says it has a pear vibe, Marcus says butterscotch, to me it tastes like strawberries.

"Just one more," I say, knocking it back like Yoplait.

"One of our guides says it acts like truth serum because the alcohol part sneaks up on you."

I notice that Gareth sets down his glass even quicker than me.

"Hey, Amy." Charlotte slurs slightly as she twirls the cork-screw. "Did you ever get your mattress? You were on a mission before the wedding…"

Great. Yet another thing eluding me. "I'm still looking," I reply. "I thought I'd found The One but it didn't pan out."

I share a glance with May, the only one I told about Matt the Mattress Guy.

"I got mine custom-made and it wasn't half as expensive as you might think," Gareth notes.

"That's so funny, we were just talking about custom—"

"Ssssh!" I hush Jay. My boobs do not need to be part of this conversation. "Carry on, Gareth."

"Well, if you'd have accepted my offer the other night, you'd know how comfortable it is."

There's a flutter around the table.

"I slept on the sofa," I hurriedly explain. "When my mum had her fall."

"Well, you're welcome to try it anytime."

Can someone start a new conversational thread? I can feel my face getting hot.

"Did we tell you about the bed we slept on when we were glamping in Kruger?"

Oh, thank you, Marcus!

As he describes their treehouse hideaway with a big bridal veil of a mosquito net, I realize Charlotte is trying to telepathically tell me to take up Gareth's offer. And I think she means now. I let my eyes glaze over and absently reach for the water carafe. But the next thing I know she's behind me, encouraging me and asking, "Who wants tea?"

"You just had an invitation into his bedroom!" she hisses as we weave back to the kitchen. "What bigger opportunity do you want?"

"I know, I know!"

"I think this is the closest he's ever come to flirting," she marvels, definitely more than tipsy.

"Why does none of this make sense?"

"Because you won't talk to him about it."

"Why do I have to be the one? He's known this whole time—"

"Oh Gareth! Remind me where you keep the teabags!" Charlotte trills.

I reach for the fridge handle and stick my head fully inside. "Is everyone okay with oat milk?"

"Why don't you let me do this?" Charlotte nudges my rear with her hip. "You check out Gareth's mattress. I think the sooner you resolve this, the better."

"Agreed," he says. "I don't like the idea of you sleeping on a bed of nails."

Really? Okay. Here we go! I adopt a businesslike tone as I follow him into his bedroom. "So, let's talk specs."

"Sex?" he startles.

"Specs," I overenunciate. "As in specifications?" I then briskly interrogate him on what motivated his decision to go custom, how he found craftsman Aidan, the length of the construction period, yada yada…

Meanwhile Gareth unpings his fitted sheet and shows me the tufting. "You can have any pattern on this top layer, though of course it will always be covered. Hop on board!"

"It's pretty high—I think I'd need a stepladder to get up!"

"Here," he says, boosting me into position.

I think the only lift we haven't done this month is over-the-shoulder fireman style. Mind you, there's still time.

"Now you know I'm not typically a fan of technology."

"I do."

"But with all the years of stooping to tend to my plants my back demanded I try out one of the adjustable frames. Do you mind?" he says, asking my permission to join me.

"Go ahead."

"So if you lie back…" He takes the remote, there is a whirring sound and we are tilted at the head and the knees. "It is better for lower back pain than lying on a flat mattress."

"Gareth?"

"Yes?"

"I have a question."

"I know what you're going to ask. What happens if you turn onto your side in the night."

"It's not about the mattress."

A pause. "Okay…"

"It's about the wedding."

I sense him tensing.

I can't think of a single way to phrase what I need to ask so I rely on visual props—taking the photo out of my top pocket and handing it to him.

"What's this?" He frowns and then his face softens. For a moment he looks nostalgic, dreamy even. "How…"

"Apparently Marcus was sent to photograph the staircase with Charlotte's mini camera and there we were."

Still he stares at the picture.

"Why didn't you say it was you?" I ask. My voice is barely a whisper.

He looks up but not at me. "I knew I wasn't the happy ending so why would it matter?"

"What do you mean?" I try to turn toward him but the tilt of the mattress is not conducive. "Can you straighten this out? Or raise the top a bit higher?"

He fumbles with the remote, jolting us up and down. At one point our feet elevate and our heads rock back like we are on a rollercoaster designed by a gynecologist.

"Sorry!"

"Can't you just tell me what happened?" I despair.

"Amy—"

"Just blurt it all out so at least I know! You're the only one who can help me make sense of all this!"

Finally he presses the right button and we level out. I take a breath and turn to face him, telling myself I can hold it together no matter what he says, but I'm not sure that's true.

"You were tending to my cut," he begins, tracing his finger over the scar on his lip. "You got tissues from the ladies' and led me over to the stairs so you could be at the right height to see the wound. Even though you were pretty tipsy, you were taking so much care."

The memory returns to me—pushing through the girls doing their lipstick and mirror selfies, collecting the tissues from the silver box dispenser, letting the tap water stream over my fingers and half the tissues, keeping the other half dry. Hurrying to his side. Standing level with him. Holding his face steady with one hand. Dabbing with the other. Leaning in. All my attention on his beautiful mouth.

He looks down at the photograph. "There was a point when everything just sort of stopped."

Yes, I see it now—my eyes meeting his. A new understanding, a new connection. A melting sensation.

"We kissed," he says, a slight crack to his voice. "And then you started to cry."

My hand goes to my cheek. He's right—amid the flood of love, there are tears streaming down my face.

"I knew in that moment that you'd had a bad premonition. And it was over."

Over?

"So I made my excuses and went up to my room. But then I felt like the walls were closing in on me. I knew I wouldn't be able to sleep so I went out walking in the grounds."

"In the dark?"

He nods. "I got kind of lost, ended up sleeping propped up against the base of a tree. I found my way back when the sun came up."

No wonder he looked so rough the next morning. We put it down to Freya's wedding but it was me.

"When I walked into the Lilac Room and heard you had kissed all these other guys and that one of them was the good premonition…" He shakes his head. "I just wanted to remove myself from the running and get out of there."

"But you didn't say you were one of the kisses!"

"I couldn't go there—I didn't think I could play it off like I didn't care. I was still so thrown by the whole thing."

I stare at him dumbfounded.

"Charlotte even asked me about it in the car. I couldn't face any more questions so I took a flight to Edinburgh to see my dad, thinking it would all be resolved by the time I got back."

I reach forward and prod his leg.

"What's that for?"

"I'm just checking this is real and that you're actually saying what I think you're saying and it's not just me hearing what I want to hear."

"What I'm saying is…"

"Yes?"

"I'm glad it's Ben and not Tristan. But I wish it had been me. Even with a busted lip I would've kissed you because I've been wanting to kiss you since the first day I walked into that classroom and you smiled at me like you already knew me."

My heart plunges in my chest.

"Gareth…" I shuffle closer.

"Yes?"

"When I cried at our kiss—"

"You don't have to explain yourself and I'm not sure I want to know what happened in the premonition."

I rest my hand on his. "Those weren't sad tears."

He blinks back at me. "What do you mean?"

My heart is rattling with nerves as I continue. "I was crying because I was so happy. Because it was you." I feel my eyes well up with emotion. "Because it's always been you."

Gareth looks stunned. "Wait—I was the good premonition? *I* was the good premonition?" he repeats, seemingly warming to the idea.

"The *really* good premonition," I confirm.

I watch as the clouds lift from his face. His brow smooths out and his lips part. He looks like he's going to speak but instead he swoops in and kisses me with dizzying intensity.

I feel light-headed. For once I can fully surrender to a kiss, free of dread, free of disappointment, fully able to feel the love.

"Amy," he whispers my name as we come up for air.

For what seems like minutes we just look into each other's eyes, taking each other in in a whole new, enchanted way.

As he smooths back my hair, I feel myself smiling, then really beaming. And now he is too. And then he's kissing me again and this time my whole body gets swept up in the bliss.

"Are you decent?" Jay bursts in, then jumps back. "Jeez, when you invited her to test the bed…"

"Did you need something?" Gareth asks, cool as a cucumber.

"What? Oh! There's some guy at the door, I'll tell him to come back. You're clearly busy."

"Some guy who?" Gareth calls after him.

"Some next-door guy."

Gareth and I look at each other and then scrabble to our feet, lunging past Jay and charging down the corridor.

"Mr. Atkins!" we cheer in unison.

"I just wanted to ask one more time, just in case—"

"Yes, yes!" we fall over each other. "Where do we sign, what can we do? Do you need us to go to the bank now?"

"Really?" He looks amazed. "You two are on the same page now?"

"Yes!" Gareth asserts.

"Finally!" I sigh.

He beams back at us. "That's all I needed to hear. We can sort the paperwork tomorrow."

"Oh, thank you!" We reach forward to hug him.

"Now, now, there's no need to get carried away," he chuckles. "I'm just glad my home is going to a good home."

"It is! We're going to love it so much!" Our arms instinctively wrap around each other like we've been a couple for years.

We watch him leave and then turn to face each other.

"Did we just buy a house together?"

"This is the best day ever!"

In my excitement I jump up into his arms, wrapping my legs around his waist, and we succumb to our most ardent kiss to date. We have so much lost time to make up for. My hand slips under his shirt, eager to connect with the warmth of his skin—

"Excuse me!"

We look up to see Charlotte beside us. I'd forgotten we had company.

"I'm sorry, but you guys have got the rest of your lives to do that. Like, literally. We need you in the garden."

Gareth and I look confused but when we get there we see May and Jay and Charlotte and Marcus gathered around a bottle of champagne.

"Where did that come from?" Gareth frowns.

"I hid it at the back of the fridge when we first got here." Marcus gives me a wink. "I had a feeling we'd be celebrating."

I beam back at him and then at each one of my friends before snaking my arm around Gareth and cheering, "Pop that cork!"

29

I wake up the next morning alone in my own bed.

For a moment I think I dreamed the whole thing. The conversation in his bedroom, the kiss, the euphoric decision to buy the house next door, the champagne toast from all our friends that made my heart almost hurt with joy...

Is it really possible that, after all these years of feeling love was out of reach, I can actually move forward into this new life? I hug the pillow to me. Even the deflated, prongy mattress doesn't bother me anymore because it's temporary and I know my new bedroom will have a balcony with sun streaming in and gauzy curtains that will waft in the breeze.

I spring up and instead of groggily stumbling to the bathroom, I find myself singing. And it's only five a.m.

I had set my alarm extra early so I would have time to update the pitch for Noble Skincare. My intention is to do such a great job that the directors look at each other with open-mouthed amazement and then cheer, "We love it!"

Of course, part of me wanted to stay with Gareth last night and spend every minute reveling in the wonder of him but as he said, "You have an opportunity to become a Noble Woman, take it!"

I feel extra fired up knowing this man wants the best for me. And there's no rush when it comes to our relationship. I want to savor the build-up to our first night together, which will now be Sunday night after the party. On the one hand, this seems an age away; on the other, it gives me the chance to go shopping for some decent underwear. It's time. Not that I think Gareth would even notice the difference between a sports bra and a lacy balconette from Agent Provocateur. Or maybe he would. That's a whole new side of him to discover. Either way, it's so unbelievably freeing to be with a man who digs the raw, flawed you. I think of my alternative existence trying to please men like Tristan and it just makes me shudder.

I hone the pitch wording as I lather up in the shower, flipping through font options as I blow-dry my hair, and then sit down with a large mug of coffee and my laptop. This is the most motivated I've felt in ages. I pace the flat perfecting the inflections of my presentation and then hop aboard the bus, sitting with nervous excitement, listening to motivational tunes and feeling way too fired up for its slow and creaky progression.

Isn't life fascinating? I think to myself as the doors open and close. Ever self-renewing. You can feel so flat and bored and disenchanted one day and then something gets you fired up and suddenly the world is filled with possibility again.

I ding the button for my stop.

Okay. Take a breath. Composure.

I cross the street, head into the building, grab a glass of water and in I go.

The presentation goes perfectly. I don't falter or trip over a single word and as I deliver the segment on donating 5 percent of the profits to a charity of the customer's choice I almost hear myself underscored by stirring, righteous music.

Becky's visuals look stunning and as she flips through each option, I see the representatives from the company nodding and whispering in an animated fashion. There are the two men we met with before, both of whom applaud as we conclude the presentation. And then there is Big Boss Man Cooper—whether this is his first or last name is irrelevant because apparently this is all he goes by.

"I love everything about this except the five percent, that's too big a chunk of the profits."

I nod. I was expecting this. Worth a shot.

"The thing is," he continues, "if you word it as 'a percentage of profits,' you never actually have to specify the amount. I mean, 0.005 percent is still a percentage."

"Well, you obviously wouldn't want to go that low," I counter.

"Why not?"

"Because it would seem misleading and exploitative."

"Excuse me?" He looks affronted.

My boss Lindsey goes to speak but he holds up his hand to halt her.

"We are donating money to a charity who didn't do anything for it and yet we are exploiting?"

I don't know where to begin with this—*a charity who didn't do anything for the money?* I'm starting to feel slightly sick. I sit forward to make my point: "I mean that you want to make the donation in good grace and good faith, not purely with an eye on profits."

"Are you telling me how to run a business?" he sneers. "Do you run the finances of this agency?"

"I do not."

"Well then, why don't you focus on what you are good at and I will do the same? Unless you don't want our account?"

"Of course we want your account," Lindsey simpers.

"I just feel that if your brand is Noble Man, you should walk the talk."

"Amy, can I see you outside for a second?" Lindsey gets to her feet and opens the door.

My face feels hot as I walk through.

"I think it's best you sit out the rest of the meeting," she whispers intently as she guides me around the corner.

"But this is my idea, my concept."

"And you are paid for your ideas, which in turn become company property."

My shoulders slump in frustration. "Are you happy with what this Cooper is saying?"

"It's not about me being happy, it's about the client being happy."

"At what cost?"

Her eyes take on a steely, if exasperated glint. "I'll speak to you after."

I stand stunned for a few minutes and then head back to my desk feeling teary and deflated. How did that all go wrong so quickly? I didn't even say that much! I push my keyboard out of the way. I can't bear the thought of Cooper taking people's money on false pretenses, especially thanks to me. Just the other night at dinner I said that the brand's intentions didn't matter but now I very much feel that they do. I reach for my phone, unsure of who to text first—May for outrage, Gareth for calming, Charlotte for pragmatism, Jay for a fantastic put-down to keep in my back pocket, should I encounter Cooper again. "You peculiar little man!" has served me well over the years.

"What a dick."

I look up to see Becky returning to her desk, giving me a sympathetic look.

"Is Lindsey still in there?"

"She's gone out for coffee."

"With them?"

"I don't know. She said she wouldn't be long."

I tap the desk nervously. "Do you think I'm going to get fired?"

"Noooo, of course not," Becky assures me. And then her phone starts to ring. "I should probably get that, I'm expecting a call from the printer's."

"Of course. Go ahead."

What if I just walked out? Stood up for my principles? I so want to work for a company I believe in and to do meaningful work but then again, if I lose this job, I won't be able to pay the mortgage on the new house, Gareth won't be able to open his cafe and our dreams of doing good through that will be over before they begin.

If I do get to stay, I would at least want to know a bit more about this Cooper character and his business dealings. I pull the keyboard back toward me and begin feverishly googling.

"Amy?" I jump as I hear my name. Darn Lindsey and her stealth shoes.

"Yes?" I try to sound casual.

"Can I see you in my office?"

The sense of doom deepens. Today is not going according to plan.

I sit down opposite her desk, avoiding eye contact. I always try to be bright and receptive and enthusiastic but right now all I feel is disillusioned and crushed of spirit.

Lindsey clasps her hands together. "Cooper suggested I let you go."

I look up with a jolt. "From the account?"

"From the company."

"What?" I gulp. My heart thumps noisily. I'm not sure how me having a good idea that everyone loves could end in, well, the end.

"I know you've been wanting to go in a different direction for a while—"

"Yes," I hastily cut in, "but I wanted to incorporate that new direction with the work we do, not replace it."

"I know." She inhales a long breath. "I think it's time…"

Oh god, here we go! I close my eyes to brace myself.

"…for us to take on some non-profit clients."

I look up in confusion. "As in…"

"As in, we offer our services to a non-profit. For free."

I can't believe it. "What makes you say that?"

"General disgust at Cooper and then realizing that while he's talking about donating 0.005 percent of the profits, I don't even do that."

"Oh."

"I just had a 'What is my legacy?' moment."

"What kind of coffee were you drinking?" I ask, wondering if the rumored CBD cafe has, in fact, opened.

"Actually, I wasn't getting coffee, I wanted to call our lawyer about withdrawing our Noble Man pitch."

"Seriously?"

"I mean, I like irony as much as the next British person but I think it's a step too far aligning Cooper with that brand."

My mouth remains open. "I can't believe this."

"This was not how I was expecting today to go either. But…" She takes a breath and raises her jaw. "It feels good. I'm turning forty next week and I don't want another decade of kowtowing to bullish clients. It's time to try something new."

"I want to hug you!"

"Not that new," she grimaces.

I laugh, somewhat deliriously.

"So, next step, I want you to bring me a list of people you think we could work in harmony with—but do a bit of digging about the company ethos, find out who is at the head and the heart. We can afford to be picky."

"Right, right," I nod, getting to my feet, eager to get started. "Thank you so much!"

Lindsey gives a light shrug. "Sometimes a 'no' can lead to an even bigger 'yes.'"

I walk away from her office feeling like I've just been handed the title for my autobiography, should I ever feel the need to write one.

30

It's Sunday. Party day. And the gang is all together.

"Ready?"

We're huddling up for a group photograph before entering the nursing home. The camera is balanced on the brick wall and May is making one final check on the composition before she presses the timer.

"Here we go!" she calls before scurrying to join us.

I pull her close as she channels Robin Williams from *Mork & Mindy*—thumbs hooked in her rainbow braces, arms clad in a stripy T-shirt, legs hidden beneath baggy, peg-pleat trousers.

"I can hardly bear to look at those!" Jay tuts, setting the pearl drop in his headband a-jangling.

He switched his outfit choice at the last minute to Rachel from *Friends* in her opening scene wedding dress. I think we all secretly knew this was going to happen but we oohed and aahed nonetheless because he'd clearly gone to so much trouble with the embellishments and even has wet-look hair.

Charlotte and Marcus have stuck to the script as Margo and Jerry from *The Good Life*, even if they are now spiritually more on a par with Tom and Barbara.

Gareth is doing his best with an Irish accent to convince as Father Ted but visually looks much more like James Norton in *Grantchester*. I am not complaining.

As for me, I ended up as Polly from *Fawlty Towers*. The outfit is fairly simple—a pale blue dress with a white pinny and bow—but I'm loving the bulbous bouffant bun of my hair. I feel like a cross between a seventies perfume ad and Barbra Streisand in *Hello, Dolly*. Gareth leans in and nuzzles at the bare back of my neck, causing me to shiver-shudder in delight. I find myself constantly reaching to touch him, even though every inch of him is covered up, from his black boots to his clerical collar.

"Oh look!" Charlotte cheers as we enter the building. "The Vicar of Dibley!"

"I have to get a picture of you two!" May positions Gareth directly behind the female vicar so that their heads and dog collars align. "Perfect!" she cheers then asks the woman's name so she can send her a copy of the pic.

"Geraldine," she replies.

May hesitates. "Is that your character name or your actual name?"

"Ummm…" The woman looks anxious.

"Not to worry," I step in. "You look wonderful, that's all that matters!"

"May I escort you to the dance floor?" Gareth offers her his arm.

"Oh, yes please!" she beams up at him.

"I'm guessing there's going to be quite a bit of identity confusion today," Charlotte notes as we follow behind.

"Either that or they'll end up recognizing more faces than normal," Marcus counters.

There's certainly going to be plenty of musical recognition with the sitcom soundtrack Lidia has compiled—everything from *Last of the Summer Wine* to *Cheers*. Apparently music is especially good for conjuring memories in dementia patients. And everyone else for that matter...

"They're playing my song!" Jay cheers as we enter the community lounge to "I'll Be There for You."

We immediately start dancing with imaginary tambourines, feeling a rush of good vibes, reaching for as many soft, crinkly hands as we can.

The nursing home typically feels like a sleepy, tinkering-along place, with the odd bit of squabbling or commotion and a tinge or two of melancholy. Today guests are buzzing and eager to get moving, grooving and, well, *confessing*.

"Just go with it." I give Gareth my blessing as another little old lady tugs at his sleeve, eager to whisper her secrets to him.

The rest of us have decided we want a copy of the playlist, loving all the cozy, familiar feelings it is conjuring, until the jangly piano of *Will & Grace* strikes up and May clutches at her heart.

"Oh my god, this reminds me of Mum."

Jay looks equally wistful. "Remember how we'd all do the bare tummy bump at the start?"

"I miss her so much!" May cries out.

"Can I get you two a drink?" Marcus asks, eyes full of concern.

"I'll help you," Charlotte offers. "I know what they like."

I guide the twins to the side of the room so they can take a moment.

"She would've loved today," May sighs, leaning back onto the wall. "Seeing everyone dressed up and playing a part."

"That was her favorite bit of modeling," Jay nods. "Never knowing who she was going to be at each shoot."

I can already see how the costumes are bringing out a different side to the residents, from the excessive flirtiness of les Blanche Devereaux to the puce-faced bluster of assorted Captain Mainwarings.

"I certainly saw your mum in a whole new light when I was getting her ready."

I frown back at Jay. "You were here earlier?"

"I wanted to help her into her outfit."

I'm about to say, "That's very nice of you but she can still zip a skirt!" when I catch sight of a woman dropping jaws and widening eyes in her black satin corset, mid-thigh leather mini and over-the-knee PVC boots. Her hair is a wild, tousled mane. All that's missing is a whip.

"Oh my god!" My hand goes to my mouth as the recognition hits. "What did you *do* to her?"

"Exactly what she asked for."

"Jay, she wanted to come as Roz from *Frasier*!"

"That is Roz from *Frasier*," he insists. "In her Halloween costume from season five, episode three."

I stumble toward her in shock. "I can't believe you talked her into this!"

"This was all her," Jay protests, hurrying after me. "She had reference pictures on her wall and everything."

"So Lidia knew?" I can't believe this.

"She said she'd spoken to you about it."

Hmm. This actually rings a bell. I think she did try to broach the subject at the hospital...

"Honestly, if you'd seen her laughing when we were backcombing her hair..."

"Really?" I soften. "She does look happy."

"And super hot."

"Maybe a little too hot. I'm worried about Malcolm's ticker."

"It's not his ticker you should be worried about," May chimes in. "Anyway, you reckon she's only been with your father, it can't hurt for her to take on the persona of a powerfully promiscuous woman for one afternoon."

"She really does seem to be in her element," I concede, watching admirer after admirer sidle up.

"Here!" Marcus hands me a plastic cup.

I knock it back in one, only to splutter at the burn.

"I meant to say—I topped off our drinks with my flask."

"Really?" May takes an appreciative sip and then eyes Marcus. "You know, you are almost impossible to dislike."

Marcus looks chuffed, seemingly understanding what a compliment this is coming from May.

"Ooh—she's finally free!" I break away to catch my mum en route to the refreshments. "Mum! Mum!"

She turns around to face me, frowning as she looks me up and down. My heart sinks.

"Polly?" she finally speaks. "Polly from *Fawlty Towers*?"

"Yes!" I cheer.

"Oh darling, you look lovely with your hair up!"

"And you look amazing with everything up—and out!"

"I've never had so much attention!" she beams.

"You deserve it. Oh, watch out—incoming Marty Crane!" I step back to allow the silver-haired chap in a red check shirt to make his move.

When she accepts his invitation to dance he boldly casts aside his aluminum walking stick and clutches her to him, as if merging for a tango.

I watch transfixed as the pair of them traverse the floor with surprising coordination and intensity.

"May!" I beckon to my friend. "Could you get some snaps of my mum dancing?"

"I'm way ahead of you, kid," she says, showing me the latest images on her phone.

"Oh, look at the pair of them!"

"Adorable," she agrees. "An elderly lumberjack cutting a rug with his dominatrix."

I can't help but smile.

"Check out these gems." May scrolls through a selection of the slightly surreal moments happening all around us.

I tilt my head. "Why May Day, have you got your mojo back?"

"How do you mean?"

"You said you were tiring of fashion girls..." I prompt.

"This could be my new project!" she gasps. "I could have an exhibition right here on all these blank walls."

"I bet Lidia would be all for it, she's been dying to jazz things up. I haven't seen her yet. Wait!" I do a double take.

As does May.

The woman we have only ever seen in her plainer-than-plain work uniform has the I Dream of Jeannie outfit down to perfection—platinum blonde ponytail, petite red velvet bolero, gauzy pink harem pants and ruched bikini top with a tantaliz-ing tassle. The tattoos are a surprise addition, all her own.

"She seems to be having trouble opening that bottle," May notes.

"Ironic for a genie," I mutter.

"I'm going to help her."

I watch as May makes her approach, opens the bottle in one deft move and then pours two glasses of cider. Lidia blushes alluringly as they clink.

"Well, what do you know..." I mutter to myself.

"They make a cute couple." Charlotte is quick to catch on as she joins me.

"I actually think this could be a match," I concur. "Lidia won't put up with any nonsense and May wouldn't have any trust issues with someone as genuine as Lidia."

Charlotte smiles. "Our family is expanding!"

"It is, isn't it?" I sigh. "There was May worrying that we're fragmenting when really we're just adding new members."

"Come on, girls, it's time to do-do-do the conga!" Marcus jollies us along.

"Is this wise?" I frown. "If one goes down, they all go down!"

"It seems to be more shuffling than kicking. Plus, they're interspersing the younger folk to add some stability to the chain."

"Come on!" Charlotte finds an opening and we shuffle along, coordinating every once in a while from sheer chance, getting more hysterical with every step.

As the music changes, it occurs to me that so much of what we need to be truly happy is right under our noses. We might believe sipping a cocktail on a Tahitian beach is the goal but there are a lot of surprisingly satisfying alternatives. Take Gareth. As much as I'd like to have his hands on my hips right now, it's giving me even more pleasure to watch him slow-dance in the corner with a stooped woman who barely comes up to his chest. Her eyes are closed as if she has "Moon River" playing in her head.

I go to move toward him but Malcolm blocks my path.

Well, actually it's Malcolm as David Brent from *The Office*, complete with fluffy yellow Emu costume.

"Gosh. Malcolm. That's quite a look."

"Yes, yes." He pushes past me to get to Jay. "Are you one of those transgenders?"

Oh dear.

"I'm just a human who likes to dress any way I please."

"Hmm," Malcolm grunts. "I heard you got Sophie in that outfit." He looks lustily in her direction.

"I did. And you're welcome," Jay smirks.

"Could you do the same for me?"

"Well, I was going to say those PVC boots don't come in your size but I actually know a place that has them up to a size 14."

"Really?" His eyes light up.

"Wait, are you serious?" Jay gasps.

"I've just always wondered, you know, what my drag alter ego would look like."

"Well, it's going to take more than one flourish of my magic wand to make that transformation," Jay informs him, eyeing his beard. "What have you got hiding under here?"

As Jay starts foraging for a jawline, Malcolm seems startled by his touch. "I—I don't know. I've had it for as long as I remember."

"Do you want to find out what is underneath? Together?"

Malcolm's usual bluster evaporates and his watery eyes fill with concern.

"I know it's scary showing the world who you are, trust me," Jay soothes. "But I think it's time."

Malcolm looks back over at my mother. "Do you think it could make certain people look at me a different way?"

"It would be a start," Jay encourages. "There might be a few behaviors you can shed while you're at it. You know, leave it all on the barbershop floor."

Malcolm nods and then leans in. "Can we do it now, before I lose my nerve?"

"My clippers are already vibrating," Jay assures him. "Come on, show me your room."

Gareth joins me to watch the unlikely pairing totter off, Malcolm graciously offering Jay his arm so he can scoop up the excess of his wedding dress with his free hand. "There's some kind of magic in the air today, isn't there?" I muse.

"Speaking of air, would you like to get some with me?" Gareth takes my hand.

"It's a shame Claire has locked the staircase or we could go up on the roof," I note as we head out the door.

Gareth raises an eyebrow. "We should probably check that lock."

"It's just along here…" I point down the corridor.

"Can you keep an eye out?" He motions for me to turn back toward the party.

"What are you doing?"

"Give me two minutes."

I lean on the wall, trying to look casual while humming along to "Hooky Street" from *Only Fools and Horses*. "This market banter is a bit like a cockney rap, isn't it?"

"Amy!" I hear Gareth hiss my name and turn to find him beckoning me through an open door.

"How did you do that?" I gasp as I hurry over.

"There are still a few things you don't know about me."

"Like you're a cat burglar on the sly?"

"Or maybe that my uncle is a locksmith."

"A likely story," I tut as we climb up to the roof. "I am so getting you a black polo neck for Christmas."

"Oh wow!" Gareth stalls as we emerge, taking in the shimmering cityscape, the park treetops, the flowing river, the gracious bridge and the most pleasing of breezes.

"Isn't it beautiful up here?"

He steps toward the railing, surveying our kingdom. "It's funny, this is my neighborhood but I've never seen it from this perspective before."

"Mum always seemed so blissed out here—like she'd given her cares the slip," I say, snuggling under his arm.

Gareth is quiet for a moment. "There might be a way for her to feel like that again."

I shake my head. "Claire would never allow it after her fall."

"I was actually thinking about down there on the water—a sunset cruise along the Thames…Do you think she'd find it relaxing, gliding along, watching the sky change color and the bridge lights come on…?"

I sigh with delight. "Yes!"

"There's just so many things we can do together now." Gareth sighs contentedly. "You said we were properly old in the premonition?"

"Super wrinkly," I confirm and then tilt my head at him. "Is that a tad daunting?"

"Not at all," he assures me. "It's what I've always wanted: to have one true love—and to have that one true love be you."

For a moment I lose myself in the warmth of his eyes and then melt into his kiss. Familiar yet new. Thrilling yet comforting.

"There is one question I have about your sneak peek into the future..." he says as we take a breath.

"Yes?"

"Did I still have my hair?"

I burst out laughing. "You're going to be a total silver fox!" I insist as I forage in his soft curls. "But everything else that happens between now and then, that's for us to discover together."

"Like whether we'll have plant-themed latte art at The Botanist?"

"You know, just this morning I watched a YouTube video on how to etch a cactus in the froth."

"We're golden then," he beams. And then he gets a very particular look in his eye.

"What are you thinking?"

His hand slips to the small of my back, pulling me close so that our hip bones bump. "I'm just wondering how it will feel sleeping beside you tonight..." I can feel the heat between us, the magnetic, pulsing charge. My head starts to swirl—the anticipation of skin on skin is too delicious—but then our phones start buzzing in unison. We leap apart, as if a mild taser has been applied to our groins.

"That'll teach me to try skipping ahead," Gareth chuckles as we reach into our respective pockets.

As suspected, we are being summoned back to the party.

I'm torn. I want to prolong the heavenly sensation of being in his arms, but I also want to see Malcolm's chin and add my name to my mum's dance card.

"We can do it all," Gareth assures me. "Together forever, one minute at a time."

"I love that!" My eyes light up. "Do you think we should get that tattooed?"

"Maybe in our seventies."

I smile back at him. This is going to be so much fun...

As we rejoin the party I realize that my mum doesn't yet know that Gareth and I are an item. I can't wait to tell her.

"Finally!" She heaves a sigh of relief as we present ourselves. "All this talk of mystery men at the wedding had me worried."

"What?"

"You don't need a premonition to predict a happy future for the pair of you. I never wanted to say anything in case you got all contrary like I did when my mum insisted Pete was The One."

This makes my shoulders slump. "To think you could have had a true love all this time."

"I did," she says. "I do."

I sigh. It makes me sad that she still thinks of Dad that way.

"For over thirty years I've had you," she continues.

I force a smile. "Well, I'm glad I can be something of a con-solation prize."

"You are not second best, Amy. You were my first choice. I chose you, you know that, don't you?"

I look to Gareth and then back to her. "How do you mean?"

"When I kissed your father I knew he was going to leave me – I saw him walking out the door, but I also saw you."

My stomach drops. "What?"

"I saw you in my vision. And I felt a love for you like nothing I had ever known. You were my girl. The biggest part of my heart. If I didn't go forward with Jimmy, I knew I would never get to be with you, never get to hold you in my arms as a baby, never get to hear you call me Mum, never get to see your life unfold. And that would be a far greater heartbreak for me."

"But, but…"

"I didn't say I didn't love him. I did. I do. Because he gave me you."

Now my eyes are tingling and the tears start to flow.

"I love you, Mum!" I say as I fall into her arms.

"Oh sweetheart," she talks into my hair. "I know it's hard for you. To see me come and go. But you have to know my love for you is eternal."

And then she reaches out and pulls Gareth into the hug. I could happily stay in this embrace forever but a certain exaggerated cough is trying to get our attention.

"Yes, Jay?" I say, noticing he has also assembled May, Lidia, Charlotte and Marcus, who is distributing a fresh round of drinks.

"So I need to present Malcolm to you but not as the tall blonde

353

from *Third Rock from the Sun* as I originally intended. There are two reasons for this: firstly, it turns out he has a hot nephew living in Manhattan so I am going to string this process out."

"Okay."

"Secondly, well, you know how he previously had grooming skills on a par with a highland cow?"

I can't help but chuckle—it's a fair comparison, such an unruly mess of hair and facial fuzz.

"Well, now he looks like a rather more distinguished Scottish icon."

He steps aside to reveal what is essentially Sean Connery circa *Entrapment*.

We blink in disbelief.

"Malcolm?" It takes my mother a moment to recognize him. With a mix of curiosity and wonder her hand reaches to touch his face, running her manicured fingertips over the area where his raggle-taggle beard once was. "I didn't know you had a mouth."

"All the better to kiss you with," he says, somehow managing to sound more sincere than wolfish.

My mother raises a brow and then looks at me. "Do you dare me?"

I gasp. And then bite my lip. "Why not?" I encourage. What's a party without a party trick?

We watch spellbound as she raises up on her tiptoes, gently guiding his face to hers. As their lips meet, his eyes close in rapture and I watch nervously as my mother experiences the rushing, warping intensity I know so well. I prepare to steady her but then her face lights up.

"Malcolm," she breathes as she takes a step back. "I had no idea!"

"What did you see?" I squeal. "How did it end?"

Mum turns to give me a knowing smile. "I think we've had enough talk about endings, haven't we?"

She's got a point.

I reach back for Jay, without looking where I'm putting my hand.

"Oi!" He smacks my wrist. "I'm saving that for the honeymoon!"

"Sorry," I chuckle. "I just wanted to thank you for transforming my mum and Malcolm—and for adding a whole new dimension to their time here."

"Well, you know me, I live to liberate."

I give him a kiss on the cheek, careful not to tangle with his veil, and then sigh as I look around the group. "Now I'm done with the fast-forwarding aspect of my life, you know what I wish I could do?"

"What?"

"Press pause, right now."

"No you don't."

"Yes, I do—everyone I love is in one place, everyone is so happy…"

"Yes, but if you paused life here, then May and Lidia would never get their first kiss, you'd never get your first night with Gareth—"

"Oh!"

"We wouldn't find out where Marcus and Charlotte's philanthropy leads or whether I make it in New York. And your mum wouldn't get to experience for real what she just got a flash of in her premonition…"

"Well, when you put it like that…"

"If you're going to wish for anything, why not wish to fully embrace the present moment?"

"Okay, wise one," I nod. "I'll drink to that!"

"You'll drink to anything!"

"Cheek!" I say, then urge everyone to raise their plastic cups in a toast.

"What are we toasting to?" May wants to know.

"To embracing the present moment!" I cheer, adding, "And each other!" as I catch Gareth's eye.

He smiles dreamily and pulls me into his chest. Then just when I think my heart can't swell any more, I realize a mass hug is layering around us—vicars and genies, husbands and wives, mothers and daughters, friends and lovers, all forming one giant embrace. I take a long breath in as I nuzzle deeper, knowing this is the feeling I want to carry with me for the rest of my life.

Acknowledgments

Every book has its own set of muses and influences and with *Skip to the End*, I am especially grateful for the creative mind of Molly Powell—thank you for sharing your imagination with me! I'd also like to make a champagne toast to editor deluxe Emma Capron, who brought a multitude of insights and ideas to this story, including shining a spotlight on a key emotional moment that, left to my own devices, I would have completely overlooked!

The entire Quercus Team have been a dream—Ajebowale Roberts, Ellie Nightingale, Ella Patel, Georgina Difford, David Murphy, Chris Keith-Wright, Isobel Smith, Rachel Campbell, Frances Doyle, Georgina Cutler, Hannah Cawse, James Buswell and Violeta Mitrova. In addition, the lovely Emma Thawley has worked so diligently on foreign rights as well as liaising with the fabulous Emily Hayward-Whitlock, who has brought a whole new chapter of excitement to the publishing process! Thanks also to the wonderful cover designer Mel Four.

Of course, there would be no acknowledgments for me to

write without my champion James Breeds, the first person to believe that I could write a novel. Over twenty years on, it's an honor to be your ride or die.

Finally, I have to give a little wink to the mystery mattress salesman who inspired the opening scene—and all the people who contribute without even knowing it! Writing may seem like a solitary pursuit, but in reality, it is a major collaboration!

About the Author

A former magazine journalist, **Molly James** is the pseudonym of an author behind twelve escapist novels, including multiple bestsellers. Excited to take her writing in a new direction, Molly now brings a twist of magical realism to her heart-based humor, creating worlds the reader will want to return to over and again…

Find out more by following @mollyjamesauthor on Instagram.

Molly James's

Skip to the End

Reading Group Guide

Reading Group Questions

1. Do you consider Amy's ability to see how a relationship ends from the first kiss a blessing or a curse? If you had the option of experiencing it, would you take it?

2. Have you ever stayed in a relationship even though you knew it had no future? What reasons did you give yourself for staying? What lessons did you learn?

3. Were you able to guess the identity of Amy's true love? If so, what clues did you pick up on? When were your suspicions confirmed, and did knowing his identity impact your reading of the rest of the novel?

4. What would you see in Amy's visions that would make you turn away from a person? What would your ideal vision be?

5. The story is told from Amy's POV. Do you wish you could

have heard any other character's thoughts? At any specific moments?

6. Each of Amy's friends has a unique personality that helps them to balance out the others. Which role do you think you play among your friends? Who could you most relate to?

7. What strategy would you have taken to figure out who the right guy was? Do you think Amy made the best choices or would you have tried something different?

8. Both Gareth and Amy deny a connection on the basis of their friendship. What do you think are the pros and cons of falling for a friend?

9. At one point, Amy says "My biggest concern is making the wrong choice." How do you deal with risk-taking in your life? Are you risky or cautious? What is a risk you've made that has paid off, or one that has not?

10. Do you ever find yourself writing your own futures for book characters—your own version of skipping to the end? Do you believe Gareth and Amy make it to old age? What do you think happens in between?

11. Much of this book—and much of romance in general— revolves around the happy ever after. Do you think there is

too much pressure on happy endings? Do you think our definition is too narrow?

12. When Amy and Ben speak about their family members with dementia, they note that sometimes you grieve something before it's gone. Do you think this is true? Can you relate to what they were feeling?

13. Amy and Gareth help each other with their goals, such as working on the flower shop. What are your current goals, and how important is it for your partner (or future partner) to support them?

14. Amy gets advice from many people on how to approach her situation. Who do you trust with your love worries? Or do you prefer to handle things yourself?

15. Amy laments on how "They say the course of true love never did run smooth but *really*?" Do you think love always comes with obstacles? What was Amy's biggest one, and how would you have dealt with it yourself?

Author Q & A

1. Where did the first spark of inspiration for SKIP TO THE END strike you? Did you know right away it was going to be this book, or was it a process to find Amy's story? What comes first for you—the plot or the characters—and why?

Typically the idea or concept comes first, then plot ideas start to bubble up, often influenced by the story setting. The characters form as I write their dialogue, so I try and do that at a clip, letting them banter back and forth without controlling what they are saying. Gradually their quirks, traits, and heart's desires reveal themselves. So many times they surprise me and are not at all who I had in mind—May had a sharper tongue than I anticipated, but I loved that it became keenly apparent how loyal and vulnerable she was beneath the surface.

2. Did having a magical element make it harder or easier to tell the love story?

Having an element of magic amps up the playful aspect of your imagination. It's great fun thinking through scenarios that have never crossed your mind before—as in, what would the impact really be if you knew how a relationship ended before it had truly begun? I did lots of pondering and ruminating as I wanted it all to sound as believable as possible, as if this really was someone's life. Even if the magical element is fanciful, I wanted the emotions to be relatable.

3. What was the most challenging part of this book? Was there a specific plot point you had to write over and over?

This book did take an awful lot of finagling over a two-year period, mostly to do with the dynamic between Gareth and Amy, but the wedding scene was also written dozens of times in dozens of ways. One of the best additions was having Amy stay with Charlotte at the venue the night before the ceremony. I found their exchange quite moving! Generally I think friendships come more naturally to me than romance.

4. When you're writing, do you write in chronological order? Does the ending come first—that is to say, do you SKIP TO THE END?

I tend to write whichever scene is closest to my mood! If I'm feeling peppy and energized, I'll run with some character banter; if I'm blue I'll ruminate on a more poignant aspect, like the mum's dementia. Other times I might spend a whole day tinkering with the description of a location, like the tumbledown cemetery, in the hope that it really conjures the setting for the reader.

As for the ending...I never write the final scenes until I've completed the whole story. I know what I'm aiming for, but I always want to feel that I'm tying up things in a very tailor-made way, and I can't do that until I have experienced every aspect of the characters' shenanigans as they often surprise me. I always want to end on a happy heart high—the kind that has you clasping the book to your chest with a smile and a satisfied sigh.

5. The three kisses all have different personalities. What were your priorities in creating the right guy for Amy?

I want to be an advocate for the good guys of the world! I've fallen foul of the charm of the glamorous bad boys too many times, so I hope to show just how sexy someone understated and honorable is, especially when life gets tough. Gareth made me swoon when he did the *Dirty Dancing* lift with Jay during gym class at school.

6. Friends to lovers can be a tricky trope—how did you decide to make Amy's magic kiss someone she was close to? Did you have any difficulties crafting their dynamic? What was your favorite moment between them?

It was indeed tricky getting the balance right. You want the readers to fall madly in love with the heroine's friend but also find appeal in the other contenders. (Personally I still have a massive crush on Ben!)

I liked the first moment Gareth swoops in and catches Amy as she is about to fall into the mud, plus the coziness when he rustles up dinner for her when she's wearing his oversize pajamas, because I think comfort is such an integral part of a dream relationship.

7. If you could personally have a different power that helped you in your life, what do you think you would choose?

I definitely would have benefitted greatly from skipping to the end of my relationships and sparing myself insane amounts of heartache and disruption, but I think one real-life power that could have been just as effective is self-esteem! I used to be so grateful for a scrap of attention from a suitor I would overlook innumerable red flags. The wrong relationship choices have such a horrible knock-on effect to other aspects of your life, I really feel there should be classes on this at school.

8. SKIP TO THE END is about the chase for a happy ending. Is there a happy ending scene in a book or even film that is your favorite? One you wish you had written?

Interesting question! Two of my favorite films—*Thelma & Louise* and *Roman Holiday*—don't have conventional happy endings but are all the more brilliant for it because they show the perfect conclusion to their specific stories, and stay absolutely true to their beautifully crafted characters.

For all the feel-good vibes, it's hard to beat *The Holiday*—so satisfying to see Kate Winslet and Cameron Diaz (with their respective beaus Jack Black and Jude Law, at the very peak of his handsomeness!) celebrating New Year's Eve together after spending the entirety of the film apart—all the ends are tied up so well and you can't help but long to join in the tipsy dancing!

9. If you were to write a spin-off about a side character, which would you pick? Did you imagine the endings of all the other kisses/Amy's friends?

I'd pick the sister-bro combo of May and Jay in a heartbeat! I have oodles of extra background on the pair of them growing up in London's garment district, the tragic loss of their model mom, and the evolution of their bonding with their rough diamond dad. I feel that Jay has much more to give and I loved May's edge. Being a people pleaser by nature I find their liberation a tonic and I love their distinctive style!

10. If someone asked you to *skip to the end* and summarize your ideal takeaway for readers, what do you most wish they learned/felt?

In essence the message would be to really appreciate all the goodies that are in your life right now, however imperfect it is. I've always been a future-gazer and love making plans for new adventures, but I think there is great value in pressing pause and taking time to make the most of your friendships, as they are such a source of joy. There is also much pleasure to be had in communing with neighbors and people on the periphery of your life, like the gang at the nursing home.

I know one reader found Jay's words of relationship wisdom significant and something they wanted to carry forth:

> "When you're with [someone], ask yourself, *How does being with this person make me feel about myself?* If you feel like the bee's knees, that's great; if you feel in any way 'less than,' move on. It really doesn't need to be any more complicated than that."

YOUR
BOOK
CLUB
RESOURCE

VISIT
GCPClubCar.com

to sign up for the **GCP Club Car** newsletter, featuring exclusive promotions, info on other **Club Car** titles, and more.

 @grandcentralpub

 @grandcentralpub

 @grandcentralpub